ORIGINS

HEIRS OF NO EMPIRE
BOOK 1

TONY AZZI

ORIGINS

Ada is a quirky, seventeen-year-old senior trying to get through high school the only way she knows how - no drama, good grades, and lots of Shawarma, heavy on the garlic sauce. At least, that was the plan until she blacks out and starts seeing all sorts of disjointed visions.

Ada's world is thrown into total chaos - or a "polycrisis" as her and her best friend Didi call it - when she discovers that her visions are part of a larger cosmos (like, literally) of events. She is shocked to learn that, ever since her mother was pregnant with her, an oppressive regime called the First Rank from the world of Unitas has been hunting her. They want something from Ada: a source of power she never knew she was born with.

With the help of her ride-or-die, Didi; the enigmatic basketball star, Axel; the mysterious Winter, who is not all as she appears to be; and her all-time frenemy, Ellen, Ada must either take the fight straight to the First Rank or surrender her powers to save her loved ones.

But decisions have consequences. And Ada's ultimate decision will
alter worlds and destinies.

UNITAS. PRESENT.

It was a terrible idea. Staring up at the marble altar of the Empress Walk temple, Helma of Kanz knew this could be the most important discovery of her life. Or it could be the last day of her life. She had never set foot in the Empress Walk before—for the obvious reason that she had no intention of ever leaving Unitas and porting to Earth.

Helma had slipped inside during the changeover of the guards. The First Rank was likely patrolling just outside, as they always did. One sound—one squeak of the tiles underneath her feet—would echo through the rotunda and alert the First Rank intelligence agency, the Infernum. If she were caught, the First Rank would sentence her to death for her unauthorized access to the sacred temple, along with any other crimes they could fabricate.

In her satchel were the green roots of random wild violets she had plucked from the Hills of the Fallen. It had been an arduous journey. The odds had been that she wouldn't even make it without being captured by the First Rank. Fortunately, she had help from sympathizers, who'd opened the gates into the hills and given her safe cover back to the Empress Walk.

A luminescent residue from the roots spotted the satchel. Helma held out the shimmering weeds. Green elixir trickled down from the roots to form pools by her feet. Her eyes widened in amazement as their glow intensified. She could have sworn they hadn't been this bright when she'd plucked them from the hills.

"The Agoge," she whispered in astonishment.

She had dedicated years to searching for the source of this tremendous power created from the Emerald Elixir by the First Empress, Sala of Legio. It had gone missing five years ago. The pulsating energy of the elixir radiated throughout the Empress Walk. Tendrils of green flares wrapped around the walls and marble columns of the temple, reaching up to the oculus above and out through its round, bronze-lined opening.

But the spectacle didn't go unnoticed.

Infernum officers, clad in matching black uniforms, burst through the door, their scepters aimed at Helma.

"Treasonous scum!" shouted one. "Under the Elimination of Subversive Threats Directive, and the authority vested in me by the Father of Unitas, Chancellor Nygaard, I hereby order your arrest and sentence you to death."

The officer snatched the glowing roots from Helma and hurled them to the marble floor. Both their gazes followed the streams of green that flowed toward the altar to form an outline of a figure.

"A host for the Agoge is on—earth?" Helma gasped in disbelief before the base of a scepter struck her temple, knocking her out cold.

CHAPTER 1
EARTH, AMONG OTHER THINGS

ADA LORHAM WASN'T REALLY that superstitious. Don't get it twisted, though—it wasn't like she tempted the fates either. Not that she would go out of her way to open an umbrella inside or break a mirror, but she just wasn't convinced that walking underneath a ladder could ever change the order of things in her world.

Basically, she went about her life assuming the universe had a plan for her, and it was going swell, if she may say so herself. She was exactly where she supposed to be and among the family and friends she was meant to be surrounded by. No amount of throwing salt over her shoulder to ward off bad luck could change all that. Everything made sense, from her being born on September thirteen, to her having wildly uncooperative curly brown hair, black eyes, five feet, six inches tall, neither thin nor curvy, and living at 154 Rutgers Place, New Jersey, United States of America. Things were exactly as they should be.

On September 4, at 154 Rutgers Place, Ada woke up at six thirty in the morning without her screeching alarm. Instead of a high-pitched, repetitive beep jarring her awake, the nervous murmurs of her parents traveled from their bedroom to nudge her from her sleep. The walls muffled their voices, but she could still hear a fuss brewing. She slithered out of bed and ran a hand through her thick, tangled hair. Her parents' voices were agitated, sort of panicked.

Guided by curiosity, she tiptoed to the far end of the upstairs hallway. Her parents' door was shut. She inched closer and bent down to place her ear by the tiny space between the bottom of the door and the floor. Despite the awkwardness of lying face down on hardwood, Ada could, with more clarity, make out the uneasy discussion between her mom and dad.

"Zeina, seventeen years ago, he said the Agoge would come alive when she nears her seventeenth birthday. You don't think I've been thinking of a million ways to prepare her for that?"

"*Ya Marcel shu a'am tihki!*" Ada's mom's reply came quick in Arabic, although Ada's American dad often had no idea what she was saying in her native language. "Genuit showed up at our house all these years ago. He said he'll come for it when she turns seventeen. Since then, nothing unusual has happened. We did the tests. The doctors never saw anything out of the ordinary."

"I'm not taking that risk," Marcel shot back in a panic. "She will wear that pendant when she turns seventeen next week. I'll tell her it's a birthday present."

As Ada peered through the narrow gap between the floors and the base of the door, she could hear her father's footsteps growing louder, closer. She sprang to her feet and retreated to her room, leaving her door half-open, then resumed her position in bed and pretended to be asleep. She heard her father pause at her door. After a few seconds, his footsteps pattered back down the hall, and Ada detected the soft click of him shutting their bedroom door.

What were they talking about? Her eyes narrowed as she tried to fit the pieces of the puzzle together. *Who is Genuit? The Agoge?*

"It's probably nothing," she muttered. "Or maybe it is something. Nope, it's probably nothing." She blew out a puff of air.

She reached for her glasses on the bedside table and put them on. Blinking a few times to adjust her eyesight, Ada peered through the window. "Still there," she whispered with excitement.

This was the day Ada would finally drive a car—her own car—

to her first day of school. She'd worked six days a week all summer at Keats Ice Cream Parlor, down the shore, and had tutored middle-school kids to save up enough money to buy a 1993 Chevy Blazer with racing stripes, no working speedometer, a punctured washer-fluid tank, and a radio with a blown-out rear speaker. The front of the car was embraced by a slowly corroding metal front guard. The car was a death trap. She called it the Blaze. If others saw it as a prime candidate for the junkyard, she saw the Blaze as a flawless piece of art. She loved that car with all its imperfections—and there were many.

Ada then haphazardly threw on a vintage, oversized, crew neck T-shirt with Thundercats in bold caps splattered on the front. She put on the first pair of jeans in sight. They felt slightly tighter than they had at the end of the school year, the last time she'd worn jeans before breaking for summer at the shore.

"Hmm, a bit snug. They must have just been washed. I'll go with that theory." She looked through the shoe rack at the bottom of her closet to carefully consider which of her six pairs of reasonably well-maintained sneakers she wished to wear for the first day of school, and she landed on a slightly creased pair of high tops. "Jordan 1s for day one. Seems appropriate."

CHAPTER 2
NOPE

On her way to the kitchen, Ada paused in front of her parents'
door again. It was too tempting not to. That cryptic exchange she
overheard replayed on a loop in her head. She tiptoed closer to
their door and lowered herself onto all fours, pressing her ear to
the gap between the door and the floor, as she'd done a little
earlier. She pushed the pang of guilt for snooping on her parents
down into the pit of her stomach and scrunched her head as close
to the door as possible, straining to catch a word—anything that
would give her more information.

"Grapes! What the heck are you doing?" Roman, her brother,
exclaimed from a few feet behind Ada.

When Roman was a toddler, he took to calling his sister by her
first and middle name, Ada Grace, as her parents would sometimes do. His speech was still developing, and so he would
pronounce it Ada Grapes. The name stuck, and he'd been calling
her Grapes ever since.

"Oh, Roman. You're awake!" Ada sprang to her feet as acrobat-
ically as her uncoordinated self would allow. She adjusted her
glasses—an appropriate finale to her poorly executed, ungraceful
attempt to perform the basic physical act of getting up off the floor.

"Yeah...you keep wandering around the hall for no apparent

reason. I'm hungry…*labneh* sandwich?" He scratched his forehead then extended his palms forward as if to inquire what his older sister had been doing taped to the floor.

Ada placed her arm around Roman to hurry him to the kitchen, still preoccupied with what she'd overheard earlier that morning.

"Hey, Roman, did you hear Mom and Dad talking this morning?" she asked him casually.

"They're up?" Roman mumbled.

"They were talking about my seventeenth birthday next week. I think."

Roman flipped his head back. "We know you love your birthday. If this is your way of reminding me and everyone else in your life that your birthday is September thirteenth, don't worry—we got the memo the first one hundred thirty-seven times you dropped a hint this week. Everyone knows—trust me. Only the moon landing was better documented than your birthday is."

"Well…it is my birthday next week. Just in case you didn't know. But that aside, do you know anything about a pendant?"

"Nope."

———

They were packed for school after Roman wolfed down his *labneh* sandwich and Ada picked at some za'atar with pita bread. Standing in the foyer and ready to leave, their father's voice rang from upstairs. "Ada, Roman… you're gonna leave without saying goodbye?" He trudged down the stairs.

Their father was tall with broad shoulders. Streaks of gray cut through his thick hair held in place by glistening hair product. He was dressed in a slightly oversized olive-green suit Ada's mom had pressed for him the prior evening.

"We figured we'd get a head start. Catch up with friends," Ada responded, still analyzing him for anything out of the ordinary.

"You catching up with the homies?" Her dad swayed his hands from side to side.

"Did you say…?" Roman tilted his head, and his lips slightly parted. "'Homies'? I am so thankful you are a vice principal at Carey Public School and not ours. Otherwise, I'd asked to be homeschooled."

"Hey, twenty minutes away from Clifton High School, in the less-than-glamorous end of Jersey, is still close enough for me to show up with a marching band at your lunch hour."

"Well, I think it's cool you teach there, Dad," Ada replied, tapping him on the shoulder. "It's super diverse. I could have picked up some Arabic there instead of begging Mama to teach me."

"You're not going into that part of town. We work hard to make sure you live in a good school district."

"Mm-hmm. Easy on the elitism, Dad. We said we were gonna work on this." Ada trotted closer to hug him goodbye. "Good luck on your first day of school, Daddy."

"Thanks, kid. You too."

Both the children had yet to say goodbye to their mom. Usually, she was the first one awake and would get a head start on researching and drafting her editorials and articles for the overseas press. As a journalist, she would often have to meet both North American and overseas deadlines, splitting her efforts across different time zones. That morning, though, Zeina Tannous, the journalist who reported across all time zones, was still sidelined in her room.

"Mama, we're going now!" Roman yelled, still standing by the door, with one hand impatiently gripping the knob and the other on the dangling strap of his backpack.

Zeina came rushing down the stairs in a hurry. "*Shu* already leaving? *Ba'ad* too early. You still have time. You eat your breakfast? I didn't even make you lunch. Akh, we didn't buy this turkey breast for Roman." She glanced over at Marcel, looking concerned.

Ada sensed her mom's unease. Zeina was clearly preoccupied with something greater than meeting her children's daily nutritional requirements. The conversation between her parents came flooding back.

"Mama, first day of school. Free lunch today. Remember?" Ada said, eyeing her mother suspiciously.

Her mom strolled over to Ada and hugged her tightly for a prolonged moment, muttering, "Just be safe *habibi*, okay. Be safe."

Not fighting her mom's bear hug, Ada asked, "Mama? Is everything okay?"

"What? Yes, yes. Just promise me if you feel sick or feel anything out of the ordinary, you'll call me right away. Okay? Keep your phone on you, and make sure it's fully charged. *Het tanshuf*, let me see." Her mom swiftly took Ada's phone from her hand to check if her battery was full.

"Umm, okay. Don't you worry about a thing. We'll message you at some point today." Ada slowly pulled the phone from her mom's grip and placed it in her pocket.

"Can we go now? Come on, people. I have a legion of adoring fans that want a piece of me this morning."

"You two go ahead," her dad quickly said, cutting short the awkwardness between Ada and her mom. "Love you Roman, A."

"Love you too," Roman said from outside the door.

"Bye!" Ada flashed her patented large smile. She hugged and kissed her mom and dad and left the house.

Upon opening the doors to the Blaze, Ada and Roman were greeted by a flow of dust and a timeworn aura of junk. Roman scanned the car's interior, then the exterior, and lightly kicked the front passenger tire.

"Hello, social suicide!" He took a deep breath, composed himself, and declared, "Okay, let's do this," before climbing into the creaky seats of the Blaze.

Ada, meanwhile, carefully entered the car, willfully oblivious to its defects. "It's a wolf in sheep's clothing," she said to Roman, rubbing the steering wheel as if it were a genie lamp and turning the key. A roar of the engine burst out.

"More like a sheep being clubbed to death by a pack of wolves," Roman said with an exaggerated look of fright.

"You know, I heard the New Jersey bus system is also great," Ada teased.

"I considered it over this… thing. But the one to school runs once an hour. I missed it this morning."

"You shouldn't get so sentimental over public transportation, Roman." Ada slapped her knee. The punch line fell flat. "Get it? Because you 'missed' the bus. Like, you are 'missing' it."

She waited for Roman to explode in laughter. He was visibly unimpressed, slightly groaning.

"I can barely deal with Dad's bad jokes. Don't go down this dark path of puns. Please." He yanked the seat back and closed his eyes.

While Ada was pulling out of the driveway, she caught sight of something peculiar six houses away and instantly slammed the brakes. Over at the home of her best friend, Diana Mendoza—or Didi, as everyone called her—she saw someone she vaguely recognized, a boy her age, standing on the lawn. He wore a white T-shirt, slightly faded ripped jeans, and sunglasses. Ada strained to remember where she'd seen him. He couldn't have been from the neighborhood. Everyone knew each other on their block. She could not connect him to the Mendozas or think of any conceivable reason why he would be there, all alone in the early-morning hours, with his arms behind his back, staring in Ada's direction.

Startled, Roman asked, "Grapes? What are you doing?" The momentum from Ada suddenly braking had propelled him forward when he'd just about dozed off.

Ada looked over at Roman and back to the Mendozas' house. She saw no one this time. The boy had vanished. The noises of cars, birds, and plentiful early autumn leaves ruffling came rushing back.

"Okay. No big deal. That's two totally not absolutely weird things so far today, and it's not even…" She checked the time on her phone. "Yep. It's not even eight a.m. yet. I thought I saw some-thing. Or someone. Never mind." Ada yanked the shift by the steering wheel down to Drive and drove off.

CHAPTER 3
CLIFTON HIGH SCHOOL IN ALL ITS GLORY

THE DRIVE to school was otherwise uneventful. Roman occasionally bobbed his head up to see how far out they were. He'd then check his phone and close his eyes again. Ada glanced at her phone when stopped at traffic lights. A few moments went by before Ada decided to lightly cross-examine Roman about football.

"I don't know," he responded with his eyes still closed. "I think I'll play it by ear and hear out some offers. I still have a few years left."

"Wherever you decide to play college football, I'll try to be nearby to wake you up at ungodly early hours for breakfast." Ada tapped him playfully on his shoulder before placing her hand back on the steering wheel.

"I have no doubts, Grapes." He grinned.

They pulled into the school grounds, where the large marquee sign on the front lawn said Welcome Back. Ada noticed the pack of boys and girls converging like puddles at various locations around the parking lot. "Clifton High is a scene today."

"Yeah, let me out here. Before you go into the parking lot," Roman coolly said.

"Aw, come on. This car isn't that bad."

"Willful blindness suits you well, my ostrich sister," Roman responded with a wrinkled smile. He swiftly opened the door, reached around to the back seat to grab his backpack, and hopped out of the car.

"You gotta put some torque into it!" Ada snaked her body toward the passenger seat. "Like you're shot-putting an anchor. Otherwise, it won't close."

"This whole vehicle is unacceptable," Roman grunted before winding up to slam the door shut. He peeked through the window to flash another quirky smile at his sister then shook his head at her. Roman checked his phone, clocked the school grounds, and sped off toward a few freshmen gathered by the steps.

A subdued sentiment crept in now that Ada was alone in her car. She was still rummaging through the catacombs of her thoughts, trying to piece together the morning's events. She bounced back and forth between her parents' conversation and the strange boy out on the lawn. No plausible theory sprang to mind that would explain either incident.

The chime from her phone jolted her back to the present.

Didi: *Oy, meet at our spot?*

Ada: *Cool just parking.*

Didi: *Yalla vamonos!*

Ada: *Don't Yalla me. I'm coming.*

She hustled out of her car and into the bustling halls of Clifton High School. Successive glimpses of friends and acquaintances followed. Spotting Jojo's backward hat, she frantically tried to avert his line of sight.

"Ada. Where you been, girl? Wow, you really filled in this summer!" Jojo hollered from across the hall.

She'd been spotted. Jojo removed his sunglasses and established eye contact. His frame, short but difficult to elude, hemmed Ada into his orbit. She looked down at her phone and quickly punched a text to Didi.

Ada: *D, where are you? Polycrisis. Full send.*

Day one, and she'd already been flagged by Jojo. She took a deep breath, gave a deliberate exhalation, and directed her eyes back up at him. Jojo wore a backward Yankees fitted cap, a crisp white tee, and relaxed-fit jeans over a pair of tan Timberland boots. His smaller stature made him look like someone who'd blown straight past the part of puberty where a boy's body filled out and had fast-forwarded to facial hair and acne blemishes. The thick silver chain hanging from his neck didn't help whatever streamer-turned-rapper look he was going for.

"Yeah. Hey, Jojo. Thanks, I think?"

"No, no, it's a good thing—you bringing that thickness to senior year." He rubbed his hands together approvingly.

Ada pressed her lips together and swayed back and forth. "Umm, I'm not sure what that—"

"Stop rubbing your hands like that." Didi's voice flew past Ada toward Jojo. "It's mad creepy."

"You're so mean it's hot." Jojo glared at Didi.

Ada wrinkled her forehead and shuffled from side to side.

"Don't you have somewhere to be, Jojo?" Didi asked while Ada idled beside her, unsure of whether to grin in support of Didi or gaze down the hallway so as not to pile onto Jojo.

It wasn't Didi's physique or heels or muscular yet curvy frame that made Jojo seem to have shrunk. It was the way she held herself with a straight and assured posture. She was the picture of confidence, with her neon green hoop earrings, long, jet-black hair, and big eyes.

"I'm exactly where I'm supposed to be." Jojo tried to maintain a relaxed demeanor.

"*Pero no*. I mean, shouldn't you be laminating a fake ID for one of your patrons?" Didi indiscriminately pointed to the first few students who walked past them.

"Which, by the way, you're doing great at. The attention to detail is spot-on," Ada quickly interjected to ease Didi's onslaught against Jojo.

"Thank you, Ada. Game recognize game." He bowed apprecia-tively at Ada. "Business has been good. You know, Jojo's got the plug. And I'll have you know, Jojo was out here slaying this summer." He paused, looked around as if he meant to tell a secret, then leaned closer and loudly whispered, "Older woman. Recent divorcée… she would have been the one, but she took her husband back. Investment banker or something. Something about him financing her needs."

"I'm trying to help you here, Jojo. You gotta work with me, dude." Ada curved her mouth into a dismayed frown.

"Ain't no helping this fool, A," Didi said. "Like, first of all, the third-person talk. It's mad weird. Stop with it. Second, congrats, Jojo. You may be onto something with a marriage counseling gig. You might get women to realize that it could be worse out there for them—so bad that they'd go running back to their husbands. You should add that to your expanding list of side hustles."

Ada hunched her shoulders and tightened her lips into a straight line. Even if she could have thought of such a witty response, there was no way she could have brought herself to say it to Jojo, despite his less-than-tactful ways.

"Hm… hmm, harsh. Don't sleep on Jojo. It's only a matter of time before Didi sees what she's missing," he said to Ada and paused.

Ada knew the punch line was coming. And judging by how Didi was rolling her hand in a circle as if fast-forwarding a film, Didi knew it too. It was one Jojo had recycled numerous times around them.

He looked suggestively at Didi, licked his lips, and asked, "How do you like your eggs in the morning?"

"Unfertilized." Didi had been armed and ready this time.

Ada let slip a snort as Jojo inhaled through his teeth before lowering his head in disappointment.

"You are cruel and sexy," Jojo said.

"Jojo, like always, this whole encounter has been low-key worrisome," Didi said.

"And mildly unsettling," Ada added under her breath.

Before he could say anything else, Didi yanked Ada's arm.

Jojo's time had expired. This was the cue for Ada to walk away and conclude the conversation.

"D! Weren't you a little harsh on Jojo back there?" Ada asked, walking in tandem with Didi.

"Aw, he'll get over it."

"I missed you," Ada said, letting the statement serve as a thank-you to Didi for saving her.

"Me too, A. Can you quit disappearing every summer? I can't handle the carnival of crazy in Clifton all by myself."

"Weren't you too busy punching people in the ring all summer? I saw the videos."

"Ey, you know the name—Diana Muay Thai Too Fly Mendoza. *Ya tu sabe!*" Didi shadowboxed a few jabs and hooks.

"Let's make this year count, D. Good times, good grades, good vibes," Ada proclaimed without breaking her stride.

"I'ma take two of those three, thank you."

"Alert." Ada's eyes popped out toward the flock of muscle-clad boys heading their way. "Twelve o'clock. Straight ahead."

"Okay, okay, just act cool, D." Didi's breath escaped in rapid, short bursts.

The boys weren't so much walking their way as they were gliding—suspended in air—toward them. The unaware aura of ripped jeans, fresh fades, uncreased sneakers, and whey protein coursing through their veins veered toward Ada and Didi.

"Hey, D." Mikey Fay nodded at Didi with minimal effort. The highly touted five-star basketball recruit had a first and last name that naturally had to be said together.

Ada clutched the straps on her bags tighter, her form contorted, and shyly acknowledged the boys as they came to an almost orchestrated stop to greet them.

"Hey, friend," Didi said.

"Friend?" Mikey Fay asked.

"*Friend* is a flexible word, papi."

The few boys surrounding Mikey Fay fixed their lips to silently exhale an inaudible *ooh* in reaction to Didi's witty response. Ada marveled at how seamlessly Didi piloted her way through flirtatious small talk with boys, always remaining one stride short of scandalous. The boys glanced at Mikey Fay. It was a sport to make fun of their own whenever one of them crashed and burned with a girl. Especially when it happened in front of them.

"Hey, Ada." A voice emanated from the pack of boys.

"Hi… Axel?" Ada pointed back at the boy. Her fingers formed a gun gesture, with her thumb protruding at a ninety-degree angle to her index finger.

Despite her brain's attempt to tell her thumb to retract, she found herself in a frozen pose, pointing at him like a used car salesperson in a '90s cable commercial, with an inflatable dancing blow-up man behind him.

"Oh, no. What do I do with my hands?" she muttered to herself. "Thumb. Recede. Come on. Okay, play it cool, A. Be cool. Like you are. Cool."

Her other hand willed itself over her other gun hand, in a vain attempt to lower her thumb. In trying to, indeed, *play it cool*, she raised and lowered her thumb repeatedly, slowly, like she was shooting air bullets at him.

"Ahh-ha, yeah, okay… I'm actually doing this," Ada said through gritted teeth.

"Are you… okay"? Axel asked.

"Yeah, no, yeah. I'm good."

"You're still shooting at me." He pointed to her hand.

"Oh. Yeah. I'm still…" She lowered her voice, slumping. "Still doing it." Ada quickly shook her hands out then placed them in her pockets.

Didi quickly intervened. "Axel, weren't you chillin' at the shore this summer too?"

"Yeah, I thought it would be nice to spend a summer away from here."

"You should have pulled up… to see what's good with Ada down there," Didi teased, slipping in a wink to Axel then tilting her chin suggestively at Ada.

"I would have, but I feared for my welfare. I didn't want to catch a stray bullet." Axel put both hands up like he was being apprehended while letting slip a satirical smile. Well built and toned, Axel had a Mediterranean complexion like Ada's. Loose curls, cooperative enough to be styled, accentuated his chiseled jawline.

"Well, New Jersey is now concealed carry. They no longer require you to, and I quote here, 'demonstrate a justifiable need to carry a handgun,'" Ada explained, expecting to draw a collective gasp of shock from her audience. None was forthcoming.

"No, A. Read the room. These boys ain't exactly the variety to pick up what you're putting down. We not dealing with PhD candidates here, *tu sabe*?" Didi tugged at Ada's arm for the second time that morning.

The boys looked on unassumingly. Or blissfully. Or a combination of both. They were busy mock punching and wrestling Mikey Fay down, accompanied by verbal jabs about crashing and burning with Didi.

"But it's important to highlight the—"

Didi cut Ada off, hooking her arm around hers and swiftly steering her out of the gathering between them and the boys. "Ey. You." Didi winked at Mikey Fay. "I'll catch you later."

"Bye, Axel." Ada shrugged and half waved.

As they walked away, she could hear them teasing Mikey Fay. "Day one, and he's already taking Ls."

"Did you…?" Ada robotically swiveled her head back to Mikey Fay and then to Didi. "When did this happen?"

"A few weeks ago, at Sam Johnson's birthday party. Just fooled around. Nothing crazy." A coy smirk formed on Didi's upper lip. She strutted a little more emphatically down the hall.

"Diana L. Mendoza. Well, I never…" Ada pretended to be flabbergasted.

"Those boys are children, A. You know how your girl gets down. You have to put them in their place from time to time. It's like a yo-yo with them. It swings one way, but you gotta remind them that it always swings back to you."

"Day one, and you're already preaching the gospel." Ada fluttered her hands to the heavens. "Thanks for the save back there with Jojo."

"Jojo's polycrisis for real. Most definitely needed a full send on that," Didi affirmed.

In her peripheral vision a few classrooms down from them, Ada spotted Ellen Liu holding court with a pack of aspiring social climbers. Ellen was wearing a sleeveless designer top Ada assumed to be European. Her petite frame could have been mistaken for fragility, but with her unquestioned confidence and the definition in her arms and legs, Ellen was a presence. Jaw-length hair emphasized her blushed cheeks. Her eyeliner, painted a precisely calculated distance from the eye's tip to just shy of her temples, punctuated what could have been an algorithmically designed portrait of someone with an elevated social status. Or a spoiled brat who was very rich.

"Man, I ain't ready for her yet, A." Didi nodded across the hall.

"In case you haven't heard, she was in Europe. Just in case you missed the first 6,347 posts on her socials." Ada braced herself, approaching Ellen like a platoon that suspected an imminent ambush. She forcibly altered her mood as soon as their line of sights collided. "Ellen! Hi! How was your summer?"

"What's good?" Didi barely raised her chin at Ellen.

"Oh…" Ellen scanned Ada from head to toe with just her eyes, keeping her head in a fixed position. "Hello, Ada. Diana." She abruptly pivoted away from the adoring junior-year girls encircling her. It was the girls' cue that their time with Ellen had expired, and Ada and Didi were on the clock.

Ellen Liu. The child of Gavin Liu. He'd made his money by purchasing distressed homes in lower socioeconomic neighborhoods, evicting the tenants who lived there, and redeveloping the buildings into high-end lofts and condos. Ellen was an unofficial spokesperson for every European fashion house. A woman of the people, she once claimed to Ada that she would readily wear discount clothing, only the thread count made her skin break out.

"And how did you two summer?" she asked with a slightly condescending emphasis on the word *summer*.

"Why we using *summer* as a verb?" Didi muttered.

Not waiting for them to answer, Ellen went on. "You two, let me tell you what I did. Barthelona. June. Private preview of Loewe's upcoming fall line. Naturally."

"Naturally," Didi said in a low monotone, skipping her brow up for a brief second.

"Barthe—Barcelona?" Ada asked. "Never been to Europe, Ellen. From the Jersey shore, to Clifton, to the Middle East. It's all I got."

"Oh, Dubai?" Ellen asked.

"Nope. Lebanon," Ada replied.

"Hmm," Ellen replied with a raised upper lip. She quickly shook off her disappointment to continue regaling them with her summer recap. "If you've spent time there, Ada, you would know. I spend so much time there, like, I wouldn't really go back if I didn't have to go to the influencer thing in Barthelona."

"I'll be sure to armchair tour the place on my next Google Street View vacation." Ada nudged Ellen, failing to provoke laughter or a comedic response from her.

"Honestly, you two never fail to underwhelm me." Ellen pointed at them with a limp wrist. "Anyway, you obvi got my text about the homecoming party at my house this Friday?" Ellen adjusted her hair behind her ear with just the tip of her finger. "You know, I do it big every fall. Like, valets and culinary concoctions inspired by countries most of these serfs couldn't locate on a map. But I am a woman of the people." She lowered her head to feign humility before raising it again. "And please don't wear that. Whatever you think is appropriate, just wear the opposite."

"Yeah, I gotta bounce to class. Malek's Shawarma after school?" Didi asked Ada while scrolling through her phone to ignore Ellen.

"We're going to do our best to be there, El," Ada said. "I gotta run to class too. Oh, and yes, definitely Malek's." Ada pointed at Didi.

Ellen raised her voice as they walked away down the bustling hallway. "The universe has big things for you, Ada. Just manifest it... or just, I don't know, don't be yourself, and it will all work out."

Later that evening, Ada called Didi.

"Day one down." She said on speaker as she perused her modest collection of Jordan 1's in her closet.

"And Ellen is already doing too much," Didi replied. "But yo, that shawarma was hitting after school."

"Malek's is definitely the spot," Ada quickly replied. The whole time at Malek's, she'd been wanting to ask Didi what was really on her mind but kept getting sidetracked with their usual gossip rundown of everyone they saw on day one.

"That toum extra was–" Didi started.

"D, I gotta ask you a question," Ada hurried to say. She took her phone off speaker and brought it to her ear. "This morning when I was leaving my driveway—I thought I saw someone standing on your lawn. Watching me."

"Like, this morning?"

"Yeah. It was like he was there... for me. Watching me or something."

"Um, I don't know, A. There's a lot of creeps up in Clifton. Maybe he was a drifter or something. Shady stuff in our town." Didi was a fast talker, but her reply came a little too fast.

"And then this morning, my parents were talking about a pendant. And someone—I can't remember his name—and an Agoge or something. It was all... strange."

Silence filled the line.

"Maybe it's nothing," Ada remarked, scrubbing off a scuff with her thumb from one of the sneakers at the bottom of her closet.

"But… I don't know. That's a bit concocted for my parents to be going into those details. My mom is an award-winning journalist who reports facts. She can't fabricate wild tales like the one I heard in their room this morning."

"I'm sure it's nothing, A,"

"Ada, *Habibi!*" Ada's mom called from downstairs.

"Ooh, gotta go. Journalist mom probably wants the dish on the first day of school."

"Aiight. I'll hit you tomorrow morning," Didi replied. "Peace."

When Ada hung up, she replayed her parents' conversation one last time before heading downstairs: *he said the Agoge would come alive when she nears her seventeenth birthday.* Her father's voice resonated in her memory.

As soon as she was about to head downstairs, the door was suddenly flung wide open, and her dad appeared. "Hey." He took one step inside Ada's room then closed the door behind him.

"Yeah, Dad?" Ada did her best to act cool.

"Stop going to Malek's without telling us first." He winked.

"How did you…?" Ada checked her phone, scrolling through her location tracking to ensure that it was turned off.

"I just know." He stepped out of the bedroom, leaving the door open.

CHAPTER 4
THE EPISODE

THE NEXT MORNING, Ada showered and threw on another vintage shirt—Dungeons and Dragons, this time—and drove Roman to school.

"Drop you off here?" Ada stopped a few yards away from the parking lot.

"Yep." He jumped out of the car and slammed the door. He grabbed his shoulder as if it were injured from the force he'd just exerted. "Thanks for the ride, Grapes!" he yelled as he walked away.

Ada's driving skills were still a work in progress—it normally took several attempts for her to back into a spot. She drove toward the far end of the parking lot, where the number of cars had thinned out just enough for her not to endure the trial of parking between two cars.

"Okay, Ada, just like we visualized. Here we go." Ada waved her fingers toward her face as if drawing whatever vibes she was putting out back into her. Her first attempt to back in between the lines was not successful. "Yeah, that's not going to work."

Fortunately, there was no one around to witness her pep talk. It was still relatively early, and there were no parked cars to her left or right yet. As she pulled in for the confirmatory second and final attempt, her fingers tingled. Then they went numb. The sensation spread to her toes. All at once, an invasion of voices, colors, faces, and indiscernible images flooded her. She was a spectator within her own mind, watching incoherent visuals and noises race by. She saw the faces of people she knew. She saw her dad holding an unblinking stare right at her, then her mom—a younger version of her. She looked pregnant. Then there was a woman, not young but exuding youth, with long, silky flowing hair and a linen robe adorned with embroidery. The woman was in a temple or a museum of some sort. Another image flashed of this same woman with a single tear streaking down her cheek, looking at a girl with eyes so purple and bright-white hair, holding a bloodied dagger.

Then it was over just as quickly as it had come on. The disjointed spell of Ada's delirium was swiftly replaced with a soothing light. A lone figure approached from the light and extended his arm toward Ada. His hands were coarse but comforting. She couldn't make out any more detail beyond recognizing the sunglasses folded into his V-neck shirt.

The light then instantly disappeared, and Ada awoke to find herself slouched back in the Blaze. A fading image of the boy persisted. Ada squinted a few times and blinked aggressively to will the image back to clarity. The spectacular light had radiated so brilliantly that it still loitered even after she'd opened her eyes. Ada could hardly concentrate on the person in front of her. When she finally looked up, the dissolving silhouette of the boy came into sharp focus. He was standing before her.

As the episode came to an end, the tingling in her fingers and toes dissipated, and she could feel her extremities once more. She adjusted her glasses, which were sitting off-kilter. The Blaze was still set in reverse, but the two rear tires of the SUV had jumped the curb in front of the parking spot and were pressed up on the curb, blocking the car from going any farther.

"Who are you…? What happened?" was all Ada could muster.

The boy unclicked her seat belt, placed her right hand over his shoulder, and lifted her out of the car. Although she was still in a daze, she was struck by the ease with which he picked her up. A small crowd of students had gathered around Ada's car. Gripped with embarrassment, she averted the gaze of onlooking students. A few passersby surveyed the half-mounted car on the lawn.

The boy gently lowered her onto the grass by the curb. Ada was now sitting with her feet resting on the asphalt and her backside on the faded public school grass. Her hands were placed at her sides to brace her from falling over. The boy towered above her.

He crouched on one knee, at Ada's eye level, and interrogated her with urgent attention. "You need to tell me what happened."

"I saw... I..." Ada pressed her tongue to the roof of her mouth, preventing any more words from escaping. "Nothing. I just blacked out. I'll see the school nurse."

He leaned in and glared at her. "Listen to me, Ada. You were nearly convulsing. What happened? Did you see anything?" he asked quietly, glancing around at the remaining onlookers.

A pendant slipped out from behind his V-neck as he bent a little closer. It had a diagonal bar with three vertical lines cutting through. It was as big as a thumbnail, but there was something alluring about it—it didn't shine but instead emitted a vivid, invisible beam. The pendant was drawing her closer to the boy. He gently placed his hand on her shoulder to reestablish the space between the two of them then quickly tucked his necklace under his shirt collar.

Ada had by now somewhat regained her senses. She could see him clearly. It was Axel. The same Axel she'd had that awkward encounter with a day earlier in the hall.

"I told you. I just blacked out. I don't know. I just blacked out. And I'm fine, by the way. Thanks for asking." She became hyperaware of her gestures, expressions, and breathing. Her right leg began to tap quickly.

"You don't seem fine. Now, I need you to describe what happened." The reflection of his pendant played on his face.

The crowd began to disperse. A group of remaining boys called out in their direction. "Yo, Axel. Let's go, man. You're gonna be late for the players-coaches meeting before the welcome assembly."

Axel initially ignored their calls but finally said to Ada, "We'll pick this up later. You need to be careful from now on."

He quickly altered his demeanor from urgently demanding an answer to cool and unconcerned as soon the awaiting group's attention fell on him.

"Um, thanks?" Ada remarked to a departing Axel, who had already turned his back to her and was making his way over to his friends. She shook herself off and sprang back up. Reaching out to close the Blaze's door, she noticed her phone lighting up with a message.

Mama: *Hayete how's school? Everything OK?*

Ada: *Everything is great so far! Just catching up with friends.*

CHAPTER 5

ASSEMBLY REQUIRED

ADA: *Where you at? Call me ASAP!*

Ada punched her message with nervous, twitching fingers then locked her phone. After barely a few moments had passed, she unlocked her phone to text Didi again.

Ada: *Oy, call me. Yalla. Polycrisis.*

Didi: *Calling you now.*

Ada's phone lit up again. She swiped to answer and skipped the formalities. "Didi, okay something absolutely wild, like beyond belief, just happened. Like more beyond belief than when I faked a bicycle injury in front of Tommy Carlucci's house hoping he'd come out to rescue me, only to have his mom come out in Cookie Monster pajama pants to make sure it wasn't on her property for liability purposes while he stayed inside playing video games."

"Tommy Carlucci, the one whose mom would drop him off in February in basketball shorts while crushing one of them extra-large energy drinks?"

"Okay, well, whatever. Listen, the wildest thing just happened."

"What happened?" Didi asked.

"You're not gonna believe me."

"Seriously, what went down? Did you sell photos of yourself in bunny suits on the internet, but you accidentally showed your face in one of the pictures, and now we gotta figure out how to get them back?"

"What? Why would I? Is there even money in that? No, listen. I'm freaking out here."

"Okay, okay, *cuentame*."

"So I get to school, right. I pull into a spot. Parked it between the lines, in case you were wondering."

"I was. Proceed."

"Then boom. I black out. I see all these things. My mom pregnant when she was younger, my dad, another woman, then someone else, real creepy vibes, who looked like she stabbed her with a knife. I don't know… then I woke up to Axel of all people."

"Axel. Like the football player you air gunned yesterday?" Didi asked.

"No need to recall that tragic incident, but yes. That Axel. He was grilling me about what I saw. Like he knew it would happen. Or he knew more than he let on."

An awkward pause filled the line between them.

"Didi?" Ada asked. "Hello?"

"Yeah, my bad, I'm just busy with, you know… anyway, listen. Meet me at the welcome assembly thing, and we'll figure it out," Didi stammered. "Also, who does a welcome assembly the second day?"

"One, valid point. Two, um, okay, I guess," Ada replied, not sure what to make of Didi's response.

As she made her way inside, Ada consciously avoided meeting the curious stares of other students as she navigated the hallways, occasionally glancing up at the pockets of students gathered. After her embarrassing parking episode, she expected chatter, mumblings, occasional pointing, and giggles. To her comfort, the other students barely noticed her.

The ringing of the bells reverberated through the school speakers. The assembly was about to begin. She hunched her bag a little tighter and picked up her pace, walking briskly toward the gymnasium that doubled as the assembly hall. Ada took a deep breath and exhaled to shake out the images of events she had either witnessed or experienced. They felt real—as though she was living in them. With one final inhalation, she composed herself to a manageable state and entered the gymnasium. It was loud and brimming with commotion. Rowdy students jostled to sit beside their friends, while annoyed students with no interest in engaging in the social gymnastics of high school were sitting alone, impatiently waiting for the assembly to begin so it could finish. Then there were the self-anointed fashionistas at the top bleachers, amalgamating, showing off their clothes and accessories. It was a scene.

"It kind of looks like my socials algorithm. I'm not proud of it." Axel's voice beamed through.

"What?" Ada hadn't noticed him on the way in. She'd been too busy skimming the cast of characters at the assembly while trying to look like someone who had not just had an out-of-body experience.

"The... whatever that situation is up there." He nodded toward the upper quadrant of the assembly, where the fashionistas were still bragging to one another about their summer acquisitions.

"Was I that obvious?" Ada asked rhetorically.

"You have a terrible poker face." Axel paused before fixing a stern gaze on Ada. "We still need to talk about what happened back there," he whispered guardedly.

Even though he was the one seeking answers, Axel asked in a way that suggested the answer lay with him. Like he was the guardian of a breadcrumb of info about what had happened to Ada earlier. She bit her tongue and slowly closed her mouth.

The timely sighting of Didi peering down at her from the bleachers with a mischievous grin presented the perfect exit strategy. Ada bolted toward Didi instantly, leaving Axel on an island by himself.

"Good talk...or lack thereof," she heard Axel mutter behind her.

"Okay, A, I see you putting in work with Axel. Check you out —leveling up for real." Didi elbowed Ada, who had nestled in beside her. "What was that about, anyway?"

"We need to talk. Like, ASAP," Ada replied through gritted teeth.

"Aw, Ada is flustered. I can see how this would be an entirely new experience for you, Ada. You know, with boys of a certain prestige taking a sudden interest." An eavesdropping Ellen injected herself into the conversation.

"Ellen, what are you even wearing? You look like you supposed to be at a racetrack betting on a horse called Mystic Sunrise or some ish," Didi said, circling her finger at Ellen's loud yellow jacket and matching beret.

"Um, excuse me, this is couture from Spain. God, New Jersey is so proletariat." Ellen pinched the brim of her yellow hat.

"Aren't you from Newark?" Winter Johnson said, springing in from directly behind them.

"Why you sit with us, anyway? Why ain't you sitting with Ally Lindsay and them Barbies up there?" Didi swept her gaze to the fashionistas at the top bleacher.

"And be seen mingling with off-the-rack bargain hunters? No thanks. At least you own your clearance-rack look."

"Winter! I didn't see you on the way in." Ada contorted herself towards Winter, then quickly turned back and leaned into Didi. "I really, *really* need to talk to you," she force-whispered.

"After this assembly," a stone-faced Didi replied.

Winter, in the row of bleachers behind Ada, appeared to have no interest joining the discussion. She remained transfixed on the microphone placed at the center court of the gym. An awkward silence ensued before she acknowledged Ada's pleasantries.

"Nice to see you too, Ada," she said without reciprocating a smile. Winter held still, keeping her gaze on the center court.

"And I live in Montclair now, Winter. You should visit sometime. It would be a welcome change from, you know…" Ellen swirled her hand in the air. "This."

"Stop big timin' Montclair like you're from there. You just moved there junior year, and you're, like, the only Asian person in the area," Didi said.

"Okay, Didi, easy on the racial overtones. We have a lot of different people in Montclair. And, like, my family's always embraced diversity. My dad even donated to the Obama campaign once, Winter."

Didi jerked away from Ellen, cringing, while Ada grimaced with embarrassment and said, "Ellen, really?"

Winter shifted her eyes to Ellen without moving her head then blankly responded, "Please thank your dad for the endorsement."

Ellen, flustered, changed the subject. "So, my party this Friday. Winter, obvi you should come too. You never come out to these things."

Ada threw Didi a glance and flicked her brows towards the exit. After her episode in the parking lot, the last thing she cared to talk about was Ellen's party.

"Didi and Ada, you can come too. Just, please, don't embarrass me. Especially you, Ada. So *pauvre*," Ellen muttered before returning to coolly texting on her phone. "Mikey Fay will be there." She melodically dragged the name out in a high pitch.

"Whatever. I'll see," Didi said.

Winter did not respond to Ellen's invitation. She continued to watch the clock straight ahead of them. Meanwhile, Didi gave Ada a questioning look.

It wasn't Ada's racing mind that caused her to fall silent; something else was happening. The sensation from earlier in the parking lot was creeping up on her. Again. That familiar numbing took up residence in her fingers and hands. A sonic wave of high-pitched frequency pierced her. The muscles in her neck tensed up. She was jolted by a shock that surged through her spine.

Confident that this was not happening in her head, she asked Didi, "Do you hear that?"

Before anyone could answer, the shrill sound was muted. There was utter silence. Everything went still. The entire gym slowed to serenity. Ada took it all in with a heightened consciousness. She inhaled deeply, only hearing her breathing.

It was not fear or anxiety that gripped her—only a peaceful feeling. She looked at the girls sitting with her—Didi, Ellen, even Winter. Every blink, movement, and speck of dust encircling them was slowed down. The bustle of the welcome assembly stopped. Nothing but Ada and the sedated stirring of the staff and students remained. Her vision gracefully swept to the far end of the gym, to the upper-right corner where a group of ninth graders were sitting. Three students came into clear focus. She could now see every detail, from the small YKK written on one of the boys' zipper jackets to the hair follicles growing from another's peach-fuzz mustache.

And again, it all stopped just as quickly as it had come on. The competing sounds of the assembly rushed back to Ada. The ninth-grade boys at the far corner were now a blurred image. Principal McGinley's stern instructions for students to find their seats echoed all the way to her. A few moments earlier, Ada had felt like she was alone on an island. Now she was hurled back into the reality she'd stepped out from.

The girls said nothing. Their mouths weren't moving and neither were their hands, but she could hear them all at once. They were not speaking over each other. Each girl's voice could be heard distinctly despite them talking simultaneously.

Ellen: "Oh my God, what is wrong with her? Seriously, she shouldn't even come to the party if she's gonna keep acting weird like this."

Didi: "Mikey Fay, where you sitting? I've been trying to get at you all morning."

Overwhelmed by the influx of competing voices, Ada raised her palm toward the girls. "Stop! Everybody, please just stop. Ellen, if you don't want me to go, then just say it. Didi, he's sitting over there, three rows down." She gestured toward Mikey Fay, seated next to a few of his teammates.

Didi and Ellen fell silent, frozen in embarrassment, their faces flushed with confusion. Ada covered her mouth, now questioning whether they'd even said anything to her. Maybe these notions—and perhaps that was all they were, notions—had never been spoken.

"I didn't say anything, Ada." Ellen quickly looked at her phone as if to make sure she hadn't unintentionally sent a text to Ada that was meant for someone else.

Didi gave Ada a deliberating look. Winter pulled her eyebrows down to give Ada a thorough once-over. Ada gasped behind her still covered mouth. She was again conscious of her every move.

"I... I need to go." Ada gathered her backpack and rushed down the bleacher aisle in an uncoordinated stumble.

"Really, Ada?" one disgruntled student said when she brushed past him, nearly knocking over his phone.

Ada apologized mid-stumble. "I'm sorry, Jojo. I have to go. I love your sweater!"

The assembly had commenced. The portly Principal McGinley had taken his position at center court, facing the twelfth-grade section, and was rolling through the formalities of welcoming the students back. Ada's sprint-like departure caught the attention of a few students. She darted down the aisle in general direction of Principal McGinley, who seemed unbothered by this mad child wildly flailing her arms while running down the steps.

Ada secured her way to the bathroom without bumping into more students. Exhausted from failing to piece together what had just happened, she replayed the events in her mind, crashing into each other in no particular order. She briefly thought about calling her mom or dad. There was nothing her younger brother could do for her. She did not want to burden him. It was just her, alone in the bathroom with the pervasive scent of Pine-Sol cleaner.

CHAPTER 6
GONNA NEED A MINUTE HERE

THE GIRLS' bathroom a little past eight thirty on this Wednesday morning was the only place Ada found solitude—away from the visions, sounds, episodes, questions, internal debates, Ellen, Axel, and even Didi. She took a moment to rest both hands on the bathroom sink, her head slouched in submission. The dash from the bleachers to the bathroom, coupled with the compounded ordeals of the morning, left her spent. Drops escaping from the tip of her chin landed on the sink and streaked down. As she brought her hand up to wipe her forehead, the bathroom door cracked slightly open. Two low voices from the other side could be heard.

"You can't go in there," whispered one.

"Listen, you just stay here and make sure no one enters," retorted the other.

"Fine," the first voice said. "But if I see someone coming through, I'm going in. You're not about to get her caught up in no trouble if someone catches the two of you in there."

"Listen, lady, calm down. No one is getting in trouble. You think I like to hang out in the girls' bathroom to console distressed girls? Stay here. I'm going in."

A whiff of stale air pushed through the door as it swung open. Ada remained hunched over the sink. It was Axel with another perfectly timed intrusion. He inspected the bathroom stalls for any unwanted listeners. Then he took a hard, pronounced swallow, like someone reluctant to speak. With a last scan around the bathroom, Axel pressed his lips together, shook his head, and ran his hands through his hair.

"What the hell was that?" he asked.

There was something both annoying and sympathetic about the way he stood upright and placed his hands on his hips.

"Listen to me," he continued. "You're going to get yourself killed. Along with many others. I need you to tell me everything."

Ada failed to gather the strength to pick her head up. She remained slumped over the sink, with both hands resting on its edge for support. Her breaths were more deliberate. Only the ominous dripping sound from a loose faucet and a muffled scraping from the air vents occupied the space between them.

"Okay, if you're not going to speak, then I will." Axel stepped toward Ada. "You're not imagining it. Whatever happened to you this morning is real. What you're going through is real." He closed the gap between them. "You are different. You were born different. Sometime around September thirteenth, you will start to realize the full potential of who you are. It's important that—"

"September thirteenth?" Ada spoke into the sink.

"Yes, your birthday. Happy early birthday, by the way." Axel said.

With her head still hung over the sink, as if hoping to find a clue in its corners and crevices, her eyes danced from one side to another. "How do you know what's happening to me?" Ada muttered, still not lifting her head.

"I'm...still not sure. But I just know you're different."

Ada decidedly released her hands from the sink and used what little energy she had to stand up straight before rotating to face this boy who she'd only spoken to for the first time the previous day.

"Who are you?" she asked in exhaustion.

"I am a Senazi - no different from humans in many respects. Yet different in many others."

"What... what is a Senazi? Are you ... European or something?" Ada massaged her temples to dispel the confusion.

Axel raised his hand abruptly to keep Ada from interrupting again. "You have something inside you. And the First Rank wants it. They've sent the Infernum to Earth to retrieve it. The more of these episodes you have, the more exposed you become." Axel shifted a little closer. He brushed his coarse hair back and rubbed his face with his palm.

"Who? I don't have anything." Ada turned over her palms to exhibit that she had no information to surrender.

"Yes, you do. The Agoge. Brave Senazis from our fallen Republic risked their lives to get it here. I don't know why or how, but you were chosen. After the fall of the Republic, Nygaard established the First Rank, and he has ruled Unitas ever since." Axel hesitated. "You're not the 'chosen one' but, you know, like, chosen for this."

"The Agoge?" Ada thought back to the conversation between her parents.

"I know it's a lot, but you have to – " he started.

"How do you know about any of this?"

"You are the host of the Agoge, Ada."

"You're not giving me much here," Ada said, flailing her hands and bobbing her head forward to elicit more details from him.

"Shortly before Chancellor Nygaard came to power and committed mass atrocities, Genuit and others retrieved the Agoge from him and fled here with it to escape Unitas. Ever since, Nygaard has been obsessed with finding it."

Ada jumped at hearing the name her parents had uttered the previous morning in their bedroom. "Genuit. How do you know that name?"

"Every Senazi knows Genuit. But there's a lot I don't know, Ada."

"You seem to know enough. Whereas I don't know who you people are. Or what this Unitas is. But if this Chancellor wants this Agoge, let him have it. I want no part of this." Ada skipped past Axel toward the bathroom exit, with her mind set on leaving.

"It's not that simple. If you don't take this seriously, you will die."

Ada stopped one step short of the door. "So, yeah, no pressure," she said over her shoulder.

"You're making light of this because you don't think it's true. Whatever you're going through is real, Ada. It's real—"

Axel was interrupted by a sequence of aggressive knocks on the bathroom door. Within seconds, it swung open again, and Didi rushed in. "Quick, you and you. Everyone's dipped from the assembly. Some girls are rollin' up. Axel, either split or find a spot to hide ASAP!"

The fable Ada had heard left her too bewildered to improvise— or even move. Axel seemed unfazed by the impending herd of female teenagers who would soon bulldoze through the bathroom.

"You need to go home right now and wear your Aegis. We can help you so long as you wear this." He untucked his pendant from underneath his shirt, clutching the chain just above the pendant itself. The diagonal bar intersecting the three vertical bars swayed from side to side. "We can try to protect you for now. Your parents will know. They will know."

"Aegis..." Ada recalled her parents' conversation again, this time glancing at Didi, who showed no surprise at Axel's cryptic advice. "How do you know my parents' name?"

Didi seemed both nervous and composed. Her eyes rested on Axel while she nibbled on her lower lip. Axel, meanwhile, gave a deliberate exhalation like someone about to engage in physical combat with the horde of invaders at the castle door.

The footsteps of approaching students blended incongruously with shrill laughter. At any minute, girls would walk into the bathroom to find Ada, Didi, and Axel inside. Ada was convinced the pack about to enter would assume the worst. The fear of being caught with a boy in the Clifton High School bathroom was more compelling than the tales of Nygaard and the Senaz that Axel had just described. Her current situation was more real. More imminent.

"I've been saying it." Didi wagged her finger at Axel. "Ooh, I've been saying it. If you drag my girl into a mess, there's gonna be problems. And you don't want these problems. Don't none of this matter right now. Everyone is coming through, and they're gonna see me, you, and Ada and start assuming all sorts of wild things."

Didi squarely faced off with Axel, who, instead of meeting her hostility, was checking himself out in the mirror directly above one of the sinks. He whistled a tune and adjusted a loose strand of hair. A moment before, he'd been visibly anxious. Now he was effortlessly playing it cool, continuing to absorb his own reflection. He idly finger combed the prickly strands of hair along the side of his head.

Time was not on Ada's side, so she went with the first reasonable thing that came to mind. She flicked her chin to Axel to hide in the stall. "You need to get in there before you're caught."

Axel shrugged. "I really don't see why this is necessary." He tucked his pendant back in, entered the bathroom stall and closed the door behind him. The distinct clicking of the lock gave Ada and Didi temporary relief. "But sure. This is somehow less embarrassing than being caught out there," he said from inside the stall.

A band of giggling girls barged into the bathroom. It was Ellen and a few of her leachers. They stumbled in, howling while shuffling around Ellen, holding her phone out for them to see something. Too consumed to notice the presence of anyone else, Ellen pointed at the phone, wriggling with an arrogant laugh.

"Oh my God, look at her rumbling down the stairs like an escaped hog. She's so weird," one of the girls commented.

The entourage froze as soon as Ellen raised her eyes to Ada and Didi. The three girls recoiled when Didi snatched the phone from Ellen's hand, their expressions transformed from animated giggles to shock and back to forced smiles. Didi and Ada glanced at Ellen's phone playing a video of Ada's clumsy dash down the bleachers and out of the assembly.

"Look, she didn't post it or anything. Come on, she wouldn't do that to Ada," one of the girls said defensively.

"You." Didi studied the girl who had committed to come to the defense of Ellen. "Who's this social climber?" she asked Ellen.

"Are you girls serious?" Didi seethed at them. "You know, Ada might let all this nonsense with what Ellen's little ducklings say about her slide. But not me. You and you and you—beat it."

Didi's reproach compelled the regiment surrounding Ellen to scurry out of the bathroom then whipped the phone back at Ellen. One raised her palm in an unconvincing display of grievance before leaving. Ada fixed a distracted stare on Ellen, who didn't leave with them, then glanced back at the corner stall. Ellen followed Ada's gaze. She glared at Ada for a clue and scrutinized Didi, holding the gaze of each, and occasionally breaking away to inspect the room. Ada consciously tried to dodge Ellen's prying eyes.

"Wait, is somebody here?" Ellen tsk-tsked. "What are you girls up to? Who's in there?"

Her finely tuned radar for juicy tidbits on full alert, Ellen took one deliberate step in the direction of the stall. If Axel was discovered, Ellen would rerun this episode to anyone willing to listen. Over and over again.

"Listen, Ellen, it's not what you think." Ada hastily slid between the stall and Ellen, obstructing her path.

"It really isn't," Axel said, his voice torpedoing from the stall, breaking the short-lived silence.

Ellen's entire face sprang into an intrigued grin. Didi pinched her nose and shook her head. Ada resigned herself to staring at the ceiling in defeat.

Axel panned into view as the door eased open. He was still adjusting the belt on his pants. He neatly tucked his shirt in and flushed the toilet. Ellen, who wore a look of neither shock nor satisfaction, just tilted her head, perplexed.

"Okay, wait. Did you actually go to the bathroom while waiting in there?" Ada asked.

"I mean, it's so much cleaner in here than in the boys' bathroom," Axel casually said.

Ellen wore a look of disgust. "Yes, okay, so I have questions here. One, who opens the door and then flushes?" She scrunched her face. "Two, what are you doing here?"

"I had to go. I didn't know how long you and the tribe of girls suckling at your social bosom would be in here." He waved his hand at the door the girls had scurried through. Then he clapped his hands as if to signify the conclusion of this gathering and made his way to the sink. "My work here is done." He broke his stride and tapped Ellen's shoulder with a yet unwashed hand.

"Did you just… and right after you…. oh my God, eww, wash your hands." Ellen gave a shiver of horror while Axel barked a laugh, grinning in her direction. As did Didi and Ada. There was something about the precision with which he'd manufactured Ellen's reaction that they found enjoyable.

"It's all love, El. All love." He snickered, washing and drying off his hands. Taking a crumpled tissue paper and mimicking a dibble motion, he assumed the tone of a play-by-play commentator. "At six-foot-one, from Clifton High School, Axel Mosley." He then pretended to jostle for position with Ellen, spun around Ada, and finally sidestepped Didi before launching the makeshift ball straight into the garbage bin. "Bang!" he exclaimed, raising both hands in a gesture of victory. "It's been a pleasure, ladies. I shall see myself out. Ada, do you accept gift cards for your birthday?" Axel turned to Ada, shielded his face from Ellen, and mouthed, "Go home." Then, he flung the door open and strode out of the bathroom.

"When I die, I want to come back as a guy." Didi pointed to the door that was swinging shut. "Zero self-awareness and supreme self-confidence. I can get with that."

When Ellen didn't engage, Didi clenched her jaw. Ada curled her fingers into a fist and then flared them out as wide as she could. One way or another, they would have to negotiate their way out of Axel's discovery in the bathroom—by Ellen, of all people.

"Relax. I've had my fair share of scandals. Ada, you never mentioned anything to anyone about the time you saw me with... you know." Ellen flicked her wrist to wipe away a past memory.

Didi raised a curious eyebrow.

"Um, excuse me? What the hell is a mansion party?" Ellen swiped her hat off with one hand, shifting her attention to her phone in the other. She was visibly upset. Scrolling frantically, she scanned the corners of her screen. "Someone just forwarded me this message they got from a Lamia Melaina. Who is that?" Ellen was now speaking to her phone. "Twelve-thousand-square-foot house. Catered. Okay, big deal. Valet," she rapidly spat with each scroll of the thumb. "Whatever. I did it first... it's the party of the year. Ditch your Friday plans and tell only your best friends." She continued to skim through her phone, barely pausing. "Do either of you know who this girl is?"

Didi giggled.

"*Mira*, maybe it's one of your underlings. Like a new anti-hero?" Didi asked, half amused, half uninterested.

"And she's having it this Friday! Like, everybody knows Friday is the day of my party," Ellen continued, ignoring Didi's sarcastic commentary.

A slight vibration of her phone rippled in Ada's jeans pocket. She read the notification with curious interest then looked up at Didi, who was also perusing something on her phone. They glanced at each other to confirm that they were reading the same message. Both girls then shot a glance at Ellen, who had returned her phone to her purse. She was standing before them, left foot tapping, arms crossed, impatiently waiting to be clued in. Ada hummed quietly to herself. Didi coughed to clear her throat.

"Ah, Ellen, did you get an invite?" Ada cautiously asked.

"What invite? Is this another one of your weird Kigurumi Society events? It was a hard no the first time."

Didi glanced down at her phone again then hit Ellen with a

satisfied grin. "You didn't get the invite, did you, El?" Didi said, repeating Ada's question, this time with intensified indulgence and a joyful smirk. "Talking about her exclusive influencer parties in Barthelona, and she can't get no love right here in Jersey." Didi pinched her fingers and brought them up over her head to pretend to wear a fancy hat like Ellen. "It seems our new friend—actually, no, Clifton High School's new friend—sent us an invite and… wait, refresh your phone." Didi stretched her neck out and perched over Ellen's phone, wide-eyed. "Checks notes. Nope. And you ain't get one. Oh, *pobrecita*! Or should I say, *pobrethita*."

Ada lifted her shoulders and burrowed her head into her neck. She toyed nervously with her fingers. "I mean, she's not our friend, El. We don't even know who she is." Ada extended her palms to Ellen in consolation.

"Oh, but she is our friend, fam. This is what equality feels like! We are all now as cool and exclusive as the great Ellen Liu. It's like we're all living that communism. Everybody is on the same social status." Didi was unrelenting.

"Why? I try so hard every year!"

The intensity of what she heard caused Ada to freeze. Didi was still savoring the moment, with both hands on her hips, her shoulders visibly bouncing up and down from laughter. Meanwhile, Ada studied Ellen further. The force of what Ellen had said—or what Ada had heard in Ellen's voice—cut through her, but Ellen's lips never moved. They never uttered those words. It was as though it came from nowhere but from everywhere all at once.

She looked at the ceilings and walls of the bathroom for another source of audio – a speaker, an intercom, something – then to Didi, who was still enjoying herself at Ellen's expense, and to Ellen again, only to find a blank expression on her face.

Ada shuffled back toward the door, unsure if she wanted to leave or stay. When both Didi and Ellen finally noticed her slow migration toward the exit, Ada said, "I…I have to get to class."

"I'ma go ahead and RSVP for this mansion party… wait, Ada, hold on!" Didi called to Ada, who was now halfway out of the bathroom, with the door swinging closed. She hurried to catch up to Ada. "Oh man, did you see her face in there?"

Ada couldn't match Didi's energy. She couldn't shake Ellen's voice. What she'd heard had been clear. So was the impact of the raw emotional force with which she'd felt Ellen's plea: "Why! I try so hard every year!" Ada shifted her jaw from side to side, replaying those words in her head.

She reached out to grasp Didi's arm, bringing her to an abrupt halt and leaned in close. "Didi, I think I heard Ellen say something…" Ada searched for an appropriate way to frame what she was about to say next. "But she didn't say it."

"What's that mean?" Didi responded without the slightest bit of presumption.

"I mean, I think I may have read her mind. Or her thoughts. Or her. I don't know." Ada took a deep breath and held it, waiting for Didi's reaction. "I know it sounds crazy, but I felt what she was saying. It's like she was deeply hurt. Like she was calling out to be heard."

Didi shook out whatever amusement that had followed her from the bathroom. She focused on Ada. "*Mira*, you need to listen to Axel and go home and ask for that pendant."

"Are you not listening? I heard her say something, but she didn't actually say it. Why is none of this fazing you?"

Didi clicked her tongue and formed a straight line with her lips. "I mean, it could have been anybody. You know how they be talking all loud in the hallway anyway." She avoided eye contact with Ada.

"No, I know what I heard. It was her voice. At this point, I don't know if I'm mentally deranged or telepathic. Either possibility is one I'm not prepared for."

"Listen, just go home. Message me if you need anything."

Ada blew out a puff of air and swayed her head from side to side. Finally relenting, she said, "Okay, okay. I'm gonna head home. I'll text you later."

"You need a ride home, or you good?"

"No, I'm good," Ada replied.

Didi leaned skeptically closer.

"No, really, I'm good." Ada repeated.

"For real, call me if you need anything." Didi peeked up at the clock then reluctantly departed.

Ada's head sagged as she darted through the rush of students hurrying to class. She was counting the hallway floor tiles, unwittingly repeating herself. "I'm not freaking out and it's not real."

"What's not real, Ada?"

Winter's question summoned Ada back to alertness. She hadn't realized she'd crossed the entire east wing.

"Oh, Winter, hi."

"Where are you going? Shouldn't you be in class?" Winter inquired with a hint of curiosity. Her lips tightened in the way they always did when she was awaiting an answer.

Ada watched the bustling of students coming and going. She opened her mouth but couldn't bring herself to say anything.

"You ran off quite abruptly back there in the assembly. Everything okay?" Winter asked.

Ada felt Winter's presence towering above her. "Yeah, I just, I didn't feel so well. That extra-garlic shawarma… you know how it goes." Ada shifted back from Winter's orbit.

"I don't know how it goes. Never had one," Winter said.

Not that Ada had expected her to understand. Their rare conversations revolved exclusively around school and extracurriculars.

"I'll take you to Malek's one day. It will change your life," Ada proposed, seizing on the small crack of a window left open by Winter to talk about anything other than her ordeal.

There was always something different about Winter. She was aloof but not unapproachable. Yet she was always scrupulous. She gave the impression that the intellectual bar was set high when it came to getting her approval. Ada never mistook her stiffness for arrogance. It was more of a silent confidence—a sense that Winter had always set her sights on a goal beyond the reach of fellow classmates and would do whatever was necessary to achieve that goal.

"So, you're not going to AP Bio now?" Winter asked.

"Ah, no. But do you know if they released an online syllabus for the class yet?" Given the events of the day, Ada was hard-pressed to convince herself of the importance of a syllabus, but she couldn't exactly talk about reading minds and whatever backstory Axel had dumped on her earlier.

Winter raised an eyebrow as she continued to scrutinize Ada, who grew uneasy. She self-consciously noticed the way her arms were folded, her posture, the way her feet were positioned, and the what-do-I-do-with-my-hands way she was fidgeting. All Ada could bring herself to do was crack a forced smile.

"Yes, the syllabus is available," Winter finally replied, still concentrating on Ada.

Ada wondered whether Winter even noted her answer or if she was merely ticking the box to get to the next question.

Before Winter could resume her cross-examination, Ada excused herself abruptly. "I gotta go. See you later. We'll get that shawarma."

"Wait, Ada..." Winter called out as Ada sped out of the school.

CHAPTER 7
BACK AT THE HOUSE

In the Blaze, Ada pulled up to the house. She rushed out of the car and into her home. "Mama? Hello?"

"Ada?" Her mom's voice drifted up from the basement.

"Mama, I need to talk to you." Ada rushed down the stairs to meet her mother in her basement office, where she was typing furiously on her computer.

"Ada, *habibi*, you're home." Her mom was glued to her screen, focused on a draft of a document with comments in the margins. "Sorry, I had my headphones in. I have to submit this editorial by —" She abruptly swiveled her chair toward Ada, eyeing her curiously. "Why are you home?"

"Mama, listen, you need to tell me everything. Is all this real? This morning I... I mean, yesterday, I heard you and Dad talking about the Aegis and an Agoge. I thought I heard things today at school. Like it was all in slow motion."

The entire drive home, her brain had been racing through what she would say to her mother—how she would break down what had happened in a coherent, structured manner. That was her plan. But now that the moment had come, she lobbed a disjointed set of facts at her mother without any real beginning, middle, or end.

In the drawn-out silence following Ada's word-salad, her mom looked like she was contemplating something. She tilted her head one way then in the opposite direction, as if considering different courses of action. Finally, she arose from her office chair and ascended the stairs.

"Wait, Mama, can you say something?" Ada trailed behind her mother, tugging at the space between them, all the way to the master bedroom on the second floor.

Her mom opened the bedroom closet. The top rack was neatly organized, with three metal boxes for storing accessories and household items. She stood on her tiptoes, fully extending her hands and fingers up toward the back of the elevated rack. Her hand rummaged through what her vision could not reach. Zeina's search grew more hurried. More panicked. She grasped up the first box and hurled it onto the bed. Then she flung the second one somewhere behind her. It landed near the contents of the first box, which were now scattered on the bed and the rug. She tossed the third and last box over her head, and it bounced off the side of the bed and onto the floor. Zeina fell to her knees and shifted from box to box, throwing random objects out.

"No, no, *keef, mabifham,* it must be here." Zeina's voice shook. She balled up her hand and lightly tapped the floor, looking around the room as if waiting for something to materialize out of thin air.

"Mama, what is it?" Ada nervously asked.

"Take that lamp down and bring that nightstand over." Zeina pointed to the corner of the room.

Before Ada could process her mother's command, Zeina rushed to the nightstand and lifted it, causing it to fall onto the bed, releasing a puff of dust that had collected on the bulb. Zeina ungracefully thumped the nightstand onto the floor by the closet and hoisted herself onto its base, bringing her eye level with the now empty closet rack.

"How could this be? *Ya rabbeh* it was just here. That's impossible. We took it out yesterday. Where are the other papers? There were stacks of them." Zeina stared into the vacant space.

"Took what out?" Ada's anxiety mirrored her mother's. Stiffening, she folded her arms and clenched her jaw pensively.

Zeina broke into tears. She could barely collect herself to speak. "It was here. It was just here. Where could it have gone?" She was breathing heavily while continuing to rummage through random drawers and corners of the bedroom.

"You're talking about the Aegis, aren't you?" Ada rested her hand on her mother's shoulder.

"We knew this day would come. You have to wear it. It's the only way to protect you. Marcel told me they will stop at nothing to find you." Zeina's despairing voice trailed off. She failed to catch her breath as she kept searching for the pendant.

"What have you and Dad been hiding from me?" Ada asked, tilting back slightly to leave enough space for the weight of her mother's response. "These past two days, I've been piecing little truths brick by brick. There must be another brick to all this."

"*Leish*. What happened to you today? How do you know about all this?" Zeina covered her mouth with her hands.

"Look, right now, I don't care about the Aegis. I just need to know why no one told me this before and what else I need to know. What is going on?" Ada held her breath, waiting for an answer.

"I didn't… I don't know. *Maba'ref*, I didn't think this would be real." Zeina resumed her frantic search.

"Real? I wish this was all a fictional tale. I really do. But the line between reality and fiction is starting to feel a little blurry here." Ada lowered and raised each hand like she was balancing a scale.

"It's not fiction. It's true. You are not the only one going through this, Ada. We have been living through this ordeal since I was pregnant with you."

"Okay, Mama, some details would help so I'm not—"

There was a knock on the front door. The ominous tapping carried through the house.

Ada's hand shot out to stop her mom from leaving the room. "Stay calm. I'll see who it is."

Zeina sidestepped Ada. "I'm coming with you."

Ada hurried out the bedroom but instinctively slowed to a tiptoeing pace as soon as she reached the staircase. She took the stairs lightly, gripping the railing tighter than usual. Her mother followed closely behind her. At the bottom, they took a deep breath and peeked their heads out and around the wall separating them from the foyer.

Ada knew the muscular physique of her unannounced guest immediately. He loitered in the doorframe, cautiously stepping into the foyer. Axel casually looked around Ada's home. In her rush to interrogate her mom, Ada had forgotten to close the front door.

"Not exactly hunkering down with safety precautions, I see." Axel gestured toward the open door. His demeanor had reverted to that of the guy at school who basked in the attention of others. He shifted past them and over to the fridge, whistling a tune.

Axel took no initiative to introduce himself to Zeina when he went digging through her fridge, with bread in one hand and a packet of turkey breast in the other. He reached for a few more condiments then sat down at the kitchen island, in the same chair Ada had sat for breakfast that morning, and carelessly applied mustard to a slice of bread.

Zeina looked on with impatience. "Who's your friend, Ada?"

"Good morning, ma'am. I just came by to see how she's doing. Beautiful home, by the way."

"How she's doing?" Zeina asked suggestively, looking past him and out the kitchen window. Then she folded her arms and snapped a contemptuous glare at Axel. "The hardwood is decades old and so is the kitchen. Can I help you?"

Ada gulped a pocket of air when she saw Zeina taking notice of the breadcrumbs tumbling to the floor from the untidy sandwich Axel was hopelessly trying to make. She bulged her eyes and whispered, "Axel, what are you doing?"

With a mouthful of turkey breast sandwich, Axel reached for the roll of paper towels, tore off a strip, and hastily wiped his mouth. "I'm sorry I failed to introduce myself. I am Axel. I go to school with your daughter. She wasn't feeling so well today and had to come home. Change of weather probably." He chewed the remaining little bit of sandwich in his mouth and swallowed with forced emphasis.

He swiped a glass, filled it with tap water, gulped down the entire amount, and went back to sit at the counter.

"Ah, Mama, yeah, this is Axel. We go to school together. I mean, we're friends, but not, like, *friends* friends." Ada jumped in between her and Axel, gritting her teeth and muttering, "dude, what the hell?"

Zeina puffed out her chest and cocked her head. "Listen—Axel, is it?" She had clearly reached the limits of her hospitality. "Now is not a good time. We're in the middle of someth—" She froze at the sight of the pendant around Axel's neck then took a quick step backward. The diagonal bar intersecting with the vertical bars on the pendant seemed to stand out more with Zeina's eyes bearing down on it.

Axel put down his empty glass, and with his index finger, he wiped the side of his mouth. "You know what this pendant is." Axel pulled his gaze down to glance at the pendant.

"Where did you get that?" she asked accusatorially, her voice rising a few octaves.

"And you know why I wear it. Or why Ada must wear it."

"I'm not going to ask you again. Where did you get that pendant?" Zeina took a decisive step closer to Axel.

"Technically, you just did, Mama," Ada muttered. "Sorry. Poor timing." She took a step back after her mom shot her a death glare.

"We call this our Aegis. It is not just for our protection. It lets us know where the others are." He shot his gaze toward Ada.

"I know what it is. Answer my question," Zeina persisted.

"This was made for me at birth by a Talisman. Ada's too, I assume."

"Mine?" Ada jerked her head forward.

"Yes, yours, Ada."

"Hi, me again—Ada." Ada raised her hand like she did in class when she wanted to ask a question. "Can we go back to the part about… everything, really? Who are you? Who is this *us* you keep referring to?"

"Me? I'm a nobody. Us—Armor—tasked me with watching over you."

Words formed in her mouth, but they remained trapped on her lips. She slowly shook her head, rubbing her temples.

"We need you. More than this world does," Axel said.

Zeina immediately pulled Ada closer to her. "I don't know what she is to you. But she is my daughter first. When my husband comes home, he will handle this." she said firmly. "Now, if you don't mind, Ada and I were in the middle of something." Zeina punctuated her statement by gesturing toward the door.

"Hi, still here. Quick follow-up: need me more than this world does? What?" Ada flared her hand out at Axel. "And, Mama, you've known this for how long now? I'm assuming Dad knows as well. And you couldn't have bothered to tell me—maybe leave it on a Post-it note on the fridge?"

"If the stakes weren't so high, we would have discarded that Aegis and those boxes years ago, but we couldn't leave your life to chance," her mom countered, unable to meet Ada's gaze.

"Leaving my security to chance. You sound like a reporter on the front lines. I need you to be my mother right now and tell me what his pendant means. What is happening to me?" Before she could allow her mother to answer, she swiftly turned to Axel. "What if I don't wear the Aegis? What if it's either lost or I choose to not wear it and help these people of yours out? Okay, I'll admit, weird things are happening. The blackout, the telepathy, the gymnasium, what you said in the bathroom…"

Zeina frantically interrupted. "Blackout? Telepathy? *Ya* Ada, didn't I tell you to message me if anything was wrong? I know I said that."

"Did you say telepathy?" Axel asked.

"Sure, these supernatural occurrences are definitely weird," Ada continued. "No offense—I think they're really neat. But this is my senior year. I just want to do well in school, participate in extracurricular activities, focus on my college applications, and who knows, if I'm lucky, make another athletics team to boost my college résumé. I don't know, maybe field hockey or something."

Axel folded his arms. He was sporting an intrigued smile, as though he had found Ada's entire proclamation borderline entertaining.

"Ada, are you even listening to what I've been saying?" He paused again to let his question sink in. "Nygaard will flood the Empress Walk once they learn where you are."

"The Empress Walk? What am I supposed to do with that information?" Ada looked at her mother, who averted her gaze again.

"It's the portal that allows us to travel to Earth and back. We believe it was built hundreds of years ago by the Mother of Unitas —the Empress Sala of Legio. Legend says that was where she led Unitas to defeat the invading hordes. The temple where she resided was called the Empress Walk. She built it as a way for our people to flee to Earth safely in case invaders sought to destroy everything she had built. No one imagined our destruction would come from within." Axel recited the history in the methodical manner of someone who had learned it by rote in class.

"Well, that's… a lot." Ada swayed her head from side to side. "So…" She held up her hands to mimic a scale. "Column A." Ada lifted her left hand slightly higher than her right. "It's undeniable that what happened to me today was not ordinary. Totally outside the realm of conceivable reality. I'll give you that much. Column B." She lowered her left hand and raised the right. "The idea that the fate of a world depends on me is implausible at best. I can't even run the two hundred without huffing and stopping to question all my lifestyle choices, let alone help you people out."

"Now that you kind of mimed it out, yes, it does seem a little outlandish." Axel angled his head down. "But this is bigger than you. You just happen to play the most important part right now. And for that, we need to keep you safe, Ada."

"You're saying I need to be safe. But you haven't shown me any real danger. I am not hurt. No one is after me. The First Rank, Infernum—whatever you keep talking about—is not at my door. I'm good so far." She pointed up and down to herself. "But fine, let's entertain this idea and say I need to wear my pendant or else this all-out war of good versus evil will descend on us."

Axel interrupted her in a manner befitting a person who could no longer sit and listen to someone talking about something they knew nothing about. "All-out war of good and evil. Good and evil." He played back Ada's remarks with a contemptuous shake of his head. "Those are absolutes."

Ada flared her nostrils. "You don't even—"

"Do you think Nygaard believes he fights for evil? In your world, do you think a soldier or freedom fighter ever fired a rifle under the banner of evil? They all have their own idea of good. Nah, Ada, it's all about keeping a grip on their power. Everybody is in it for themselves. Self-preservation." Axel slumped back down on the stool. His question still rested in the still air of the kitchen.

"So, is this about your self-preservation?" Ada asked with a hint of skepticism.

His voice softened. The arrogance had dissipated. "There's a lot I don't know. I just know we need to keep you safe and find your Aegis. We can feel each other's presence if we're wearing it."

"Listen, Axel, you've been truthful to us. At least, I hope you have. I think we must be honest with you." Ada flashed a look at her mom. She was about to do what she knew her mom was hoping she wouldn't do.

Zeina forcefully shook her head at her daughter.

"We…" Ada tipped her head as if to redo that opening word. "*I* don't have the pendant. It's lost, and we can't find it."

"Ada, *habibi,* no. What are you doing?" a startled Zeina asked.

"Mama, it's okay. I trust him." Ada eyed Axel suspiciously. "I think."

"I don't know even know him. I never heard of him. Why hasn't Marcel mentioned anything about you?" Zeina's eyes bulged out as soon as she said the name.

"Marcel?" Axel asked with intrigue.

"*Yii* Marcel! I have to tell him. He will know what to do." Zeina sped off back upstairs to retrieve her phone.

"Why would Dad –?" Ada started.

"Back to the part about the Aegis being gone. How do you lose it?" Axel flung his hands out like someone waiting for the answer to be deposited into his palms. He then groaned before aggressively slapping those outstretched hands over his face in a defeated gesture. "I'm gonna get in so much trouble for this. You had one job, Axel. One job."

"One job? Were you sent here to watch over me or something?" Ada examined Axel, offering him no sympathy.

"I—yes. They tasked me with looking out for you as you got closer to September thirteenth."

"You mean, my birthday?"

"Sure—birthday, let's call it that. Semantics aren't my primary concern right now," Axel said flippantly.

"Is that why you spent the summer by the shore? I randomly saw you everywhere." Ada glared at him.

"Yes, that and the rich daddy's girls. It's like that place is a hotbed for girls who never fail to engage in hedonistic displays of poor judgment." Axel's lip twisted while he stared longingly out the window. He chuckled lightly before returning his attention to Ada.

Ada grimaced. "Okay, gross. Not interested in your summer escapades."

Ada traced her cheek with her index finger and stared pensively at Axel, deliberating something she'd only just then pieced together. She opened her mouth to speak before electing to prolong the silence a little longer.

Finally, she removed her hand from her face and pointed at Axel accusingly. "So, it was you who was watching me yesterday morning from Didi's lawn, wasn't it?"

"You were watching my daughter *enta*?" Zeina had rejoined the discussion at the worst possible time. The last thing Ada wanted was to worsen her mom's peak-level anxiety.

"I mean, I feel like there are matters of larger importance at hand. Of primary concern is what happened to your pendant. Second, we still need to sort out the facts of how you could read thoughts. Third, there's this whole saving-our-world thing." Axel rounded his shoulders and protruded his head forward to solicit any possible bit of sympathy.

With Zeina's petitioning looks fixed on him, Axel raised his finger again to explain. From the glint in his eye, he appeared to be enjoying the rapid-fire interrogation. A repository of anger shot out from Zeina. Ada was doing her best to sympathize with both of them but could only manage a nervous smile and knitted brow.

"Fine. I shall address the matter of the lawn incident." He finally dropped his shoulders. "I figured Ada may have seen me. I have been instructed to look out for you this week, Ada. Make sure no strange happenings occur. Believe me, I would much rather sleep in than wake up way too early to creep on you. I probably could have been stealthier, but that would have been super creepy. So, I figured the only thing to do was stand on their lawn and pretend like I was delivering the paper or, I don't know, cleaning up poop after my dog. I don't have a dog, by the way." He chuckled lightly. "I've already taken a beating from Didi once. Why implicate myself with another household?" he said in a brief moment of reflection. "Besides, you're lucky I was trailing you this morning. After you blacked out behind the wheel, you could've driven that crapshoot you have parked out there into a pole."

"Blacked out? Ada?" Zeina asked.

"What do you mean implicate yourself with another household? What happened with Didi?" Ada asked, ignoring her mom's inquiry to pounce on the chance to extract more information from Axel.

"Let's just say there's some sensitivity between me and the Mendozas." Axel scratched the back of his head and averted her gaze.

"Sensitivity? She tells me everything," Ada said, feeling a hint of concern.

"Listen, we do our homework. We've been waiting for this—for you—for a long time." Axel began to flip through a random magazine from the stash on the counter. "Are we good now, Zeina? Can I call you Zeina?"

Her mom was still visibly unimpressed. "It's Mrs. Tannous. And how do you know my name?" Zeina shot him a piercing look.

"It's right here. On the subscription." Axel smirked, tossing the magazine back on the counter.

Ada puffed out a defeated sigh. This exchange between her, Axel, and Zeina was clearly heading nowhere and would likely escalate to more accusations by Zeina and whimsical defenses by Axel.

"Mama, listen, I know it's a lot, but for what it's worth, Axel has been of help since yesterday morning. I didn't tell you I passed out in the parking lot because I didn't want to worry you. He also was there after I felt..." She struggled to find the appropriate language to describe that scene in the assembly. "After I felt weird."

"All this aside, right now, we need to find the Aegis. Zei—I mean, Mrs. Tannous—tear up this house if you have to. Ada, I'm going to take you back to school, where you can be among people. It's in public. There's safety in numbers. I'd rather you be there than leave you here alone like a sitting duck."

"Mama, he's right. There's nothing you can do for me at home. I'll be safer at school," Ada said. It wasn't that she didn't want to be with her mom—she just needed to restore a grain of normalcy to her life. And school offered that glimmer of a routine that could at least accommodate the regular order she'd been enjoying up until the previous day.

Zeina clicked her tongue in rapid succession under her breath. She shifted her weight from one foot to the other and back again. "Okay. Okay. Ada, you go to school. But you're not driving after what happened to you yesterday. I'll drive you there."

"I'll drive her. I need to keep a close watch. It's still early. We can get you back by next period," Axel said.

Her dad is gonna kill me once he finds out I lost the pendant. I need to find it.

Ada glanced over at her mother. "Did you say something, Mama?"

"Me? No," Zeina replied.

"Axel, you drove here, right?" Ada returned her focus to Axel.

"Yup." Axel pointed toward the curb, although the living room wall obstructed the view.

Not bothering to tidy up his sandwich mess, Axel hustled to the door. Ada was slowly following him when she felt her mother's shivering hand grab her forearm.

"It's all right, Mama. I'll call if anything is wrong. You can release that death grip," Ada half joked.

"Anything, *habibi*—you see anything out of the ordinary, and you call us. I'm gonna try your dad again." Her mom finally loosened her grip.

"Bye, Mrs. Tannous. Don't worry—Ada'll be all right. What's the worst that can happen, right?"

Zeina shot him a death glare.

"Don't answer that," Axel said.

"Bye, Mama, it's gonna be alright. I'll text if anything happens," Ada hugged her mother then slung her backpack over her shoulder. Both she and Axel exited the house and whipped out their phones as soon as they stepped outside.

Didi: *yo you good?*

Ada: *Loaded question.*

Didi: *?*

"This is how you blend in on Earth?" Ada glanced up from her messages and noticed the slick sports car parked in her driveway.

She looked up and down the street to ensure that the red Mercedes coupe hadn't drawn any unwanted attention from the neighbors. Her mother's Camry was often the sole vehicle in the driveway. This ostentatious exhibit would certainly have nosy neighbors murmuring among themselves.

"The people at Armor lived well before they fled Unitas. Who am I to question their expensive habits?"

"Yeah, they're really struggling with this whole First Rank refugees thing," Ada said.

"I don't know. They gave me a car, and they registered me at this school and told me follow you around."

Ada laid her hand on the passenger-door handle. The fluidity with which the door opened to welcome her to this enclave of luxury, the way it swiveled gracefully, the way she sank into the seat, and the smoothness of the armrest—all were so different from the Blaze.

"Who else was in your home yesterday, today? Did anyone come over? What about your brother? Does he know about the Aegis?" Axel had backed out of the driveway and was driving at an alarming speed through the suburban backstreets.

"Roman wouldn't know. My parents never mentioned anything. No one has been over this week. Honestly, I don't know. And slow down, Lewis Hamilton!" Ada waved her hand at Axel. "For someone trying to protect me, you seem to be trying to get me killed."

"Sorry, my sensory abilities are more heightened than yours. I see and process things a little faster." Axel eased off the pedal to a speed slightly faster than was reasonable.

"You mean, you can see things faster?"

"No, I see things the same way you do. But I can process them quicker than you. Basically, it's like there is a bullet train from my eyes to my brain, computing information," Axel explained proudly.

"Um, that's not that fast. You do realize that regular earthling neurons travel much faster than a bullet train, right?" Ada caught herself making a raised eyebrow face. "Back there, you said that you and the Mendozas weren't on good terms. Do they know who you are? Does Didi, like, *know*, who you really are?"

A fleeting upturn of the corner of Axel's mouth formed as soon as she brought up Didi's name.

"That's a conversation you should probably have with Didi." Axel kept his focus on the road, one hand resting lazily on the wheel.

"Wrong door. I'll take supernatural abilities for two hundred dollars. Next question." Ada hesitated, not sure whether she wanted to know the answer to what she was about to ask.

Axel sat up slightly in his seat, looking amused.

"How did you know I was passed out in the Blaze?" Ada continued.

"The what?"

"Ah, so you didn't do your homework. You don't know everything about me. The car. My car. The Blaze."

"Oh, the Blaze. You call that dilapidated two-ton paperweight the Blaze. How… cute." Axel chuckled.

"At least I'm not driving the company car. How did you magically appear outside my car window?"

"I happened to be there."

"So you were following me?"

"I prefer the term *synchronizing my orbit around you*. But yeah."

"That doesn't make me feel better." Ada allowed herself to be consumed by the soft leather of the car seat before snapping back to the conversation at hand. "Look, despite your morally nebulous ways, I'm going to trust you. For now. I don't know why, when we're sitting in an absurdly expensive car purchased with probably laundered-out-of-this-world money. Which, by the way, if I get implicated in whatever RICO charges they slap you with for any of this money-washing scheme, I will take the first plea they give me."

"After all I've done for you, Ada Lorham, you would rat me out to the feds so quickly?" Axel beamed, showing a glimpse of most of his teeth.

"Jokes aside, I can respect your honor-among-thieves thing, but you gotta tell me more than 'I am in danger and these people are out to get something I have.'" Ada lifted her head from the cushioned headrest.

"Honestly, I don't really know more than what they told me. All we're trying to do is keep you safe."

"You keep referring to *we*. Let's start with that. Who is Armor?"

"After we fled Unitas, we scattered across the Americas. All that was left was a group of resistors to Nygaard. They called themselves the Administration for the Restoration of Morality and Reason—ARMOR.'

"Armor…? You people really workshopped that abbreviation, did you? Was Justice League taken?"

"Really? Because your entire military defense in America is named after the geometric shape of the building," Axel shot back. "But yeah, Armor. That's who 'we' are. We did not concentrate Senazi Armor in one state or country, out of fear of being found out. The more dispersed we were, the less of a threat we could be to other Senazis fleeing the First Rank. Their Infernum continues to hunt us down, but our resistance holds. But if Nygaard finds out you're here, he will flood this place with Infernum and Phalanx. Many Senazi in Unitas will die because of that. Blood for blood is what the Empress Walk demands without the Agoge."

Ada spun her head around toward Axel. "Blood for blood. What does that mean? Phalanx? What… what is that?"

"It means for every Infernum or Phalanx that is teleported to Earth, Senazi blood must be sacrificed into the Empress Walk to open the portal. And the Infernum are the secret police operating in the open. The Phalanx is the army. The First Rank is the party that commands them." He let his explanation rest in the ensuing silence.

"You said back there you were asked to look after me this

week. Does Armor know who I am? Did you know who I was this whole time?" Ada asked.

"Me? No. But Armor knew. I received the instruction to monitor you. It wasn't my place to question things among the Armor ranks," Axel said, not taking his eyes off the road.

"Okay, follow up question: why can't I read your mind but I can read…" Ada deliberated whether to tell him about hearing Ellen's thoughts. Or her mother's. She decided that the more she could learn, the more she could hope that the deluge of confusion in her head might recede. "I read Ellen's mind. And my mom's. At least, I think I did." She quickly shot her hands up defensively. "But it was one thing only. Like, one sentence."

"I honestly don't know. Legend says that the first and only Empress of Unitas, Sala of Legio, had the power to read human minds." Axel navigated one-handed with a casual grip on the wheel. He leaned his head on his free palm, his elbow casually resting on the edge of the window.

"It seems to only happen when someone is experiencing a strong surge of emotions," Ada continued with a tiny smile, satisfied at having drawn that conclusion by herself.

"What do you mean?" Axel's resting hand now took the wheel. He leaned into Ada, his brows contracting toward one another.

"I don't know. It's not like there's a manual for how to deal with the telepathic complexities of interspecies interaction. Not yet at least." As they drew nearer to the school, Ada checked the time on her phone. "I have civics with Didi now. Who has been totally sketch about all this, PS." She resigned herself to the uncomfortable fact that she would have to eventually question her best friend about what she knew and how she knew it.

"Listen." Axel traced the steering wheel. "She is one of the few people in this world that knows about us. And trust me, we would have preferred she never found out. It's a long story that I'm sure she'll get around to telling you." Axel resumed his casual driving position. "And no. I cannot read your mind."

"I know. Because I wasn't thinking that," Ada replied defensively.

He navigated the streets that led back to Clifton High School. Rows of houses wore the neighborhood's tranquil grayish colors. Ada's sight hopped to the window of each house as they whizzed by. She speculated about whether the families of these homes also kept secrets—perhaps not as seemingly fictional as hers but just as outlandish. Maybe every household had its hidden trove of secrets.

CHAPTER 8

CLIFTON HIGH SCHOOL— TAKE TWO

THEY PULLED into the school parking lot and wove through the thick crowds of students breaking for lunch hour. A calming sense of relief crept back into Ada at being back at Clifton High. The cracks in the pavement and faded yellow parking lanes offered a peaceful familiarity.

Meanwhile, Axel was busy scoping out the occasional scantily clad junior or senior girl on school grounds. He took extra care to drive slowly, making heads turn toward his car, pretending not to notice the students glancing through the car windows. Ada noticed how he took caution to only peek at the attractive blonde approaching on the left, whose tight skirt rode up a few inches higher than the school-mandated one-inch-above-the-knee policy.

"We're taking liberties with the dress code, are we, Roxane?" he said to the girl, who was now in his rearview.

"To think you would have denied me a front-row seat to witness firsthand the interactions of primitive species in their natural habitat at Clifton High." Ada grinned.

"I always took you for a sweet girl. I didn't know you also had a comedic side."

"There's a lot you don't know about me, Axel Mosley—if that's even your real name."

"It's not. Kind of, at least."

"Cool. We're off to a good start." Ada waved her hands aimlessly, looking for the latch to open the car door. "How do you even get out of this spaceship? Why are there so many buttons?"

Axel came to a full stop, putting the car in park. "Before you get out, I need you to be careful. You never know who could be watching us. Keep calm and be easy. And it's the latch. The one that looks like every other car-door latch." He pointed to the illuminated outline of a latch on her side.

Students looked on perplexedly as Ada exited Axel's car. The scene was a gossip factory ready to be unleashed. Curious glares locked onto her. She brushed her hair back behind her ear and paced along, counting the joints separating the concrete slabs of the sidewalk leading into the school.

"I mean, this is still preferable to passing out and driving over the curb," she muttered.

A rush of voices penetrated Ada's consciousness:

"Is that Ada Lorham with Axel? I did not see that one coming."

"They're probably just friends."

Making her way into the building, she was struggling to block them out. They were people's intimate thoughts, regardless of how misplaced, mean, or ill-informed they might have been. It was like reading someone's diary. Nothing was sacred anymore. At every turn, she was committing unwarranted intrusions into someone's innermost feelings.

She kept her head down until she reached her locker. The sounds of shuffling feet and commotion filled the halls. Ada threw on her headphones without even playing any music. She sensed a familiar presence behind her but did not bother to turn around, hoping she'd only imagined it.

A hand unexpectedly shifted the right headphone off. "Mama told me you came home because you weren't feeling well. Surprised to see you back here," Roman said in Ada's ear.

"Yeah, I wasn't feeling so hot. I'm better now, though," Ada replied.

"Don't stress yourself out the first week of the year. I mean, I'm only here to scope out the talent… and because I have to be, of course. And because football tryouts are today. Not like I need to go to tryouts. But formalities… you know."

"Okay, little bro. Try not to strain that neck of yours before the season starts." Ada noticed Roman checking out the fleet of younger girls approaching her locker.

"Hey, Roman!" they said, disregarding the conversation between Ada and Roman.

"Hey." Roman turned to barely acknowledge them with a slight nod before swiveling back to Ada. The girls lingered in social limbo.

"Fans of yours?" Ada teased.

"Hey, hey, chill out. I'll see you girls in a bit. I gotta talk to my sis for a minute." Roman coolly waved them off.

The girls departed not nearly as quickly as they'd arrived, shuffling their books, and exchanging looks of hesitation.

"You sure you all right, Grapes?"

"I'm feeling great." Ada perked up. Roman was still the only remaining shred of normalcy in her life. She was committed to keeping it that way, even if it meant withholding information from him like her parents had done to her. It was selfish, but she needed reassurance that her life was not completely falling apart.

Roman hesitated. "All right, Grapes. I'm gonna get going."

"I'll see you at home?" Ada said, swallowing the ball of anxiety ballooning in her throat.

CHAPTER 9
MR. SAM PAUL'S CLASS

ADA's last class of the day was Advanced Social Sciences with Mr. Paul. He was in his early thirties and had yet to be compromised by the throes of cynicism that often came with being a public school teacher. Mr. Paul—or Sam, as he encouraged students in his class to call him—got along well with the kids. He could carry on a conversation about social media trends, college sports, and rap music. Despite trying to be relatable to the high school seniors, he sometimes dated himself by regularly dropping Jay-Z and Biggie references to students who vaguely, at best, knew of those icons.

Instead of images of the founding fathers, the US Constitution, Congress, and the White House, Mr. Paul had plastered the classroom with photos of pop-culture characters—Tony Soprano from *The Sopranos*, Avon Barksdale from *The Wire*, and Nucky Thompson from *Boardwalk Empire*. A New York Knicks foam finger rested on top of a filing cabinet in the corner. The music playing from Mr. Paul's portable Bluetooth speaker gave color to the posters. Ada bobbed her head up and down, enjoying the beat, upon entering the class. Winter was sitting in the first row at the right side of the room. She had been the first one to arrive.

"Hi, Mr. Paul—er, Sam," Ada said. "Cool song. Is that another of the Wu-Tang?"

"Ada, good to see you! Close. It's Chef Raekwon—Incarcerated Scarfaces," Sam said, reciprocating Ada's enthusiasm.

"He throws down the gauntlet in this track." Mr. Paul turned off the song as more students filed in.

"I like that line… how he's talking about battling for cash." Ada bobbed her head to the beat.

The student desks were split into two sections and pushed to the sides, dividing the classroom into equal parts with a makeshift banner for each, Team Wall Street on the right versus Team Main Street on the left. The chairs on each side were directly facing each other, like the chambers of a parliamentary showdown, with the middle aisle vacant. The lesson in their first civics class would be a debate.

"Hi, Winter. I see you're on Team Wall Street." Ada gestured to the hastily made sign resting on the table in front of the chairs on one side.

Winter studied Ada a little longer than usual. She tapped the pencil on the notebook resting on her lap before pensively twirling it between her fingers. "You weren't in AP Bio." She kept scrutinizing Ada, alternating between tapping her pencil for a few drumbeats and rotating it around her fingers.

"Um, yeah, I was just feeling a bit nauseous. I didn't, um, have breakfast this morning. I'm good now, though." Ada scratched her head.

"Good. Good to hear." Winter continued to tap and rotate the pencil.

"Okay. Well, I guess I'll just sit on this side. Power to the people. Yay." Ada pointed to the Main Street sign and squealed in feigned excitement. She claimed a seat toward the back of her section.

"A rational desire to protect yourself from moral accountability," Winter said without breaking the rhythmic pattern of her pencil tapping.

"Okay, well. Good chat," Ada responded, unsure of whether Winter was addressing her decision to sit on Main Street, taking a jab at her personally, or being dismissive of the entire Wall Street versus Main Street exercise.

One by one, the students entered the class. Some would shuffle back and forth, while others would decisively choose a side. A few minutes later, once the class had filled up, Sam Paul cleared his throat and casually strutted through the middle aisle between the two teams. He was sporting faded jeans and rolled-up sleeves on a sweatshirt with the words Wu-Tang is for the Children.

"Welcome to Advanced Civics. By my count, there are a few more people missing, but we'll get started anyway. I am your teacher, Sam Paul. You all can call me Sam—it won't hurt my feelings. This is my second year at Clifton High School, and I think I'm enjoying my time so far, except for, you know, the commute from Hoboken every day… ah, Ellen, you're just in time." Ellen had walked in, looking mildly perplexed, and Sam gestured toward the back of Team Main Street. "Why don't you grab that seat over there?"

"How about I not slum it in Gen Pop? I'll grab that seat beside Winter." Ellen walked and talked her way to the vacant chair before gracefully sitting.

"You've probably figured out why I've split you into two groups. We're going to talk about a hot issue in America right now —the push and pull of power between corporate America and the everyday folk. The subject of this debate shall be who built America? Wall Street or Main Street? The regular folks or the large corporations? Did working people build wealth, or did wealth build wealth? I have broken you off into groups. You chose the side you wanted to be on as soon as you sat down. That is the side you were birthed into. Wall Street can switch sides to Main Street, but students in Main Street are stuck there. That is, after all, where they were birthed. I will be moderating the debate. Each team shall present its opening argument. You shall appoint one among you to speak. Each valid statement or counterargument is worth one point. Oh, and also, Team Wall Street starts with a ten-point lead. Why? Because it's not fair."

A few students on Team Wall Street sneered. Others on Team Main Street raised their hands in protest to the unfair handicap. Winter expressed neither satisfaction nor excitement. In the midst of their competing protests, Didi rushed in through the open door. She checked her schedule, peeked her head back around the door to verify the room number, and then paced toward Team Wall Street. She was about to rest her bag on the desk when Ada managed to catch her eye from across the room, gesturing with her brows to sit with her team.

Didi hustled over to Team Main Street, momentarily distracting the class with her unapologetic rustling about. On Ada's left sat Charles Simon in a beige long-sleeved polo pullover sweater, with hair perfectly parted from left to right. Didi stopped directly between Ada and Charles's desks.

She bent over from behind Charles and snaked her head to his ear. "Hey, broski, you're gonna have to move. My girl ate something funky and has been projectile vomiting all over the place. I suggest you sit over there if you're not trying to be peeling this morning's scrambled egg off your shirt."

Charles shot an inquisitive look at Ada and then Didi. He gave up his seat to relocate to the back of the class but not before shaking his head in disappointment at Didi's lack of tact. Ada turned red with embarrassment and avoided looking at Charles directly.

The subdued fuss did not go unnoticed by their teacher, who asked with an intrigued smile, "Ms. Mendoza, are you sure you don't want to sit on Team Wall Street, seeing as you evicted a resident from his desk without the least bit of deliberation?"

Didi was unfazed by Sam's request. "No, I'm straight, Mr. Paul. Evictions, shmevictions. We're all bound to get canceled for something at some point, anyway, *ya tu sabe*?"

"Now that everyone is here," Mr. Paul continued, "each team will have ten minutes to confer and come up with an opening argument. Main Street will go first, and as is to be expected, Wall Street shall have the last word."

The students immediately folded into each other. Deliberations about points, counterpoints, themes, and arguments floated around the classroom.

"Okay, so, everyone..." Charles took the lead among the huddled students. A few outliers were carrying on among themselves, unconcerned with the assignment. "I know the hot thing these days is to invoke this theory of social and institutional equality in a nation founded on actual social and institutional inequality. But I think we should really talk about how the working man is getting pushed out by greedy tech companies..."

"I gotta talk to you." Ada turned to Didi, ignoring Charles's noble outline planning for the debate.

"Anything else happened today?" Didi asked.

"Yeah, no. All good. Axel showed up at my house, but whatever. I mean, I did lose the pendant. So there's that."

Didi lowered her voice. "What? And all you could text back was 'loaded question'?"

"I don't know? I'm trying to keep it together here. Listen, I got the impression that there's history between you and Axel. I'm sorry to pry, but I think it's important that I know. You know, with all of... this going on." Ada whooshed her hands around.

The students on Team Main Street continued to confer among themselves, constructing points and counterpoints. Meanwhile, Didi's face contorted with annoyance at the mention of Axel's name. She looked at the other students, who were evidently preoccupied with the debate prep, and leaned in closer to Ada. "He broke into our house!"

"What? When? Axel?" Ada's asked loudly enough for the students in her section to take note. A few of them briefly stared down Ada and Didi.

"Like, tell me how... I legit found him in the basement going through my stuff," Didi said.

"But... why would Axel break into your house?"

Didi was looking everywhere except in Ada's direction. She bit her fingernail as she pulled out a notebook from her backpack, flipping it open to a random blank page.

"Didi!" Ada tried to recapture Didi's attention. "You're literally just writing 'Civics—Team Main Street' on the page." She flicked her eyebrows toward Didi's barely legible notes. Her voice had reached the limits of whispering and was about to graduate to audible agitation. "What are you not telling me?" She snatched the pencil from Didi.

"Okay, Okay." Didi grabbed the pencil back. "I should have told you about him and that woman he was with."

Ada leaned in closer yet again.

"Woman?"

"Remember that time my parents were out of town for my sister's soccer tournament, and I had to stay back solo because we had softball that weekend?"

"Yes. I broke a small yet significant bone in my foot that weekend, sliding into first base."

"More like launching yourself into the base. And relax, it was a bone bruise. But yeah, that weekend. We really gotta do this right now?" Didi whispered through her gritted teeth.

"I mean, at no point has my timing with all this been optimal, so we might as well." Ada hopped up and shuffled her chair closer to Didi.

"Ugh, fine." Didi cast one last glance behind her, where their fellow classmates had convened to discuss their project. "So, that night, I was in bed. Home alone. And I heard a sound. Like a bang." Didi slapped her fist to produce a popping sound. "And I'm like, 'Aw, hell nah. Not today.' I was like, 'Nah, it's probably nothing.' So I closed my eyes, but then I heard somebody downstairs. You know how I get down. I'm not about to get got in my own home. So I head downstairs right. Like, stealth mode. Not gonna lie—I was shook for a minute. But I was like, 'Today is not the day.' So I—"

Didi abruptly turned to Charles, who was shooting laser dagger stares at them, his hands apart, gesturing for them to join the debate preparation. "How can I help you, Charles?" she asked a little louder than would be deemed appropriate for a classroom setting.

Charles's haughty tone reached them from a few desks over. "Excuse me—Ada and Didi, would you care to join us, or would you like to gossip with each other like school children?"

"Go Wikipedia some facts or something. We're dealing with a situation here." She refocused onto Ada. "So anyway, where was I?"

"You're at home, and you heard something," Ada said.

"Oh yeah, so I go downstairs, right? Like legit tiptoes stealth mode. I turn the lights on and see Axel in my basement, like frozen deer in headlights. But there was this woman with him. Like, an old woman. Not old like weak or nothing. She looked like she was somebody important in her day."

Ada leaned in. "Was it his mom or something?"

"Nah, not really. Let me finish. So at this point, I'm damn near about to pass out. Like, I am terrified, right? I'm home alone. This is happening down in my basement. I'm like, 'This is how I die.' But remember our old liquor cabinet in the basement? Axel was, like, lifting it no problem. I remember my dad and uncles struggling to get it down the stairs when it was empty and talking about how it was solid wood and all.

"Then I was like, 'Wait, I know you. You're Axel. The kid from school. The guy with the car. The ball player—hooper.'" Didi flicked her wrist in a basketball-shooting motion. "And he was all like, 'You mean future-D1-star Axel, and yeah the whip. You know I got it like that.'"

"He didn't actually use those words, did he?" Ada asked.

"I mean, no, but you know how he be feeling himself. But yeah, he was like, 'Yeah that's me.' Then he said something like"—Didi lowered her voice to a deep bass to mimic Axel—"'So you got questions. How about we debrief at school on Monday. Or maybe I could put it all in an email or something.' I said, 'Nah, you're gonna tell me what's good right now. Or I'm calling the police.'

Then this is where things got weird. He was like, 'Listen, this isn't about you. It's about your girl Ada.' And the woman with her was telling him to stop—like, 'No, Axel you're saying too much.'"

"Okay, wait. Who's this woman?" Ada asked.

"Oh, yeah, yeah, the woman. She was actually cool. She was having none of Axel's antics and was damn near about to punish him right then and there. Then Axel went off about how you are in trouble, and soon when you turn seventeen, something will happen to you and how they are here to protect you and want to make sure that I'm not Infernum or something. He was talking crazy when she cut him off, Cisca was her name, and said, 'No, you say too much, young Axel.' All serious." Didi had stiffened her brows and stretched her neck up to adopt a serious demeanor.

"What?" Didi turned to Charles. "Sure, whatever. We heard that. I'm writing it down. 1811. First corporation was registered in New York. Got it." Didi pretended to jot down notes. Charles glared at her and Ada.

"So then, this Cisca—real elegant woman, like, creases on her forehead, but you can tell she moisturizes—was like, 'We are people of Unitas seeking refuge on Earth.' Talking about how they are the last of a resistance to an evil in their world. They called themselves Armor. Then she said she wouldn't be telling me any of this if you weren't my girl and that it was important to know that you were in danger. I was like, 'Cool, cool. Ya'll still need to leave.'"

"So you knew all this and never told me?" Ada said in a forced whisper, bulging her eyes at Didi.

"Wait, hold up. I still had my doubts until Cisca said something that had me shook. She was like, 'This time, the danger is closer than six houses away.' And I was like, 'Wait, what? What did you say? How do you know about the six-houses-away thing?' And she knew. She knew it all. About how when we were young, our parents only let us play from my house to yours and how we'd count them. And then she told me about how people were looking for that thing, the Agoge, inside you. And something about a fallen republic and a Chancellor and the First Rank. I don't know, I tuned that part out. The only thing I could bring myself to ask them was if Unitas was in Europe or something."

"OMG, right?" Ada quickly interjected.

"Perfectly valid question. So yeah, Unitas, Agoge, something about an Empress Walk. It was…" Didi paused while her eyes shifted from side to side. "It was all too much. Anyway, all I knew was some stuff was gonna go down when you turned seventeen. And Cisca said I should keep an eye out for anything unusual and report it to Axel. But nothing crazy went down since then, so I thought nothing about it. That and I damn near got my ass handed to me by my parents when they found out I had Axel over that night."

"Hold on, what? Mama Doralis caught you?" Ada clenched her jaw at the frightening thought of Didi's stern Boricua mama catching her with a boy at her house the first ever time they left her home alone.

"Kind of. So I'm downstairs, talking to them two, Cisca and Axel. And all of a sudden, someone knocks on the door. I'm like, 'Dang, what is it now?' So I tell them to stay where they are, and I run upstairs. I look through the peephole, and it's my *tia* Camila and my *tio* Windel."

"*Tia* Camila, the one who spent all her money on a psychic to tell her that Windel wasn't cheating on her and was not about to leave her?" Ada asked.

"Yeah, that one. Maybe the psychic should have told her that *tio* was damn near about to leave her when he found out she'd blasted through their savings for all them tarot-card sessions."

"Valid." Ada nodded and pressed her lips together.

"So anyway, they had stopped by to make sure I was cool with being all alone. Then right when I was about to close the door, I heard a bang downstairs. And I was like, ayy, Axel was going through boxes still when I told him to chill for a minute. Now my *tia* and *tio* barge in and start looking at me all serious, like I'm hiding something. I'm like, 'No, no, it's nothing,' and Axel runs upstairs and, like, launches himself from the second last step and into the foyer like he's Kalpesh making a curtain call in one of his musicals that nobody watches anyway… wassup, Kal? You good?" Didi quickly waved to Kalpesh, who had looked up when Didi said his name.

Turning back to Ada, Didi continued. "Axel was like, 'Hey, let me assure you there is a perfectly acceptable explanation to this.'" She raised her finger to reenact Axel's desperate attempt to hold off the impending barrage of questions that her tia and tio were about to launch on her that evening. "Then he looked at them both and suddenly dashed for the door, flung it open, and sprinted outside the house at, like, top speed. He disappeared while I was standing there thinking about my own funeral."

"What?" Ada sat there, mouth agape, trying to make sense of Didi's jumbled account.

CHAPTER 10
THE DEBATE

"OMG, Ada, it was the worst thing ever. I was grounded for a month. Axel pulled a ninja move and dashed out the front door. Cisca had to listen to them ream me out for an hour while she hid downstairs."

"I know they put you in a bad spot, but you should have told me."

"Yeah, it was rough. I should have told you for real. That one was on me."

"Remember that time we were kids, and we hid your sister's teddy bears for an entire year? And when your mom finally found it, we still denied it." Ada rolled her eyes back to reminisce.

"I still deny it. Taking that to my grave, man."

"Exactly. We ride together. No secrets." Ada extended her clenched fist. Didi tapped the end of Ada's fist against hers. "Wait—is that why you couldn't hang out for literally the entire month of May last year?"

"Yep. I was grounded that whole month and couldn't figure out how to tell you why," Didi said.

"Okay, but wait—how did you know that something was wrong with me in the assembly? That, you know, I was having some sort of episode?"

Ada gathered her stream of thoughts. If Didi knew something else, Ada had to know. Any clue would help.

"Yo, I don't know. I've been keeping an eye out for any weird business with you. Cisca hit me up before school started. She told me that the Agoge will be awakening in you soon. That you won't be able to hold it back or something."

"Is that why you were hovering and texting me nonstop during summer?" Ada asked.

"I feel like a narc. But I'm not sorry. I had to make sure you were straight," Didi said.

"Didi, there's one more thing. I don't know if Axel and Cisca told you."

"*Di me.*" Didi looked on curiously.

"What I was telling you yesterday since my, you know, episode. I can listen to people's thoughts. Or their feelings. Or I don't know, I'm still trying to figure it out. Like, I heard…" Ada looked back at Ellen sitting across from them, who was preoccupied with disdainfully studying the strands of hair hanging off her shoulders. Ada leaned in closer to Didi and whispered, "I heard Ellen's thoughts when she was with us in the bathroom."

A look of amazement spread across Didi's face. His eyebrows stretched back to her forehead. Her eyeballs swiveled from side to side. "Wait, you're not reading my thoughts now, are you?" Didi pointed at Ada accusatorially.

"What? No. I'm getting a blank from you." Ada put her hands up in a show of innocence.

"Good. Because I'm literally speechless. Or brainless. Or something like that. Ada, this is crazy. Ooh, you never have to study for an exam again. You just tap into whatever everyone else is thinking." Didi's excited voice drew the attention of those near them.

A few students from Team Main Street looked at them incredulously, unimpressed by their complete lack of participation in preparing for the debate.

"Go highlight some notes, Charles," Didi snapped at Charles's disapproving glare.

"That's not how it works," Ada quickly said to Didi before addressing the team. "Hi, hey, great work, everyone. Sorry, we were dealing with something. All good. Let's get this debate prepped."

"Time's up... *team*." Charles's cutting inflection warped them back to the classroom setting and out of their clandestine conversation. "It goes without saying I will be presenting our position since you two literally did nothing but chat like a bunch of preteens waiting in line at the Magic Kingdom."

"Ooh, I'm being reduced. Sick burn, Charles," Didi said, pouting her lips and pretending to be hurt.

"And it looks like Winter will be presenting for Team Wall Street," Mr. Paul said, deflecting the exchange between Didi, Ada, and Charles. "All right, everyone, are you ready to present your positions? Team Main Street will go first, followed by Team Wall Street. Team Main Street, please present your speaker."

Ada peeked over at Didi, who was preoccupied with her cell phone, and noticed she had typed, *Is it cheating if you're reading the teacher's thoughts?*

"Ms. Mendoza, it seems you and Ms. Lorham were hard at work preparing for this argument." Mr. Paul addressed Didi with a slightly humorous tone. "I think, since you worked so hard on this presentation, I'm going to move one of you to Team Wall Street. What do you say, Ms. Mendoza? Who says you can't get ahead in America?"

Busted. Mr. Paul had noticed them chatting by themselves the entire time. At least he didn't scold them in front of the class. Didi grabbed her bag and moved to one of the seats in the back of Team Wall Street without objection.

Charles gathered his notes with care, mumbling to himself. He marched to the empty seat at the front of the group, sat down, and set his notes on the lone desk on their side of the divide. Mr. Paul continued to pace back and forth in the aisle separating the two groups of students.

"Who built America?" Charles began. "Wall Street—the corporations, big industry—or Main Street, the average American? This country was founded before the introduction of laws regulating corporations and interstate commerce. Sure, there were big companies that made a lot of money, but it was us ordinary people who were laying bricks and hoisting steel. The rise of the corporation in..." Charles paused to check his notes. "In 1811, in New York, organized these people under a different name. The corporate legal entity."

"Somebody used Google," Ellen whispered to one of the students seated next to her.

Charles continued his opening statement. "But these people were still ordinary, everyday folks who made things, manufactured products. Built the bridges and tunnels in New York and New Jersey and elsewhere in America. A legal entity is nothing without its human capital. The people, that's who built Amer—"

"People? What you mean by people?" Didi interjected.

"Um, the Americans—you know, ordinary American people," Charles responded with an expression that said the answer was obvious.

"Yeah, but who's that? Women, immigrants, black people? They were grinding just as hard. And, like, they weren't even seen as American 'people' by legal standards."

"Here we go. We couldn't even get past the opening statement without making it about race," Charles whispered and rolled his eyes dismissively.

"At least the ordinary American people got paid. Black people built your Main Street and Wall Street for free," Didi interjected.

"Diana, you're supposed to be on our side, remember?" Ellen snapped.

"I pulled up for the participation grade," Didi snapped back at Ellen. "But we're talking about hustling for a paycheck, which you wouldn't know about because Daddy bankrolls your life." Didi shot a side-eye at Ellen. "Oh, and immigrants built America for nothing. A little small piece of Americana pie and a one-bedroom tenement for their whole fam. There's more than one kind of 'ordinary American,' Charles."

"Yeah, but you and your family and many others eventually moved up and out. You live in a nice neighborhood, you drive a decent car, your dad has his own business, and we all attend the same public school. Isn't that what the American dream is about? We all eventually make it if we work hard enough. Race is a limiting factor if you make it one."

"Yeah, for real, Charles—tell me more about your family's struggle with social mobility. I'd love to hear about your abuela's experience in the Bronx," Didi countered.

"Ugh, this is so performative." Ellen jumped into the conversation. "You act like you were forced into being, like, ordinary or something. Yeah, there are poor people in America. There are immigrants who come here and initially struggle. But poverty is, like, a choice. My dad came here from the mainland with nothing. Now we own buildings and a bunch of property. No one handed my dad anything. They called him the worst names in the book. Chink, slanty eye, piss complexion, gook. But he and his family— his brother, sister, and even his elderly mom—kept working and rose above it. No one is going to feel sorry for you. Get up, work, and get through it. Like I said, being poor is a choice."

"It's a choice, but it's also a choice for policymakers, Ellen," Ada said, finally inserting herself into the debate. "I hear what you're saying. But your dad came here with a family. He had generations of social bonds to draw on. What if the social bonds of the family were systematically broken? What if your dad was taken from his parents, and his parents were taken from theirs, and so on, and they were dehumanized, told by everyone that he is inferior, and forced to work for free? Ultimately, he died and was brushed aside like ashes, and then your mom was only viewed as a vessel for reproduction, then work, then more reproduction to give this country children treated like free assets, then she worked until she died only to have her children repeat the cycle."

Winter halted her tapping and twirling of her pen. She grasped her pen firmly before deliberately laying it on her desk. She quickly closed her notebook, placed it back in her backpack, zipped it up, rose, and strode across the room without bringing her eyes up. Mr. Paul watched but elected not to point out anything. It was the first time Winter had shown anything resembling a reaction at school, as far as Ada could remember.

"Look, I don't know about any of that," Charles said. "All I know is that the founding fathers intended on equality for people."

Winter suddenly stopped, closed the door, and turned to face the class. She shot a dubious stare at Charles. "Equality, hmm?" She gave a sarcastic laugh loud enough for the class to hear. "Equality means different things to different people. Social mobility is conceivable when you come here from China or India or PR. You've already bought into the American dream as soon as you set foot in America. You even came here of your own accord. You see what other immigrants before you accomplished—how they came with nothing but worked and made it. That is your playbook. It's been handed down with each generation. Then you say, 'We did it. We couldn't speak the language, and we made all this happen. Why can't they?'" She let out a low sigh. "Why can't they? Because from the moment black people came to America, they were told they were nothing. They were told they were here to work and only work. They had no previous generational examples of success. Because dads, granddads, great-granddads, and so on were all slaves. What example of social mobility do they have to draw on? They weren't sold the dream when they were born."

"So you want us to apologize for that? My parents ate locusts back home so they wouldn't starve," Ellen rebutted.

"But they were home. Among their own. Not strangers in the only land they ever knew," Winter said despondently before finally opening the door and leaving the class.

"I wish we would also talk about how Africans in Africa were directly responsible for the slave trade," Charles said. "They were capturing and selling slaves for the European traders showing up at their shores. They weren't exactly uninvolved in all this."

Ada scratched her head.

Kal, a Desi classmate, who'd been sitting on team Main Street, doodling characters in his notebook, finally spoke. "Yeah, no, we're gonna sub you out, Charles. Someone bench him."

The clock struck three. That was the cue for everyone to pull themselves out of the debate and back to reality, shifting from passionately debating to checking their phones, chuckling, and returning to their routines.

"We ran out of time," Mr. Paul said. "Team Wall Street will present next class. Good first day, everyone. Good ideas bounced around. I encourage more people to participate next time. Remember, no opinion is a bad opinion. It was John Stuart Mill who argued that the only check against our own fallibility is to promote the free expression of ideas. Not all old white guys should be canceled." He raised his voice a few decibels in an attempt to be heard over the chatting and shuffling of papers and feet.

"Ooh, that's deep. Is he on Instagram?" one of the students asked from the back of the class.

———

Didi insisted on driving Ada home after learning that she'd left the Blaze back at her house. The ride home was anything but subdued. They finally got the chance to do what they'd done their entire lives—gossip and one-up each other with tales of their random socially awkward encounters.

"Like, for real, I can't believe you complimented Jojo's sweater while you were tumbling down the stairs. Only you." Didi laughed as she recounted her experience of Ada's ungraceful exit from the assembly.

"Oh my God, I was, like, this is my nightmare." Ada shook her head and laughed.

The laughter subsided as they pulled into Ada's driveway. Ada traced the seam of her jeans with her thumbs and then lifted her head. She pressed her lips together, feeling restless. "I'm gonna be okay, right?"

"I don't know," Didi replied, surprising Ada with how forthright she was being about her fate.

CHAPTER 11
SHE THREW A PARTY. YEAH, SHE THREW A PARTY

"AND WE'RE COMMITTING to the sneakers? Even when you're going to a mansion party?" Didi nodded to Ada's Jordans as they stood in the foyer of Ada's house.

"Don't your feet revolt against you for wearing heels all night?" Ada pointed to Didi's huge heels.

"Don't ever change, Ada Lorham." Didi gave Ada a genuine smile.

Ada hugged her dad and then her mom, who was still loading the dishwasher.

Zeina froze up before relaxing again and whispering, "Be careful."

"Be home by eleven." Marcel pointed at her sternly.

"Midnight, maybe?" Ada lifted her brows.

"You want to stay home instead?" he responded.

"Fine. Eleven." Ada dropped her chin to concede then mumbled, "Thank you, Daddy." As soon as she and Didi stepped outside, she said, "I'm driving."

"What's wrong with the way I drive?" Didi asked but yielded to Ada's request by walking over to the passenger side of the Blaze.

"Because I don't want to miss my newly negotiated eleven p.m.

curfew. You tend to escalate things and get whisked away. I need an exit strategy just in case things go that way." Ada hopped into the car, sending puffs of dirt floating out of the seat. "You have to yank the door open." She made an aggressive pulling motion with her hand through the window.

As soon as they were both seated, Didi chuckled at something on her phone. "Ha! Ellen is asking me for the address now that she had to cancel her party," she said as Ada cut through the back-streets of Clifton and into Montclair, the next town over. "She just texted me."

"But I thought she wasn't invited."

"I'ma mess with her a little," Didi said with a cheeky smile while typing into her phone.

About ten minutes later, they pulled up to the mansion. This neighborhood was different. The lawns were manicured, the roads were finely paved, and even the asphalt glistened. The trees were carefully trimmed and skirted. The houses were bigger. Each one had its own unique style and symmetry. But one house—the mansion—stood out from the rest. It was an island on the block. The Victorian-style home rested in grandeur, dwarfing the other affluent ones on the street.

"I'm getting Twelve Oaks *Gone with the Wind* vibes from this house," Ada remarked.

"This is going to be epic." Didi was preoccupied with taking photos of the mansion.

Even if they weren't sure of the address, the girls surmised from the spotlights and blaring music that this was definitely the spot. From the red carpet to the valet service out front, it was like nothing they'd ever experienced.

"I'll drop you off here and park down the street," Ada said, reluctant to give possession of her revered vehicle to the people in the black tuxedos and white gloves.

"I'll walk with you, A," Didi said.

"Nah, all good. I'll find parking and head in."

"All right, I'll catch you inside. This is wild. They got a water fountain literally the size of my swimming pool in the front of this joint. Oh wow, lion statues. I bet these are the types who vacation in the Hamptons and rock white sweaters on white linen pants in July, but their rich pores never sweat."

Ada drove around the circular fountain and to the front. "See you inside," she said as Didi got out of the Blaze.

She waved off the valet, looped the car around the circle, and drove out of the majestic gates and back onto the street before finally spotting a vacant spot a block out. After pulling in, Ada texted her parents to let them know she had arrived, turned off the car, and aggressively pushed open the door. She recalled the ease with which Axel's door had elegantly opened and how, in contrast, the Blaze needed a semi-violent show of force to open.

Ada strolled by the immaculately groomed lawns outside each home. It was a lovely fall night, anyway. The reflection of the early-autumn leaves from the streetlights while bass notes and conflated teenage excitement filled the air.

"You seriously have zero protective instincts," said a familiar voice behind Ada.

She instantly knew it was Axel. He'd probably been trailing her the whole time. After hearing the story of Axel and the other Senaz in Didi's basement, she'd expected him to be close by.

"Your Aegis is missing, and you're out gallivanting out here by yourself?" he asked.

"Fancy seeing you here. We have to stop meeting like this," she said without breaking stride.

"You seem to think you have all the answers." Axel was accompanying her a few strides back.

"I've been doing okay my whole life. I'm sure if something happens, it won't be in upscale New Jersey. I'll take my chances." Ada paused. "And your cologne is excessive."

"I think I smell nice." Axel pinched his shirt and pulled it toward his nose to smell himself. "The sooner you understand that this isn't a game, the easier it will be for us to protect you."

"I'm starting to think I do not need you. But you… people need me. You know, I could just as well walk away from all this."

"I would love to see how that would work out for you, Ada. Please, go ahead and 'walk away' from all this." He maintained his distance behind her.

Ada stopped a few yards from the mansion's open gates and turned to face Axel. "I know what happened at Didi's house. That's not cool. But I'm not doing this. Not tonight. I'm gonna go into this party, hang out with friends, probably drive a few of them home, then wake up tomorrow and deal with…" She waved her hands at Axel. "You people. Because I'm sure you'll be around. Somewhere."

He raised his hand from his waist, looking like he was about to speak.

Ada motioned with both her palms to prevent another one of his long-winded rants. "And don't ever think about sneaking into my house. Even if it's for your holy war back in your world."

Axel shook his head and retreated a few steps back from Ada. The thunderous bass and treble blared distinctively down the driveway. More cars continued to make their way through the open gates.

"Cool. Cool. Enjoy your time, Ada. I didn't sign up to be a chaperone, anyway. I'm gonna go inside, maybe do a few keg stands, probably be celebrated for doing something dumb like skateboarding off the roof and into a pool, maybe, then head home and feel good about myself. You should try it." Axel sounded irritable.

"Real self-validating behavior there, Axel," Ada shot back.

"If you can't comprehend the gravity of the situation, then you may as well denounce that you're special and go in there and crush some cheap beer in red cups like everyone else."

"Maybe I will. Maybe I won't. All I know right now is you're starting to get on my nerves. I'm going inside." Ada marched briskly toward the party.

"The universe gives meat to those with no teeth," he muttered as she walked away.

CHAPTER 12
THE GIRL IN THE GREEN DRESS

ADA: *Where you at?*

Ada texted as she made her way through the grand doors of the mansion. The crystal doorknob glistening with the reflection of the lighting was hard to miss. The silver front door was splattered with more crystals in a sequential pattern. When she finally looked up from her phone, she was struck by the grandeur of it all. Soaring cathedral ceilings greeted her. The regal architectural masterpiece had a vast open space occupying the center that seemed as large as a basketball court, with elegant columns separating each breakaway room. It was a stunning royal-style residence. The floors were natural marble with onyx mosaics and gold moldings, and an absurdly large crystal chandelier dangled above the center of the room. Both contemporary and classical art decorated the walls. The second floor featured a balcony spanning the entire perimeter where, presumably, closed doors led to multiple bedrooms and bathrooms. Ornate railings graced the balconies on all four sides of the house. The ground floor was crowded with partygoers, but Ada noticed security stationed at each stairway, turning away people who tried to get upstairs.

Didi: *By this ice sculpture bar thingy. This house is wild fam.*

Ada: *There are like 3 of them in here. Which one?*

"Ellen! You found the place!" Didi exclaimed to Ellen, who was coming toward the ice sculpture at the same time as Ada.

"Real funny, Didi. Pin dropping me the location of the comic book store. They were having a local Comic-Con. I should have known it wasn't the spot when three tatted-up Powerpuff Girls asked me if I was going as 'non-appropriated Mulan', whatever that means." Ellen was clearly in a foul mood, studying the home with a frown.

Didi wore a look of extreme satisfaction.

"And look at this place. Seriously, how gaudy?" Ellen remarked.

"How did you even find the spot?" Didi inquired with a sly grin.

"Thanks to Ada over here. She texted me the location. Your friend is your only redeeming quality." Ellen nodded at Ada. "Okay, so who the hell is Lamia Melaina? I found nothing on her socials."

"Yeah, me neither. She's a ghost," Didi said.

"Shots!?" Jojo had caught up to the rest of the group. "First round's on your boy. Let's go!"

"They're literally free, Jojo," Didi blandly answered.

"Does this place have a bathroom? I've been driving around the middle of nowhere, New Jersey, the entire night." Ellen uncomfortably wiggled.

Across the room, Ada spotted someone who stood out from the swathe of people. She was holding court, surrounded by those clamoring for her attention. Her jungle-green dress with touches of blue beamed with extravagance. The dress hung loosely beneath her neck, extended all the way down below her naval, and drooped behind her, flowing a few inches short of the floor. It was open at the back. Her whole style was a definite contrast to Ada's cargo pants and vintage RUN-DMC T-shirt.

Suddenly, streams of thoughts seared through Ada's skull.

"I can't believe he's here with her."

"I'm supposed to be home by ten p.m. Okay, one more drink, and that's it."

"These heels are killing me."

Voice after voice intruded into her mind. The pressure of all those unrelenting thoughts overwhelmed her. She hunched over in agony, placing both hands over her eyes then shifting them to her ears to block the voices out. Fear, happiness, anxiety, confusion, entrancement, excitement, horror—she could sense the emotions all the way to the pit of her stomach. They bounced around inside her, pulling her down to one knee.

"Do you need to lie down somewhere?" A tepid hand reached out to Ada's shoulder.

In a moment of relief, Ada looked up toward the voice. The girl in the green dress now was standing directly above Ada, her black hair dangling perfectly, with an empathetic smile.

"I'm… no, I'm just feeling a little unwell," Ada mustered the energy to say.

"You've been feeling that lots lately. I told her to lay off the shawarmas," Jojo noted.

"Jojo, it's a woman thing. It happens to us once a month, *ya tu sabe*," Didi hurriedly said.

Ada regained her composure, took a deep breath, and gathered the strength to stand back up to meet the eyes of the girl in the green dress. She took in her flowy black hair and the glow of her bronze skin.

"I'm Lamia."

Ellen studied her closely. Didi looked on indifferently. Ada gathered the strength to reach out a hand. Lamia watched Ada's waiting hand before finally shaking it. The handshake lingered a little too long. They were the only two people in the room for a few seconds.

Finally, Lamia released her grip. "Nice shoes. Jordan 13s," she commented after glancing at Ada's feet.

Ellen rolled her eyes.

"You know your sneakers. I wouldn't have guessed," Ada said, gesturing at Lamia's gown, with its daring frontal cutout and sumptuous drape.

"I like to know things." Lamia lightly tapped Ada's sneakers with the front tip of her heels.

"Is that gown Elie Saab?" Ellen asked, hurling herself into the conversation.

Lamia threw a dismissive glance at her before refocusing her gaze back on Ada.

"I gotta give it to you—you pulled up to a catered event in sneakers. It's bold, but it's confident. Fitting in is so played out." Lamia, again, gifted Ellen a sideways glance.

"Erm, yeah, thanks. I got a thing for sneakers. That, and I can't walk in heels to save my life," Ada said.

"Funny enough, I was actually able to secure the entire Kobe 9 series last week," Lamia continued. "Every release. It took a while, but I'm pretty sure I got them all. At least that's what my shoe broker assured me."

"Shoe broker," Ada said to herself. "I didn't know that was a thing. I shall discuss that with my college counselor as a potential career path." She laughed nervously before restraining herself to keep from rambling. "You've got them all? Like, even the Kobe Grinches?"

"Yes," Lamia coolly said.

"The pink Kay Yows?"

"Those too." Lamia nodded gracefully. "I've got them all stored away in the pool house out back. I'll show you them later on tonight." Lamia looked around the party and smiled at the sight of two guys balancing wineglasses on their heads.

"I should probably do my rounds. It was nice meeting you, Ada, and you too." She gestured to the rest of them.

Their eyes shimmered with adoration at being granted an audience with the host of a party, who moved and talked like a celebrity—all except Ellen, who'd cast a sharp, questioning look at Lamia when she'd uttered Ada's name.

"We'll have a drink later," Lamia said.

Before they could reply, she glided into the crowd, floating about, parting those who had stopped what they were doing to admire her. It was as if Lamia had temporarily suspended time and space.

"Do you guys think we're actually friends now? Or am I just imagining that part?" Ada asked.

"Okay, she's my new favorite human in the world. Rocks fresh threads…" Didi counted on her fingers. "Is mad cultured, lives in a ridiculous home, and is still hella chill with everybody she meets. Basically, she's the good version of Ellen." Didi held out four fingers to Ellen like she was presenting proof.

"She's trying to come for my crown. It's a power play," Ellen said, glaring out at Lamia.

"She don't even know you're alive, El. Did you see how she brushed you off? Like, shoo, little bug, I got gold columns." Didi flicked her fingers at Ellen. "Your pops owns a couple of brick buildings."

"She's like a phantom. She doesn't exist on socials. Why even live a life of luxury if you don't post about it? It's like going to a Michelin restaurant for the food and not for content." Ellen was scrolling through her phone. "Who are you, Lamia Melaina?" she muttered to herself, fully consumed with her phone.

"Like, no, really. I'm wowed by how well adjusted a human being you are," Didi said.

"I'm going to take a look around. Something's off. But first, I desperately need to hit the bathroom," Ellen said before wandering out into the crowd.

Didi nudged Ada and whispered loudly enough for only them to hear, "*Mira*. Isn't he supposed to be on guard for you or something?" She motioned toward Axel at one of the marble-top tables, flipping solo cups and gulping back beers. He was consumed in a competitive beer-pong game with his basketball teammates and surrounded by the usual cast of high school groupies vying for his attention.

"It's better this way," Ada whispered back. "He's so preachy."

"Yeah, he was trying to do the most back in the bathroom with all that 'chosen one' talk, after your, you know, thing." Didi pressed her fingers to her temples and mimicked a brain explosion.

They watched as Axel took off his shirt and hoisted both hands in the air to declare himself the victor of beer pong before placing his arm around one of the girls, who swooned a little.

"*Pero* Mikey Fay, on the other hand…" Didi nodded at Mikey Fay, who noticed her looking over at him.

He raised his cup at her, winked, and flashed a confident smile. He was leaning against the ornate table that had been set up for beer pong.

"Someone, get me a doggy bag because I'm taking him home," Didi remarked.

"Really? And your dad will make him breakfast in the morning?" Ada asked.

"You know your girl don't got that kind of foresight."

The party had reached capacity. There was barely any room for Ada and Didi to move about. They were unable to recognize most of the faces present.

A fight briefly broke out in one of the rear corners of the house. A legion of burly men dressed in black, who were running security at the event, stepped in to quickly dispose of the belligerent culprits. It served as a gentle reminder to all in attendance that the natural result of every high school party involving alcohol—a fight between testosterone-driven boys—would not be tolerated there.

Ellen had rejoined Ada and Didi, wearing that same unimpressed scowl. Meanwhile, a most unexpected person was making their way toward them.

"Winter? What are you doing here?" Ellen asked.

"I am asking myself the same thing," Winter responded, looking around at Lamia's home. She was dressed in casual gray distressed jeans and a tank top more suitable for an evening jog than a party of this caliber.

"Hi, Winter," Ada said casually, drawing a scrutinizing glance from Winter.

"Who's hosting this thing?" Winter asked them.

"That's what I'm trying to find out. I'm getting major Jay Gatsby energy from this chick. Like, where did she come from?" Ellen quickly answered, trying to clock Lamia, who had disappeared into the crowd.

"Good book. Not his best, though," Winter said, continuing to scope out the place.

"Hmm, I agree. I'm a fan of *The Beautiful and the Damned*." Ellen said with a sly wink.

Winter raised an eyebrow of amiable surprise. "I like *Tender Is the Night*. You can't trust who you think you should." Winter restfully met Ellen's wink with a crafty smile then glanced again at Ada, who hunched her shoulders and swayed uncomfortably at that comment.

Ellen flinched just slightly under Winter's piercing black eyes. She adjusted her purse and hurriedly ran her fingers through a few loose strands of hair behind her ear. The two were silent for a moment amid the loud bass blaring through the party.

"I didn't know you read F. Scott Fitzgerald," Winter said approvingly. Her initial smile grew just slightly larger.

"I love him. The guy wrote about ambition versus loss, and money versus class. He spoke my language."

"I thought I had you pegged, Ellen Liu. I guess I was wrong about you." Winter was now sporting a visible smile.

"A lot of people are." Ellen continued to hold her smile.

"Makes two of us," Winter said. "I'm gonna take a walk and check out this..." She waved her hand around the room. "This party. I'll see you later?" She politely waited for only Ellen's reply.

Didi and Ada shared a perplexed look.

"Hey, we should, like, I don't know, get a coffee sometime or something," Ellen nervously said.

"I'd like that," Winter responded before shifting past Ellen and into the hall of the party, shooting one last studious glance at Ada.

Winter swiftly transformed her smile back to that of an unamused spectator and wove through the crowd with a severe countenance. She made no effort to even politely nod at a guy obstructing her way while taking inventory of every detail at the party, from the art to the security personnel to every column lining the halls. She was clearly not there to socialize. She was there for something else.

Mikey Fay casually strolled over to Didi. With one hand in his pocket, he said, "Who invited all these people? I thought it was gonna be just you and I." He gave a knowing laugh.

"Is that line original, or you been dropping it on other girls?" Didi asked.

"Um, yeah, I guess," Mikey Fay responded.

"Whatever. You'll do."

Ada, meanwhile, took that as her cue to pretend to talk to Ellen, who didn't even try to go along with it.

CHAPTER 13
THE POOL HOUSE, AMONG OTHER THINGS

"Allow me to show you how to work a room," Ellen said to Ada, casually waving at a few people Ada vaguely recognized.

Together, they navigated their way through the maze of mostly inebriated revelers. Ada tucked her hands into her pockets, unsure of whether to participate in the occasional small talk Ellen so comfortably engaged in. Axel was still consumed in the bravado that came with being a high school superstar athlete. His healthy dose of self-confidence only intensified when surrounded by teammates and admirers. He didn't even notice Ada and Ellen when they slipped past him as he was performing a headstand while one girl held the beer funnel for him, with a small audience cheering him on.

"Did anybody scuff those yet?" Lamia appeared at Ada's side. Regardless of how thick the crowd was, Lamia could part the throng of people directly surrounding her.

Ellen shooed away the person she was pretending to be interested in as soon as Lamia showed up.

"So far, so good. Although I've accepted it's an inevitability at this point," Ada said.

Ellen lingered, eager to insert herself into the conversation, like a kid waiting for the right time to jump into a double Dutch jump rope.

"I'm sure I have that pair in your size if that happens." Lamia assessed Ada's feet.

"Ordinarily, I would think that's a crazy thing to say, but..." Ada looked around the house in wonder. "Given the context, it wouldn't surprise me that you had multiple sizes of sneakers."

"Come, let me show you the collection." Lamia abruptly made her way to the rear patio door, expecting Ada to follow her, not sparing a glance at Ellen.

"Go ahead," Ellen mouthed to Ada then pretended to be involved with something on her phone.

Reluctantly, Ada trailed along behind Lamia. A burly security guard opened the patio door leading to the back. She and Lamia made their way out to the open air while the guard followed. Turning back to look at the security guard behind them, Ada noticed Ellen slip outside, undetected, by placing her foot in the door and waiting for the security guard to take a few steps farther before carefully opening the door just enough to squeeze through and take cover behind the cedars running alongside the path. Ada rushed to swivel her head back to Lamia, forgetting to breathe.

Ada turned again to cast another glance at the cedars concealing Ellen. She tilted her neck to see around the burly man trailing close behind them. He maintained his distance but eerily kept the same pace as the girls.

"Everything all right? You seem tense," Lamia asked.

"Yeah, all good. Just the whole security guard thing." Ada whipped her head back again, focusing her peripheral vision on the cedar instead of the large man behind them. "You really need one in your own home?"

"Not really. But since I don't know most of these people, I figured it was better to be safe than sorry. You know how that goes."

"Erm, I guess," Ada said.

"That's Darius, by the way." Lamia flicked her thumb behind her at the man trailing them.

"Hi." Ada looked back to half-wave at him. Her eyes bulged a little wider than she would have liked when she caught sight of Ellen's heel protruding from the cedar. She quickly turned around and marched with Lamia toward the pool house at the end of the path.

"Okay, so here we are. Prepared to have your mind blown." Lamia punched a four-digit code into the lock.

Two successive beeps confirmed the correct code, followed by the sound of a bolt winding open. Before Ada stepped in, she turned around one last time to spot Ellen out in the open, tiptoeing over to them barefoot while holding her heels in her hand. Ada quickly rushed in, hoping that Ellen would not compromise her encounter with Lamia.

Lamia flipped the light switch, revealing a spectacle of aisles and rows of floor-to-ceiling custom-built cabinets. Each compartment displayed a pair of shoes behind a glass case. She then flipped on another light switch to turn on the backlighting in the cabinets, prominently displaying the shoes like they were featured items in a museum.

"Oh. My. God. This is like the Louvres of shoes. I would live in this room. Like, eat, sleep, start a family, everything in this room." Her jaw slackened, taking a mental inventory of every sneaker displayed, barely noticing Darius stepping inside behind them.

"Lamia, this is amazing," Ada said, splitting her attention between Lamia and the sneakers.

Lamia glanced back at the door, which was shut. Darius nodded in confirmation. She then leisurely made her way to a small empty bookshelf. With her back turned to Ada, she clutched a crumbled-up handkerchief.

Lamia wore a sullen look of concern when she turned back to face Ada. "You didn't seem like yourself back there. You sure you're all right?"

Before Ada could answer, her eyes widened as she spotted a sliver of a shadow floating in the window behind Lamia. If she'd blinked, she would have missed the forehead and silky hair of Ellen ducking behind the windowsill just outside the pool house. Lamia quickly followed Ada's line of sight toward the window.

"Oh no. I'm just—it's my stomach. It's been weird all day," Ada quickly said to draw Lamia back to her.

Lamia slowly turned back to Ada, her mouth forming something that might have resembled a smile. She extended the hand gripping the handkerchief. "So, what's it like being the host of the Agoge?"

Lamia's question sucked the air from the room. Before Ada could process the question, two hands on her shoulders jerked her down. Dazed and lying on her back, she was now pinned down by a man kneeling above her—the security guard, Darius. His grip was unbreakable. He then picked her up with ease and bear-hugged her from behind to constrain her movements. Lamia was unflinching, as though the scene had played out exactly like she had envisioned.

"Host of the *what*?" Ellen's voice pierced through Ada.

Neither Lamia nor Darius seemed to acknowledge the presence of someone else in the room. It was still the three of them. Outside the window, Ellen's head peeked up for a brief second as Ada kicked and flailed in a futile attempt to escape.

"Your plan worked. The Chancellor will reward you greatly for your services to the First Rank," Darius said, continuing to bear hug a struggling Ada.

She was panting for breath. Overwhelmed with panic, Ada reared her head back, frantically trying to loosen the oversized Darius's grip. His arms felt like chains.

"Why are you doing this to me?" Ada asked between grunts of exertion.

"Have you always been this self-absorbed? You really think this is still about you?" Lamia's eyes were now devoid of human emotion and filled with calculating deliberation.

"I don't know what this is about. But I don't want any part of it. Just let me go." Ada was gasping for air.

"But you are a part of it, Ada. The Agoge within you is a part of it," Lamia remarked coldly, smirking above a restrained Ada.

"Please, just… let me go, please."

Ignoring Ada's pleas, Lamia casually surveyed the exhibit of sneakers along the walls. "So much work to make this whole thing believable. I had to learn every one of these shoes like a history catalog."

"I don't understand. What do you want from me?" Ada asked, kicking to no avail.

She directed her steely gaze at Ada. "From you? Nothing. What I want is the First Rank, the Infernum, to know it was I—Lamia Melaina, a once Able Infernum recruit, who clawed her way up to Learning Infernum and is now a Leading Infernum—who dispensed with this Agoge business in such a short time when the Chancellor spent seventeen years trying with no success. Such a foolish little girl you are."

"Little girl? We're literally, like, the same age," Ada said.

"And yet we lead such different lives."

"We'll keep her here," Darius spoke authoritatively. "I've sent word to General Bruton. They should arrive soon. Chancellor Nygaard will want to take no chances."

"No, Darius, I should have been the one to send word. I was the one who put this plan together. Me."

"You forget yourself, Lamia. You dare speak to a superior officer this way?" Darius tightened his grip on Ada.

"I feel like you two have some things you need to work out. Why don't you just put me down, let me walk, and externalize whatever it is you're going through together." Ada tilted her back toward Darius.

"Superior officer. And now look at you still," Lamia said to Darius. "All these years later, and you're still where you started."

"I served the First Rank. And you would be wise to do the

same, Lamia. This is not a suitable conversation right now," Darius said.

"I would be wise? I serve the First Rank in the way I see most fit, Darius."

"The consequence for insubordination is death, Lamia. You have enforced many sentences. You should know this."

"The line between insubordination and compliance is measured by success," Lamia shot back. She finally shifted her gaze to Ada.

"She's insane. This chick is insane," Ellen's voice seared into Ada's mind. "Is she a spy or something? Is Ada a spy? Is this one of those escape-room clubs Ada is a part of?"

Ellen snapped back up to catch another glimpse of the chaos inside.

"Please, help. Call someone. Help!" Ada pleaded toward the window.

Lamia, with a conceited grin, looked around the pool house, waiting for someone to pop out and come to Ada's defense.

Still gripping the handkerchief, Lamia pulled a silver pendant from it with three bars and a diagonal line hanging from the chain.

"Were you looking for something this week? An Aegis, perchance? I wonder how it disappeared?" Lamia allowed the Aegis to dangle from her fingertips.

Ada screamed in another failed attempt to free herself from Darius's hold. "Give it back to me. Give it now!" She'd never seen her Aegis but, for reasons she couldn't explain, she felt a connection to it – as though it was calling out to Ada.

"To think, this whole time, it was in a shoebox in your mother's closet."

"You've been watching me all along?" Ada asked not for confirmation but to finally accept that the danger was as real as Axel had warned about.

"Me? No, not personally. But our Able Infernum at Clifton High School has kept tabs. That's when I decided to have this party. I needed to assemble all of you in one space. To know for certain which among you was the host of the Agoge."

"An Able Infernum?" Ada uttered.

Axel. Everything he'd done had been intentionally designed to lead her to this moment. To trap her for glory. He'd told her he was moved by power and loyalty. He just hadn't specified to what cause. Perhaps he'd left her just enough breadcrumbs to rid himself of the guilt for eventually serving her up to the First Rank.

"We are everywhere, Ada," Lamia said with stony satisfaction. "Thankfully, one of the First Rank on Earth graciously allowed us to use her home. A bit too gaudy for me, but it served its purpose." She dismissively waved a hand.

Ellen's voice beamed through again. "So, she's a squatter. I knew it. I bet that bracelet was a lab diamond, too. I could see right through it."

"You don't even live here? Whose shoes are these? You see why I have trust issues." Ada's feet were still dangling a short distance off the floor.

"I thought you already had a suitor. You see, when Axel suddenly took an interest in you, that's when things got—what do you people here say? Juicy? Why would a gifted athlete, perhaps too gifted, suddenly take a liking for the girl of your caliber, or lack thereof? We knew we were close. That the Agoge was somewhere in this godforsaken town I never wish to return to."

"I don't understand. I didn't tell anyone. You can take the pendant. I don't want any of this. Just let me go." A ripple from her phone whirred in her jeans pocket. It could have been anybody at that point—her mom, her dad, Didi. Maybe Roman.

"Ah, if only it were that easy. Well, actually, it is if we just kill you. Pity those aren't my orders." Lamia said. But she couldn't seem to resist the temptation to continue boasting about her plan. "Axel caught our attention. Our Able Infernum did flag him early as possessing superior traits. And when we found him pulling you from your car that morning, trailing you to the girl's bathroom, we knew something was off. So we searched your home. So predictable of your mother, Zeina, to keep it in a shoebox in her closet. Little did I know I would uncover more than just your Aegis." She cryptically gazed out of the window through which Ada had spotted Ellen ducking.

Despite being confined by an overmatched Darius, Ada exhaled a breath of relief at the newly established fact that Axel wasn't the one who had given her up. Everyone and no one came to mind when she perused the mental catalog of people who could have been part of the secret Internum.

"Look, please don't hurt my family. I'll give you what you need, but leave them out of this." Ada gave another kick and arm flail, hoping to catch Darius off guard. She then focused all her energy on Lamia. Ada tightened her brows, coiled her fingers into tight knots and breathed slowly, desperately trying to extract any thought or emotion that could be read from Lamia's mind.

"Are you trying to read my mind? Interesting." Lamia lost herself in deep thought before rejoining her audience. "Even Sala knew it doesn't work on other Senazis. *A* for effort, though," she said, pouting.

"Sala?" Ada temporarily surrendered her efforts to escape.

"It's not story time, and I have no interest in you or your little family tree, which, I came to learn, is quite intriguing, if I may say."

"No, don't go in there!" Ellen's voice said again.

Suddenly, at the door, there were three successive knocks.

"See who it is," Lamia said.

Darius was clutching Ada with an arm so powerful he would shatter her rib cage if he squeezed any tighter. He contorted his body to move a hand over her mouth—the same one he was using to hold Ada's back to his chest. Then he reached out to open the door with his free hand. He fumbled to coordinate all these actions as he shifted closer to the door.

"Never mind. I'll do it," Lamia said with annoyance.

Without any appearance of apprehension, she opened the door, but not enough to let Ada and Darius be seen. This would be

Ada's chance to scream for help. But Darius was holding her mouth with his spare hand, muffling her helpless pleas.

"Oh, it's you. Shouldn't you be back there?" Lamia said, looking cautiously behind and around the person at the door.

"Did you get her? Is she in there?" inquired a voice with nervous excitement.

"Is there anyone out there?" Lamia asked the person at the door.

"No. No one."

"Very well. I suppose you earned the right to be here. Come in, and don't get in the way." Lamia opened the door slightly wider.

He stepped through the threshold and entered the room—tall, well-built, with brown hair, blue eyes, and a white T-shirt with sleeves just above the biceps, exposing well-defined arms. Ada's blood boiled as soon she laid eyes on him.

"Mikey Fay. You motherf—"

"Were you expecting Axel?" Lamia asked but kept her stare firmly locked on Mikey Fay. "We'll dispose of your Senazi team-mate after this affair."

"Axel is in there. Reveling in his glory," Mikey Fay dutifully reported.

Lamia's gaze flicked upward in a dramatic gesture of annoyance. "Reveling in his glory," she repeated Mikey Fay's words. "You high school jocks are all little boys who can shave."

Ada again peeked out to the window, where she spotted Ellen, mouth agape, staring at Mikey Fay. Ada quickly made eye contact with Ellen, who mouthed, "What the hell?"

In response, Ada mouthed, "Call 911." Pressing her thumb onto her fingers to mimic the act of dialing a phone.

Ellen sharply lifted her shoulders and mouthed back, "What?" then ducked down as soon as Lamia turned back to face Ada.

"Didi. What did you do with Didi?" Ada asked suddenly.

"Who knows? Who cares? Last I saw her, she was accosted by Jojo carrying Jell-O shots. So you can say it hasn't been a good night for either of you."

The Aegis dangled from Lamia's hand. A feeling beckoned Ada toward the pendant, urging her to reach for it. She had to get to her Aegis. There was no one else to rely on at this moment. No one was coming to save her. It was just her, Darius, Lamia, and now, Mikey Fay. Axel wasn't there. Ellen was ducking under a window ledge and Didi was still inside.

Ada swiped at the Aegis in Lamia's hand but only grasped air. A sinister smile formed on Lamia's lips.

"You people are cruel," Ada uttered through labored breaths.

"Cruel? Disorder is cruel. Disorder from the so-called freedoms you humans value. Ours is a society of stability. The Republic was no different from this chaos here. They filled their cups in their mansions while hunger beset the streets. Their moral perversion set Unitas on fire. The First Rank restored the glory of the Senaz from the ashes through order and justice. After all, 'order shall prevail.'" She raised her hands out front of her chest ceremoniously and connected her thumbs and index fingers to form a triangle.

Mikey Fay made the same triangle gesture with his hands. "Order shall prevail."

"Ah, okay. Happy you all found each other in this cult thing of yours," Ada said.

"Funny girl. I'm actually starting to like you." Lamia smiled wickedly.

"Good to know. If I die here tonight, I want you to love again, Lamia." Ada puckered her lips, assuming a phony look of compassion.

Mikey Fay let slip a giggle at Ada's retort as Lamia came two paces closer until they were face-to-face and Ada could feel Lamia's glacial breath on her cheeks. Her skin tingled despite her best attempt not to show she was afraid.

"You fancy yourself a wit." Lamia breathed down on her. "Well, here is a witty idea of my own. We're going to make you wear the Aegis to tell us the location of every other treasonous Senazi here."

"Lamia, those are not our directives. We are to wait here until General Bruton arrives," Darius said again, this time more assertively.

"Won't it please the Chancellor if we offer him the names of everyone else?" Although this was a question, Lamia did not wait for an answer. "Tie her up. I'll make her wear the Aegis," Lamia said. There was a cruelty in her voice that suggested she would not ask again.

"We are only to find the host of the Agoge and inform the General. If she wears the pendant, the Treasonous will know she's here and come to rescue her," Darius replied, concerned.

"Yeah, Lamia, I hear you. You are seen. But I think we should listen to Darius here," Ada said. Somehow, being tied up seemed more fatal than being bear-hugged by an occasionally reasonable villain.

Lamia retrieved a roll of duct tape from her purse then flung it to Mike Fay and flung her chin at Ada.

"Who brings duct tape to a party? Major red flag," Ada said.

Mikey Fay, who'd been looking on sheepishly, obediently taped Ada's hands together.

"Mikey Fay, I think this will kill your shot with Didi," Ada said.

"You just don't know when to shut up, do you? Tape her mouth shut," Lamia instructed Mikey Fay.

Darius continued to clasp Ada from behind. He slightly loosened his grip once Ada's hands were tied. Mikey Fay clamped a hand over her mouth. Ada bit the side of his palm. He recoiled, not uttering a sound, and that hand became a fist that flew toward her chin, knocking her glasses off her face as soon as it landed. The last blurred thing Ada saw before being knocked unconscious was a freeze-frame of Lamia's smug grin.

"Ada, no!" Ellen's voice ruptured her mind again.

When Ada awakened moments later, her feet were bound together with tape. Her heavy curls rested over her eyes to partially obstruct her blurred vision but she could still see both

Mikey Fay and Lamia standing menacingly above her as her body lay on the floor. The blood from Mikey Fay's blow trickled down her neck. Muffled screams were impeded by the duct tape on her mouth, which was pulsating with blood, and drowned out by the music outside. Darius looked on as he checked his watch and peeked out behind the front window.

The merciless low pitch of Lamia's voice was ringing in Ada's ears as she slipped in and out of consciousness. She faintly heard Lamia arguing with Darius but was still too disoriented from the blow to her head to make out what they were saying.

"Her Aegis is the key. Don't you see?"

"I won't allow it."

Ada was awakened again by Lamia's interrogation. "It seems Darius is not as useless as he appears. If you come in contact with the Aegis, your protectors will come for you. So I've decided to destroy it once and for all. This worthless piece of jewelry that preoccupied us all for your entire baseless existence will be no more."

Lamia condescendingly snarled. "You're going to tell me everything you know about Axel, about your family, about why you were chosen to host the Agoge. You, remove the tape from her mouth. Let's see if she's got any jokes left to tell." Lamia nodded at Mikey Fay, who tore the tape off.

Ada struggled to speak. "I don't… I don't know."

"If you don't tell me, I'm sure your family will. Starting with that adorable little brother of yours. Roman, is it? It'll be awfully hard to play college football with broken legs. That would be a horrible tragedy."

"No, please, leave him out of this," Ada pleaded. That was it—the trigger that shattered what fragile facade Ada was maintaining. Lamia had threatened Roman.

"Ah, not so funny anymore, is it?" Lamia seemed delighted to finally be breaking Ada.

Though they were bound, she aggressively kicked her feet, only to meet air and thump back on the floor. She was a helpless fish flopping for life, struggling to breathe, as Lamia gripped the Aegis. The pendant swung from side to side.

Ada's vision was suddenly pulled to the window, where she spotted an object of some sort whirling through the opened crack. It bounced on the floor once before landing between Lamia and Ada, immediately arresting everyone's attention. The stone bounced a few more times before coming to a halt in the center of the space. Time stood still as all of them were fixated on the unexpected interruption that had flown into the room.

"Go see what that was," Lamia demanded of Darius.

A shadow of what must have been Ellen slivered away before it disappeared into the dimly lit backyard. Darius sidestepped Ada and rumbled toward the door. The brawny man stampeded out of the pool house.

"Such a shame." Lamia looked down at Ada lying on the floor. "All that potential. All that power. Wasted on you." She leaned against the window, turning her gaze back out to the backyard.

"It was no one," Darius reported back upon reentering the pool house.

"You never fail to disappoint, Darius," Lamia said, drawing a cocky snicker from Mikey Fay.

In Darius's absence, Lamia had laid the Aegis on the floor and was scanning the room, looking for something. Her sight finally landed on the stone that Ellen had thrown into the room. "How fortuitous," she said in a low voice, reaching out to retrieve it.

With the Aegis placed between Ada and her, Lamia slowly dropped to one knee. She raised her hand, the one holding the stone, as someone would before striking a blow.

"First, I'll destroy your precious Aegis. Formalities, you know. And then, if you don't talk, I'll start with your brother. Then your mother and father. Tell me what you know. Where are the other Treasonous?"

Lamia's voice stirred a madness in Ada. The thought of any harm coming to her family—especially at the hands of Lamia, with that arrogant smile and that conceited laugh—triggered a rage. She could feel a foreign, strange sensation brewing within her. Her hands trembled. Her jaws clenched. She exhaled through her gritted teeth. She could not pinpoint the source, but an energy originated from within her and surged to her extremities. It concentrated at her fingertips. Unable to control the fantastical power, her hands shook aggressively.

Ada let out a primal roar that rattled the floor beneath her. Its raw energy manifested into a blazing green light that erupted from her hands and shot toward Lamia, Darius and Mikey Fay. They were instantly flung to the far shoe cabinets and knocked unconscious. An avalanche of broken glass and shoes descended on them.

Ada collapsed to the floor. The Aegis was just out of reach. She tried to extend her arm so she could clutch it.

Then all went dark as Ada blacked out.

CHAPTER 14
AFTERMATH

Colors and sounds spiraled. A tingling sensation spread to Ada's toes and fingers. The taste of lead resided in her mouth as she lay sprawled on the parquet floor of the pool house. Her feet were no longer bound. Neither were her hands. Tiny shreds of duct tape clung to them. The power must have gone out. Through her blurry vision, she squinted to make out a lifeless Darius and Lamia, barely visible in the darkness of night, under a mountain of sneakers at the far end of the room. Mikey Fay's limp body was an arm's length away. Through it all, she was gripping her pendant ferociously in one hand.

"Help. Someone," Ada mumbled to the floor. She willed herself to lean on her elbows before collapsing back down. Faint echoes of discord from outside sailed into the house. Her breathing, now audible and weary, drowned it out.

"Help." She groaned again.

The dull sound of the handle turning and the whiff of new air from the door opening invaded her senses. Someone entered the room. The intruder crept closer. Ada's strength again failed as she attempted to cover her face in defense. She mustered all her might to blink and refocus. The intruder said nothing. It looked at Mikey Fay's body on the floor then back at Ada. The silhouette of a hand drew nearer to Ada. In the darkness, too disoriented to speak, Ada felt that hand lift her head slightly off the floor.

"What happened? Who did this?" The voice penetrated her perplexed state.

That voice. She'd heard it before. But never like this. It had an uncanny urgency. She blinked again to identify the interlocutor. Her eyes strained a little harder before bursting open.

"Winter?" She panted. "Winter, help me." Ada struggled to get up.

"Don't even think about it." Winter shoved Ada back down with her forearm. "Where are the others? How many of you are there?" Winter continued to press her forearm into Ada's chest. The stream of her braids swayed over Ada.

"I… what just happened here?" Ada trailed off, lowering her voice as soon as she spotted the heaps of disarray in the room, from the shattered glass to the sneakers scattered everywhere. The darkness draped a blanket of confusion over everything.

She could faintly hear people from outside the pool house.

"I don't have a light. My phone is dead."

"I can't see anything."

Ada dropped her head back down to meet Winter's demanding glare.

"That green light. I've seen that green light before," Winter said.

"What green light?" Ada asked.

"Did the First Rank send you? Are you Infernum? Who are you?" Winter's voice was firm, but a hint of anxiety trickled through.

"Winter, listen to me. I am not Infernum. These people tried to kill me." Ada gathered the strength to tilt her head back up again despite still being pinned to the floor by an overpowering Winter.

"Liar. Is he with you?" She nodded in Mikey Fay's direction. "What did you do to him?"

"I don't know. They were going to kill me. Lamia and the big guy with her, Darius. She's insane, by the way." Ada drooped her head back before angling it curiously. "Wait. How do you know about the Infernum?"

Ignoring her questions, Winter followed Ada's finger, pointing to the back of the room, where the outline of two people on the floor lay under the rubble of sneakers. Winter pressed her forearm deeper into Ada's chest before decisively releasing her. She peered closely at Darius's broad, stiff body. Her leg suddenly trembled against Ada as she audibly inhaled through her mouth.

Ada struggled to speak, still lying on her back. "Where's Axel?"

"I knew it. I spotted him walking out here when I was inside. I thought my eyes had deceived me," Winter said as if seeking validation for her suspicions. "Who did this to him?" She turned back to Ada as if to physically haul the answer from her.

"I did. I think." Ada wiped the beads of sweat from her forehead. "I just don't know how."

Winter made her way through the chaotic mess toward Darius and Lamia, leaving Ada to only see her outline from the back.

"You know him? Where have you seen him before?" Ada asked.

"The last time I saw my family." Winter towered over Darius's body.

He was like a potentially ferocious bear in the woods, either hibernating or dead. Even in a comatose state, his physical stature foretold danger. But that danger was lost on Winter. She kneeled closer to his unconscious body and whispered just loudly enough for Ada to hear, "Even in your death, you will not find peace."

The door flung open again, temporarily allowing a burst of more noise from the party. Two more people hurried inside.

"Ada, are you hurt?" Axel rushed to Ada's side. "Your Aegis," he said frantically, retrieving Ada's glasses and handing them to her.

"I saw a light flash. It was this weird green, almost like..." Didi rolled her eyes downward.

"Like an emerald," Axel exclaimed.

Didi locked the door behind her. She rushed to Ada's side, glancing at Mikey Fay. Axel flashed a cursory look at Mikey Fay as well.

"It took me a minute to find Axel. Dude was half naked, letting the crew team do Jaeger shots off him." Didi thumbed Axel.

"Lamia is Infernum. So is Mikey Fay." Ada put her glasses back on and blinked hard a few times. "Also, Didi, if we ever make a burn book, Lamia is in our top three. Up there with Mary Tudor," Ada said as Didi and Axel helped her up to one knee. "Where's Ellen? Is she ok?"

"Damn. And to think she was mad chill. We'll have to bump either the guy who invented Crocs or the one who invented fidget spinners." Didi turned to Mikey Fay. "Mikey Fay, you punk-ass clown. Now you know why I got trust issues,"

"Same." Struggling to rise, Ada hunched over with her hands resting on her knees for support. "More of them are coming. They said something about a General Bruton on his way."

"What did you say?" Winter's voice rang out from the opposite end of the room. Undaunted by either Didi or Axel, Winter stormed toward Ada as Axel stepped in to obstruct her path. In a swift show of force, Winter brushed him aside, causing him to lose his balance. Axel grimaced from the sweeping blow cast by Winter. He readjusted his stance and flung himself toward Winter, this time gripping her elbow, propelling her to turn around and face him instead of Ada. Winter countered and effortlessly pinned him down. She relaxed her grip for a moment. Axel, too, eased up. They exchanged a measured look of caution.

Still caught in a submission move, he finally asked in disbelief, *"Semoni Senazi arti?"*

"Senazi artam?" Her patently guarded voice crackled in astonishment.

"Eyi." Axel nodded.

She finally released him.

"You're Senazi," Axel said.

"Hold up. You... you're one of them too? Am I the only immigrant here who's not an immigrant?" Didi asked Winter, who continued to disregard her.

"It's *artim*. Not *arti*. Your Senazi is rusty." Winter skeptically surveyed Axel before her eyes finally landed on Ada.

"I've got a bad shoulder. It's just, you know, an old basketball injury." Axel shook his shoulder and turned his gaze downward with a grimace.

"Did you say *General Bruton*?" Winter demanded.

"Yes. Darius said they're coming here," Ada responded.

Axel rubbed the pain and bit his lip. "General Bruton. We know that name. Armor told us about his barbarity. We didn't think someone that cruel would actually be real."

"He is real," Winter said, still eyeing Axel, Ada, and Didi somewhat suspiciously.

"How do you know that name, Winter?" Ada asked.

A sullen silence fell. Winter stared at the window trim where Ellen had sought refuge on the other side earlier. Ada, Didi, and Axel remained as still as the woodworking on that window trim.

"He killed my father." Winter redirected her stare at Ada. Her frame drooped just enough for Ada to assume that she was replaying a scene in her mind. Her eyes bounced around like someone watching a film on a large theater screen.

The four of them immediately perked up at the sound of Darius's low-pitched groan. Darius was not yet dead. Perhaps neither were the others. Mikey Fay began to stir as well. Lamia's choked breathing became more discernible with each passing second.

"We have to get out of here." Axel flung Ada's arm around him and headed toward the door.

Didi drew back from Mikey Fay and moved toward the exit. Winter stayed put – almost as if she were welcoming the growing stirs of the three incapacitated people on the floor.

Ada beckoned to her. "Winter, we have to get out of here."

"Winter, you'll have to give us a full download later, but you're going to get yourself killed if you stay." Axel readjusted Ada's arm around him. The muffled sounds of car engines mixed with the noise of the partygoers outside. Axel and Didi tensed in apprehension. Winter didn't.

"Let them come. I want their deaths on my hands." Winter barely even twitched. The light from a car's headlights, originating from somewhere behind the backyard fence and trees, reflected off her face.

"Listen to me. I don't know what these people did to your family. But if Bruton is here, they brought a damn army with them. You don't stand a chance," Axel implored.

"Winter, we gotta go. There are still some people inside the house. We can blend in with them while they're leaving." Ada had regained the strength to stand on her own. She peeled Axel's arm off her.

"*Oye, mira,* I'm all for throwing this bum in a river, but we're all gonna be offed for real if we stay here. This ain't the time for a full send." Didi jerked her thumb at Mikey Fay before placing her hand on Winter's arm to guide her out of the house.

Winter took one last look at the three bodies regaining consciousness and took one step forward, allowing Didi to lead her out.

"Wait." Ada limped back to the pile of shoes dispersed all over the floor.

She sifted through a few pairs before landing on some low-top sneakers. A cursory peek inside the tongue of the shoe confirmed that they were her size. Taking one last look at Lamia, she hoped—however faint that hope was—that this would be the last time she saw her. Ada scuttled back and deposited the sneakers in Didi's oversized purse.

"Real classy, you two," Axel said, unimpressed by Ada and Didi's looting.

"She promised me some sneakers if I scuffed these. I had to make sure she kept her end of the bargain." Ada noted, inspecting her sneakers, which were chafed and slightly lacerated from the struggle. A few splatters of her blood had settled onto her white laces.

"Just be cool, Ada. Let Axel hold you up like you drank too much," Didi whispered as they stepped through the patio door and back inside. "Winter, act like—I don't know. Act like you're not hell-bent on committing homicide against the people who actually want to kill us right now. Just blend."

CHAPTER 15
FLIGHT

A TORRENT of stone-faced men and women flooded through the foyer. They were jostling their way in through the mad dash of partygoers fleeing the uncanny sight of disciplined, uniformed officers barging in. Black shirts and trousers spread to each corner and room. Some canvassed the upper chambers that were off-limits to those at the party. A few splintered into the kitchen in small groups while others spilled to the backyard area by the pool house.

"Upstairs, clear," a serrated, authoritative voice declared.

Ada peeked back through the patio door to notice an increasing number of people approaching the pool house.

"Pick up the pace before they find Lamia inside that pool house," Axel whispered in her ear.

He continued to prop Ada up as she did her best attempt to recreate her version of a high schooler in their drunken glory. Axel held on to the patio door left open by people trickling into the backyard before it locked shut again. Ada felt his bicep and forearm twine from her lower back to her shoulder. He flexed hard enough to escort her out but gently enough to ensure that he wasn't pushing her along.

"Keep your head down. We're almost out of here," Didi whispered to Winter, who was striding methodically to the foyer like it was a conscious exercise to place one foot in front of the other. They were nearly at the open front door with Axel and Ada shuffling behind them.

"You there. What happened to your face?" A cutting voice halted Ada and Axel in their tracks. She was a tall, boxy figure who stood resolutely. With military precision, her legs were shoulder distance apart. She layered an inspecting gaze onto Ada's bloody lip then scrutinized Axel, who was still holding Ada up in their damsel-in-distress performance.

"She had way too much to drink and… you know." Axel forced a sheepish smile.

"I tried to adjust my bra, lost my grip, and punched myself in the face." Ada wobbled and swung her finger at the woman's chest but missed and found air only. She then placed the same finger on the woman's nose, pressed against it, and dizzily stammered, "Boop," before laughing under her breath.

The woman lifted her lip in a snarl and waved them away. Axel steered Ada along as she continued to teeter in her best fake-drunk walk.

"Maybe don't oversell it?" Axel whispered as she shuffled a few steps toward the exit.

Something was off. Winter was no longer advancing with everyone else. Her feet were planted and her posture stiff. Her jaw hardened, and her gaze was stuck on an approaching figure. Axel and Ada looked out in the general direction Winter was homed in on. Didi tried to nudge her along to no avail.

"Just keep going, Winter," Didi whispered. "What you doing? This is not the move."

Winter ignored her question.

"Okay, Winter, I feel like if you didn't really understand the assignment, you should have at least put your hand up back there or something," Didi hurriedly whispered. "Keep walking."

Winter was now squarely locked in on the approaching figure.

"Holy hell, it must be him!" Axel said in muted fervor. A twitch of his neck where Ada's arm rested prompted her to freeze.

Meanwhile, Winter's breath grew louder, more aggressive, more deliberate. Her entire body remained a sculpture, not committing to the slightest movement.

"Winter, what is it?" Ada asked, hoping to break her out of this sudden trance. But Winter had blocked out everything, like a predator unmoved by everything else around her while hunting its prey. "Winter!" Ada spoke with a little more urgency this time.

The man who Winter was staring at barked at the pool of subordinates flanking him. "What's the bloody Leading Infernum's name? Lamia? Get 'er to me now. Where's her Master Infernum?"

"Yes, General," a subordinate immediately said.

The General scowled at the mansion, paying no attention to his aides clearing out the crowd of people from the party.

"That scar," Winter said slowly. "It's him."

The scar cut down his left cheek, glistening even in the darkness. It pulled Ada in, leaving her to focus on nothing else—not even his coarse hair or the way he was trudging along with sturdy shoulders, as if the air were lifting him and dragging him off with each stride.

Stopping at the circular fountain at the front of the mansion, Ada checked for Winter, who was still scrutinizing him with extraordinary ferocity. She could see how Winter was expanding her chest outward a few inches. Winter raised her heel as if she was about to lunge forward.

"General Bruton, no sign of her yet, sir," another subordinate said, not meeting the scornful eyes of his General.

"Keep looking, you useless maggots. Now. And get these lights back on," General Bruton shouted without breaking his attention from Winter. He peered at her a little closer, tilting his head contemplatively. His tongue played on his teeth until another subordinate handed him a folder to divert his attention.

Winter visibly exhaled and finally complied with Didi's nudge to keep moving. Neither Ada nor the others had been able to penetrate her oneness with whatever moment she was having. The dance of solitude between her and General Bruton had lasted a few seconds in real time but had seemed like an eternity to Ada.

They finally cleared the mansion grounds and were out on the road. The dark wrought iron gates towered behind them. "My car is just up there," Ada said, pointing to the end of the street.

Winter took one last look back at the grounds, where General Bruton was no longer visible among the busybodies.

Didi tugged Winter. "What happened? Who was that?"

"That was General Bruton," Axel said, running his hands through his hair and breathing out through puffed-out cheeks. "We need to get out of here. Now."

"We'll take my car," Ada said.

Didi sped up to Ada. "Give me the keys. I'll drive."

Arriving at the Blaze, all but Winter turned back to ensure that no one was following them.

"You have to turn the key and jolt the door at the same time," Ada said to Didi, who was struggling to open the driver's side door.

"This whip is one way to blow out your shoulder." Didi finally managed to pop the door open. She hopped in and unlocked the doors for the others. Ada slid into the back seat and kept her head down. Axel took the front passenger seat, while Winter took the rear seat beside Ada.

"Pump the brakes first, then apply a little gas while turning the car on," Ada advised Didi. The group jiggled in their seats from the vibration of the engine. "It's a smooth ride when you put it in drive."

Didi cautiously drove away, checking her rear view. The street was empty of the Infernum. Only the gentle breeze and leaves rustling escorted them out of the area.

"Aiight, where am I going?" Didi finally slouched into her seat now that they were in the clear.

"We have to regroup. Definitely not at my house. My mom is

already on edge. She'll flip when she sees my lip." Ada traced the outline of the pendant in her pocket.

"Hell no. I am not bringing Axel to my house. I caught a proper Latina beatdown by Doralis the last time he showed up," Didi said.

"No," Winter said. Knowing her, Ada assumed she wasn't about to explain why.

I can't bring unauthorized members of Armor to HQ." Axel nodded toward Didi and Winter.

"Who's Armor?" Winter inquired.

"More like, who are you, Winter? And what was that back there with Bruton and Darius? Were you trying to get us killed?" Axel asked, raising his voice. He contorted his body around to watch for Winter's response.

CHAPTER 16
LAMIA – STAY SCHEMING

"WHAT IN THE STUNTIN' hell happened here? Where is the Agoge?"

Lamia blinked hard to make out the image of General Bruton standing above her. She had somewhat regained consciousness but was still sprawled on the floor under debris of sneakers. At the sight of the General, she swiped away a sneaker that was resting on her hip and sprang to her feet. She adjusted her dress and pulled her hair back.

To her right, Darius rose to his feet and saluted the General by forming the First Rank triangle with his hands. Over by where Ada had blasted them, Mikey Fay seemed to be regaining his senses, too, but made no attempt to rise like Darius or Lamia. Mikey Fay reached for his phone then chucked it back onto the floor, reclining and sighing in exasperation.

"Able Infernum. Rise to your feet and salute your General," Lamia sharply said to Mikey Fay.

Lamia felt Darius's scowl burning a hole through her. She knew he would be put off by her sudden devotion to duty and hierarchy. But she also knew that his penchant for decorum would make him abstain from scolding Lamia in the presence of General Bruton. Lamia quite enjoyed seeing Darius's ire manifesting in the form of a quivering scowl.

Mikey Fay vaulted up to form a triangle. He snapped to attention as he kept his salute directed at the General until Lamia shooed him away with a wave of the hand. Taking his cue, Mikey Fay scampered out of the pool house with his head down to avoid meeting the General's displeasure.

"I will not ask again." General Bruton brought his chin up and widened his stance.

"The host. We found her. We know who she is," Lamia quickly answered.

One of them had to tell General Bruton they'd found Ada and then lost her.

"Darius, perhaps it is more befitting of your status as a Master Infernum, my Master Infernum, to brief the General on what happened. I am only a Leading Infernum, sir," Lamia said in a soft voice. She pressed her hands together and deferentially bowed to Darius and General Bruton.

Darius was spared a few moments to assemble the right words to deliver his update. He had never been an orator. What respect he drew from his superiors—and supposedly from her—was due to his devotion to the First Rank. Being asked to delicately construct a narrative for the highest military general in Unitas was a task he would undoubtedly fail at. Lamia folded her arms and cracked a grin of satisfaction for the stage she'd just set.

"We, uh, identified our subject, erm, target. A, a, person. A girl." Darius stammered and fumbled through his report to General Bruton. "Uh, the, the Agoge. We have identified her home and her school."

"Have you detained her?" General Bruton's question punctured any confidence Darius was trying to project.

Lamia's head swiveled from Darius to Bruton and back to Darius, like a spectator at a tennis match.

"We, uh, not exactly." Darius deflated into himself. He rubbed his hands along his pants. "She… she summoned an ability. We held her here as ordered. Then she shot out a light from within her. It was… green."

"Are you telling me you failed?" Bruton's calloused hand shot to Darius and squeezed his throat with a viselike grip.

"General..." Darius gasped for air through Bruton's constricting hand around his throat. "This girl is powerful." He wheezed, struggling to draw another breath.

"You said it was a bleedin' green light, did you?" General Bruton finally released his grip without even sparing a glance at Darius, who lightly caressed his neck where the imprints of Bruton's fingers had been dug.

"Yes, General," Lamia patiently responded on Darius's behalf.

"The Empress Walk shook in Unitas." Bruton's words ricocheted between Lamia and Darius. "But come off it—she's a right tad too young. No trainin' to be wrangling with the Agoge's power."

"General, if I may," Lamia tapped her lips with her finger. "The plan I put together to identify and capture Ada Lorham was being executed with precision and would have succeeded had it not been for the unnatural intervention of an unforeseen power within her. The next time, we will be ready for her if you provide us with more resources. More Infernum. Phalanx. I imagine capturing her again will not prove difficult."

"No. We're not gamblin' with another chance." General Bruton barked at Lamia. "We will have to draw her out like a rat. The Chancellor wants her to hand over the Agoge with nobody hurting her. Said something about it being the only way. I reckon he has his reasons. You can do with her what you bleedin' want after we get that Agoge."

Lamia's nostrils flared, and her lips thinned as she muttered, "Yes, General."

"What triggered her use of this power?" General Bruton asked as he caressed his scar with his thumb and skeptically eyed Lamia.

Lamia set her frustrations aside to contemplate what came next, calculating her next chess move with fast math. The fact that she had flagrantly disobeyed orders and tried to destroy the Aegis would amount to insubordination, which was punishable by death. To lie to the General about her actions in the presence of another Infernum would implicate them both and be deemed an act of insubordination – punishable by death.

"We can't say for sure. But we think it might have something to do with her Aegis." Lamia gave Darius a suppressed look, imploring him to not expose her actions to the General. She could see the conflict thrashing about on his lips. He was a man of duty to the First Rank, yet to implicate himself in Lamia's scheming earlier that night would surely lead to his arrest, or worse, likely his death. He was still her Master Infernum and had to answer for her.

"Yes." Darius caved like she'd expected he would. "Yes, her Aegis must have triggered something."

"These shabby communication devices," General Bruton mused contemptuously. "Do they really think that a bloody pendant is of any use in their rebellion against Unitas? One by one, they get picked off, and still, like a bunch of blind children, they swear allegiance to a place that only exists in their minds. Unitas? What's it to them? It's a bloody idea they invented. They still think life was good back when the Republic ran things. Well, let me tell you, it wasn't. It was divided, crumbling under the fat bellies of its immoral bastard leaders."

"Why can't we just take one of those Aegises and use it to find the rest of Armor?" Lamia asked.

Her question drew the mockery of the General, who turned to Darius. "What are you teaching these young Infernum? Useless. All of you."

"I… sir, we focus on the prescribed Infernum training regimen as set out by the First Rank." Darius's response made him seem smaller, no longer a sizable, dominating presence.

"You see, young Leading Infernum, the Aegis is from the DNA of the Senazi that uses it. It's primitive technology. Every Aegis is made for a Senazi. They are linked," General Bruton explained to Lamia.

"I understand now, General. Thank you for enlightening me

with what my superiors had failed to explain." Lamia held her stare at Darius.

"You—what is your name again?" The General waved his hand at Lamia.

"Lamia of Unitas, sir." Lamia gracefully dipped her head.

"You did good here, for a Leading Infernum." He took one last meditative look around the room disarrayed by broken glass and shoes.

"General?" Lamia called.

"Ay, what is it?" he responded, slightly annoyed.

"It is the only way." She paused, thinking about how to frame her question. "What did the Chancellor mean by that?"

"You would be wise to not ask too many questions, young Infernum."

With each pacing step the General took out of the pool house, Lamia could feel the room being relieved of the unbearable mass of his arrogance. On his way out, he grazed an equally stalwart Infernum bursting through the door. Realizing that she'd nearly bumped into the General, the Infernum quickly lowered her head but not before sneaking a knowing peek at Lamia. She immediately held her stare and gave the triangle salute. With a displeased glance, Bruton dispensed with her and returned to the aides waiting outside.

"All under control?" the Infernum girl asked.

"Nothing beyond our grasp, Solana," Lamia replied. "Did you see anything?"

"Just some drunk kids on the way in. Anyway, I found these outside that window." Solana held out a pair of silver heels with a leather sole detail and an ankle strap embellished with a silver fringed accessory. Lamia plucked the heels from her hand, dangled them from her finger, and brought them closer to her face.

"I know who these belong to," Lamia said with the heels swaying like an abandoned swing set in a light breeze. "Where did you say you found them?"

"Out there. By that window, on the stones." Solana pointed to the window by the side of the room.

"Makes sense." Lamia grinned.

CHAPTER 17
GETAWAY VEHICLE

"WAIT, STOP THE CAR!" Axel exclaimed.

Didi slammed on the brakes, jerking Ada and Winter forward in the back seat. Someone was running aimlessly in the street. Didi snorted in casual laughter and accelerated a little closer to the wandering person. She rolled the window down while she made her approach.

"Ellen? The hell are you doing?" Didi shrieked.

"You! Ada. You're alive." Ellen instantly stopped her mad dash to nowhere to lean against the driver-side window frame. "Lamia is crazy. She was there…" Ellen panted. "In the pool house. She was there with another guy. And…" She took another shallow breath. "And Mikey Fay. He's no good, Didi. I mean, he's hot. But he's no good."

She dropped her head to the car window frame and brought it up again. Her hair did not resemble the silky smooth set she'd flaunted at the beginning of the party. Loose, frizzy strands went haywire in each direction. Small clumps of dirt resided under and on her manicured nails. A purple scratch ran down her right cheek.

"At first, I thought it was one of your weird Medieval Times reenactments. But it got real when Mikey Fay hit you." Ellen's breathing was beginning to slow. She looked back toward the end of the empty, dimly lit street.

"He did what?" Didi said in an elevated voice.

Axel turned back to Ada. "Did he do this?" he asked in a fiery tone.

"Yes. But it could have just as easily been Lamia or anyone else." Ada brought her hands to her lips to wipe off dense drops of blood that had formed.

"Are you part of this cult too?" Ellen asked. "They said your name. And some guy named Bruton who was coming. And... Winter? What are you doing here?"

"Get in." Ada pushed the door open. "Where are your shoes?" She asked as soon as Ellen entered the back seat. Now sandwiched between Winter and Ellen, Ada shimmied herself forward to clear some space.

"First of all, you're welcome. Second of all, I could have been killed trying to save you back there. That guy Darius is the size of three people. My phone's dead. Where are we going? I'm panicking over here."

"Save her?" Didi asked from the driver's seat.

"Um, yeah. Right here. Thank you, Ellen." Ellen bobbed her up a few inches higher. "Oh, you're welcome, like, everyone."

"Okay, calm down, Ellen. Chill." Didi lowered her face to hide a smile.

"Thanks for that advice, Diana. Didn't realize being told to calm down was all I needed to feel better. We've entered the age of post-medicine."

"Listen, we all have questions right now. Why don't we go to Malek's and regroup? No one will know to look for us there," Ada said.

"Could be the move. I could crush a shawarma right now. I'm starving." Didi made a sudden left, jerking everyone in the opposite direction.

"Who thinks about food in a time like this? Shawarmas? Isn't that something millennials who ride their bikes to those coworking spaces eat?" Ellen asked incredulously.

"You mean the ninety-nine percent rest of us?" Didi quipped back.

"What's Malek's?" Axel asked.

Ada and Didi ignored Ellen. In unison, they mockingly sneered at Axel.

"You seem to think you have all the answers. The universe gives meat to those who have no teeth," Ada said, lowering her voice in an attempt to impersonate Axel. She swayed her head from side to side and puckered her lips for emphasis.

"My blisters have blisters on them." Ellen wiggled her toes in a slight grimace.

"Give her these shoes." Axel threw Didi's purse back at Ada.

Ada hesitated and pressed her teeth together. She opened the purse and peered inside then looked down at Ellen's dirty feet smudged with dried sediment and back up at the immaculately fresh pair of Kobes reposing delicately in the pit of the purse.

"I mean, they're limited editions, El." Ada stroked the outline of the sneakers' fabric. She pinched her lips together again.

"They're not even yours. Give her the shoes!" Winter barked.

"Eyo, we commandeered them joints, Winter!" Didi shouted back, rolling through a stop sign.

"Okay, but maybe wear my socks with them. And try not to crease them," Ada said.

"Ew, I'm not wearing your dirty socks. Give me the damn shoes." Ellen dipped her hand into the purse and pulled out the sneakers. "Great, I came here in a pair of Zanotti heels, and now I'm wearing shoes that look like something a prepubescent YouTuber would wear."

Ellen contorted her legs to slide the shoes on, folding and rubbing them against the back seat, to Ada's discomfort.

It was supposed to be a simple, uneventful, curfew-abiding night. Ada was supposed to ride to the party with Didi, then, assuming Didi didn't get sidetracked with any wild extracurriculars, they would ride home together. Not to mention, she had promised her dad she would be home by eleven. All their phones had died when Ada shot out that blinding green light from her hands. For all she knew, it could have been midnight.

Missing her curfew might have been conceivable since nights out with Didi generally went sideways. Even Axel wiggling himself into the equation this evening, she could have foreseen since he'd been following her around with all that cryptic end-of-worlds talk. But at no point did Ada account for sitting the in the back seat of her own car with Ellen and Winter of all people, at whatever hour of the night, evading the First Rank after blasting them with a supernatural energy, only to regroup at her shawarma spot.

And yet, a nagging suspicion told her that this was only the beginning of events she couldn't possibly foresee – events for which she was clearly woefully unprepared.

CHAPTER 18
BACK AT MALEK'S

"Hɪ, Amo Malek. Two shawarma toum extra and three regular toum," Ada said, doing what she could to play it cool at the counter.

"*Habibti* Ada…what happened to your lip? Why it's bleeding? Who did this?" Malek accusingly looked at Axel. With his signature white towel thrown over one shoulder, he flipped his palm up to a few waiting customers. They would have to wait a little longer until he finished his conversation with Ada.

"No, no, it was an accident at a party we were just at," Ada reassured him. She threw her chin at Axel, Ellen, and Winter, who were seated with Didi at one of the three tables. "The regular toum is for those three. We'll have to build their tolerance to the extra toum." Ada grinned, hoping to veer the conversation away from having to answer any more questions about what had happened to her.

Malek reached out to the ice machine, scooped a few ice cubes, and placed them in a white linen cloth from under the counter. "Take this, *habibi*. Put on your lip. It make the swelling go down." He then wiped the few beads of sweat trickling down his face with his towel.

"Thanks, Amo Malek." Ada applied the makeshift ice pack to her lip.

He continued to study her doubtfully. "They'll be up in a minute. I help these people, okay?"

With a smile, Ada dipped her head to thank Malek and sat down with the rest of the group.

"Who wants to go first?" Didi crossed her arms and projected her question at Ellen.

"No. You people have some explaining to do. We could have had a party at my house, but instead, you flocked to the first shiny invite at a mansion and nearly got yourselves killed." Ellen crossed her arms back at Didi.

"Yeah, my bad. That one was on me." Didi said.

"She was about to get Children of the Corned for some Agoge thing they kept asking her about, and I nearly was about to go down with her. Fortunately, one of the few sports Asian parents ever put us in came in handy when I scaled the wall and out, which by the way, I think exceeds zoning height limits. It was, like, ten feet tall." Ellen raised her hand over her head to emphatically demonstrate. "Thankfully, those tall cedars hid me long enough to climb over." She caressed the scratch on her cheek.

"Didn't you do fencing or something?" Didi asked offhandedly.

"I'm talking about competitive gymnastics, Didi. But yeah, back-to-back state champ in fencing, too. They even wrote about me in the *Clifton Merchant*," Ellen gloated.

"Hmm. I'm sure it was read by tens of people," Didi said.

Ada leaned in a little closer to Ellen. "Why were you out there?"

"Oh, so now I'm going first? Okay, fine." Ellen leaned back against her chair. "I found myself outside by the pool house because, I don't know, whatever, I was just out there for some fresh air and the party was lame, anyway. That's when I heard Lamia ask you about a pendant and a Chancellor. The name sounded German or something. And then she got into it with this massive guy, Darius, who was, like, 'No, we have to wait here until Bruton arrives.' But Lamia was like, 'Whatever, I'm a boss, I'll do what I want.' Real mirror-selfie-with-sunglasses-on and out-of-context-inspirational-quote vibes. Anyway, so yeah, then Mikey Fay came in and was like, 'Nah, we're good. Axel is out there being Axel.'" Ellen pumped her fists in the air.

"Okay, I don't dance like that. But go on," Axel said.

"Anyway, where was I? Yeah, so Axel was busy dancing and partying like he just found out he's not the father. Then you were on the ground, and Lamia threatened to kill you, but then she was like, 'No, we'll make her wear the pendant,' but then she was like, 'No, no, just kidding. We'll destroy the pendant thingy that apparently is a big deal.' So I, you know, I had to jump in and save her because her real friends were probably busy doing body shots." She pointed to Axel and Didi, who threw their heads back and let out annoyed groans. "So yeah, I had to improvise."

"You didn't run away and call 911 like I was trying to tell you. You stayed to save me." Ada softened her voice. She thoughtfully played back the scenes at the pool house.

"Is that what you were saying? I thought you were telling me to take a photo of the culprits for evidence. But my storage was full, and I didn't want to delete any of my curated photos," Ellen responded matter-of-factly and crossed her arms.

"Wait, hold up. Let me understand this. You, Ellen Liu, the girl who crops out her unattractive friends from photos on social media, did a selfless thing that nearly got you killed?" Didi angled her head. "Damn, I guess there's a heart in there after all."

"You don't even know me, Diana. Go worry about blowing out your hair and finding the next two-for-one tacky-hoop-earrings sale."

"And there is she. Welcome back. We've missed you. Thought we lost you for a minute." Didi gave Ellen an approving wink.

Malek's portly frame carried a tray of five shawarmas toward them, wrapped in deli papers. Ada and the others instantly paused their conversation. Exchanging conspiratorial glances with one another, each pretended to be preoccupied with something. Didi tapped the table and puckered her lips, while Ellen made no attempt to disguise her doubts about the food offering.

"Yes! I'm starving." Ada hunched her back and slapped her stomach after returning the half-melted ice bag to Malek.

"Excuse me, can you please cut this in half? I'll save the rest of it for later," Winter abruptly said. "I'm not that hungry."

"No problem. We do it anyway you like." Malek politely set aside one of the sandwiches. "I will keep it at the cash for you in a bag. You pay later when you leave. And if you don't like, you don't pay." Malek trailed back to the counter. He then declared to a few listening ears by the cash register, who excitedly sprang up at the prospect of a free meal, "That's only for them. You pay now or don't eat."

"This night's been a wild ride." Axel took his first bite and raised his eyebrows in approval of the sandwich.

Ada did the same. While savoring the first bite, she laid her sandwich down and reached into her pockets. Her fingers crawled deeper to hook the pendant, pulled it out, and flung it onto the table. It landed beside a strip of pickle that had tumbled off her shawarma.

Axel wrinkled his forehead at the sight of her Aegis. "You have it?"

Ellen recoiled, staring at the Aegis. "That! What is that, and why was Lamia about to destroy it? She kept calling it an Aegis or something."

"Lamia was the one who took it." She spared a glance at Axel. "Look, what you heard wasn't a cult. It's not a Medieval reenactment. Although if I had to choose, I'd be more into US Civil War reenactment in Gettysburg. Did you know that the largest one was held near the original battlefield—"

"Don't care. Get to the story," Ellen interrupted.

"These people aren't from here. They're not, how do I say this, human like you and me. They're more human like, you know, Axel. And…" She glanced at Winter but elected to stop short.

"I figured Axel was involved in all this. So is he a… whatever they are?" Ellen asked.

"One week in, and you've blown my cover, Ada." Axel eyeballed Ada but seemed unbothered. He reached under his collar and untucked his Aegis. Didi, Winter, and Ellen compared the lines of the two Aegises, the one Axel was wearing and the one lying on the table. They were mirror images of each other.

"They want something. Something that I was apparently born with and that I didn't know I had. And if tonight proved anything, it's that they'll do absolutely anything to get it." Ada took another bite of her shawarma.

"What is that *something*, Ada?" Winter asked, narrowing her eyes.

Didi knew about the Agoge. So did Axel. Winter had unveiled herself as Senazi. Now Ellen was involved in all this. Ada's secret, guarded by her parents for seventeen years, had spilled out in one night. It was pointless to conceal the truth from Winter. Or from Ellen, who, despite her flaws—and Ada thought they were many —had saved her life that night.

"The Agoge," Ada replied.

"You? You are carrying the Agoge?" Winter jerked her head toward Ada.

"I guess. So I've been told. I don't know much, but I know it's doing… things inside me." Ada bumped her fist softly against the table twice—not to communicate anything to Winter or anyone else seated with her but because she didn't know what to do with her hands, or the rest of her body, after finally voicing this heavy truth that had been weighing on her chest since the first day of school.

"If you have the Agoge, that means—no. Can't be…" Winter looked at Ada in astonishment. Her mouth spilled open.

"Is the water here reverse osmosis?" Ellen asked.

"It is possible," Axel quickly said to Winter. "But we don't even know if that's a real thing."

"Oy, what are you people not telling Ada?" Didi raised her

voice again. "Enough talking in code. *Basta*. What else she need to know?"

Axel bit into the remaining piece of shawarma, chewed loudly, and said, "Well, you see, it's more than just possible … how do you say this…?"

"That she's Senazi of Legio bloodline," Winter said evenly.

"Wait, hold up. That thing inside you. I thought it gave you powers only. You mean, you…" Didi pointed to Axel and Winter. "Ada is from the same place as you and you?"

"No, I'm human. I'm me." Ada looked to Axel for confirmation. "I'm human, right? It's the Agoge inside me that gives me this power. Isn't that what you told me?"

Ellen threw both hands up.

"You're one of them too?" Ellen shot all ten of her fingers at Ada.

Axel shook his head slowly. "You know, Winter, you should work at a paternity clinic. Just inform dads they're the father without cushioning the blow first with that bedside manner of yours."

"That's impossible. My mom is Lebanese, and my dad is from New York." Ada wasn't addressing them anymore but rather herself. She wove through the catacombs of her memory to recall any instance that could have possibly given rise to any doubt that her parents were anything but human.

"It's not impossible. It's the truth. At least, that's what my—" Winter's eyes drooped for a moment too long, and her usual steadiness escaped her for a minor, passing second. She pulled herself together. "That's what my father told me – that only a Legio can host the Agoge."

"Is this true?" Ada asked Axel.

"Honestly, they don't tell me anything. I don't even know who Armor is beyond those I live with. They keep us decentralized for our protection." Axel fluttered his lips, disappointed.

"If you're a Senazi, and you have the Agoge, that means you're a Legio." Winter cast an intrigued gaze at Ada.

"How do you know so much about all this? Who are you? How did you show up at the pool house?" Ada asked. The question had been on her mind from the instant Winter burst into the pool house.

"The green light. The emerald-green light in the pool house." Winter gazed out the shop window at the city street. "I hadn't seen that green light since…" She seemed to recede into her own world.

CHAPTER 19
THE SIRENS

The Sirens wailed.

Erected around the perimeter of the Senate, the sirens wailed.

Esna had heard the reports too—accounts of how Infernum in hooded black cloaks were marching through the Square of Roses in perfect discipline, holding scepters with an emblem of the First Rank at their base: a red triangle. Accounts of how units would break off at each passing house. Of how, without warning, they would kick down doors and gather the elderly, children, mothers, fathers, and disabled. Of how they threw the children into the back of carriages guided by elosivs, who dashed off with the cracking of whips toward makeshift First Rank holding cells in the Epoch Library. Of how anyone who resisted was met with the fatal blow of scepters.

Esna's father huddled with the family in the depths of the working quarters of the Senate Records Keeper, a room located beneath the Senate. Esna was only twelve, but she still remembered how when she would accompany her father, General Romis, through these halls, he would be met with showers of reverence from senators and aides. The people had admired his honor. His troops had respected his courage. He'd always been the first on the front lines, so eager to lay down his life for the brave soldiers he commanded. Romis had visited this room often to converse with Scholast Adil, the Senate Records Keeper.

Adil had lived in the small quarters with only a bed, quill, and stacks on stacks of memorialized senate decrees, laws, and legal commentary written by prominent Senazi scholars. He'd ominously gone missing three days earlier. His disappearance happened at the same time as other senators and bureaucrats loyal to the Republic—the Treasonous, as Chancellor Nygaard called them—disappeared during the Night of No Moon, as it had since been coined by the First Rank. One by one, senators were either bullied into supporting the Cleansing or had to face death or imprisonment. Some stood fast, while political opportunists wilted before Nygaard.

"Ansa, we only have a few minutes," Romis warned his wife.

Her lips quivered in the thick air of the room they sought refuge in. Esna almost couldn't tell because her mother mostly remained composed. Ansa held her youngest son, baby Finius, close to her chest. He was hungry. Terror had frayed her biological ability to breastfeed.

"It is a natural Senazi reaction to anxiety," Romis would say in an empty attempt to comfort her. The baby's cries were drowned out by the sirens outside. Cries of tortured Senazi men and women and of children ripped from families echoed, wailing helplessly for their mothers and fathers. Crackling fires were consuming portraits of great Senazi leaders of the past. Statues of the Mother of Senaz holding her two infants—Justice and Virtue—were torn down and savagely destroyed by young Infernum thugs licensed to be kings for a day.

"Mama, I'm hungry." Vensana burrowed into her mother.

Romis ran his hand through her coarse, braided hair.

"Your sister is freezing. Keep her warm, my baby." Ansa rubbed Vensana's back, briefly allaying her hunger.

Esna ignored her roaring, empty stomach. She was hungry, but she was the eldest. Vensana was seven with a penchant for defiance. Esna wrapped her arm around Vensana and gently placed a palm on her cheek. It was cold. So was the room.

Vensana had always liked her hair unkempt. It was a beautiful web of thickness sprouting everywhere. Esna flattened the strands with the same hand, only to watch them spring right back up after she'd passed over them. Outside, the sirens still wailed.

The door to the room abruptly swung open. The family shuddered in fear. Those sirens. Their shrieking was suddenly more distinct. Less muffled. The hallway outside was dimly lit. A man occupied the entrance. His face was cloaked by a hood. The dull light left his features indistinguishable. Esna huddled close to her father, fearing the worst. She was old enough to know that he occupied a prominent position. And because of that, their capture was a premium.

"General," the man sputtered. He took a few last looks around before removing his hood.

"Anto," Romis said in greeting.

The man entered the room. Esna could now make out his face. She'd seen him accompany her father before. He was young, perhaps no more than the age of awakening.

"My family. Get them to the Empress Walk. I will join the fight," Romis ordered Anto. There was less authority in his voice. More desperation. His fierce energy was absent.

Esna pulled the creased photo from her pocket and stole a glance—Vensana, Finius, and her parents, all posing regally in front of their home. The world had been so different then. Less cruel and more promising.

Romis signaled to his family to gather by the entrance. After struggling to her feet with baby Finius still tucked to her chest, Ansa guided her two children with her free arm. Esna clutched the hand of Vensana, who trailed close behind her, still shivering from the cold. Her fever had jumped that morning and never broken. Romis was the first out to the hallway, where Anto was waiting with Romis's scepter firmly in one hand and a pile of black hoodies in another.

"My men. What of them?" Romis leaned closer to speak in confidence. "What of the battle at Stalwart Falls?" He relieved Anto of his rightful scepter.

"General, it is lost. They fought to the last sweat on their brows. To the last drop of blood."

"I... I have failed Unitas," Romis said.

Anto's declaration had depleted Romis of whatever redness remained in his cheeks. Esna knew that without Unitas, her father had little left to hold on to. The dream of Unitas as a haven for the unwanted, the fallen, and those who wished to be free to be who they wanted to be and love who they wanted to love was now scattered to ashes. Esna's father would have nothing if he did not have Unitas.

"There is no one left. Most died," Anto said. "Few were captured, and others sacrificed themselves to send their loved ones through the Empress Walk. We have to go, sir. The entire Infernum is searching for you."

"Under the cover of darkness, without even the faint light of the moon, does the Republic die." General Romis's expression grew forlorn.

Ansa gripped his arm and drew an assertive breath. "Romis, this fight, Unitas—it is finished. This family is all we have."

Romis drew a deep breath as he rested his scepter against the wall and raised his arms to neck level. He ceremoniously extended three fingers – his pinkie, ring, and middle finger – out and brought them to his heart. It was the Republic military salute. The same salute was illustrated in an engraving at the base of every scepter used in battle— three vertical bars with a diagonal line cutting across to represent the Unitas Army's Creed of *Honor, Sacrifice, Loyalty*. Mention of the Creed or that salute was now banned by the Elimination of Subversive Threats Directive issued by Nygaard and enforced by General Bruton, the new general of the Phalanx of the First Rank Army, appointed by Nygaard.

"It is an honor to have served the one true General." Anto reciprocated Romis's salute.

"Put these on. They should conceal you from the Infernum." Anto distributed the black hoodies to the family. Romis initially hesitated, retracting his hand as soon as it grazed the fabric. He gnawed on his lips. Wearing the enemy's colors would mean submission and defeat.

Led by Anto, the family moved through the narrow corridor and up an even narrower flight of stairs. At the top was a door left slightly open by Anto before he made his way down to retrieve the family. Esna still clutched Vensana's hand. She would squeeze it once when everyone stopped and twice to signal that they should start moving again. Anto peered through the door to ensure that no Infernum was still on the premises. He crouched through the door to secure the family's exit.

The opulent marble lining the historical halls and dome of the Senate caucus, which Esna would often marvel at when she would visit her father, was smeared with graffiti and char. Rubble now decorated the marble floors. They raced through the Grand Hall until they reached the entrance of the Senate, occasionally stumbling on the remains of statues and paintings. The doors to the Senate were impenetrable. At the order of the Empress Sala of Legio in the early days of Unitas, craftsmen and masons from the deepest corners of their world had traded for the finest steel and mortar to make sure no invading force could occupy the Senate. The ancestors had never accounted for someone who might invade from within.

"We can't go through those doors, Rom. It's risky," Ansa warned.

"There is no other way to enter or leave the Senate. The Infernum is on the north and south side of the Senate, clearing homes of the remaining Republic loyalists."

Ansa's eyes shifted rapidly from her kids to Romis and back at her kids. "It's going to be all right, my babies." She kissed Finius on his forehead, breathing him in. "Esna, carry your sister."

Esna picked Vensana up and mounted her securely on her back.

"We're going to play a game. You close your eyes and describe that pet elosiv you wanted for your birthday. Describe every detail. Don't open your eyes until I tell you." Esna caressed Vensana's hand.

The Senate door had been left wide open by First Rank sympathizers. Anto flipped his hood up and cautiously approached the doors. Esna stepped forward to catch a glimpse of the view. She could not immediately process what she saw from her place atop the senate entrance. In the Epoch Library, a fire billowed through one of the second-floor windows, disfiguring its ornate sills. The First Rank flag – a red triangle with a black background – was hoisted above the Square of Roses. Her father gasped.

The Senate was built on a giant elevated rock structure. The empress of Unitas had intended for it overlook and always guard its people. It offered a panoramic view of the surrounding neighborhoods. Nowhere was the First Rank's complete takeover more evident than from the vantage point of this rock. Everywhere were fires, bodies of dissenters tied to light poles, young children of "subversive threats" rounded into the back of wagons pushed by elosivs, and First Rank graffiti of red triangles with the caption Order Shall Prevail or Treasonous Will Burn covered the walls. A mob of black-hooded teenagers roamed with scepters of fallen Unitas soldiers.

"How dare they desecrate the Creed scepter?" Romis muttered.

"Sir, we will go down these stairs and through the Senate Podium. From there, we will take the lower stairs and travel along the columns of Inquisition Grounds to stay out of view of the Epoch Library. Once the area is clear, we will straddle the south side of the Square of Roses toward the stairs of the Empress Walk." Anto traced the route with his fingers.

They made their way down the stairs and through the Senate Podium. Vensana was still young, but Esna understood why it had been left unscathed. Nygaard would probably want to appear before the people as the head of the First Rank in the place where senators had once addressed Senazis. When Esna would play in the alleys of Sassine, to the west of the Senate, she would hear children talking about the promise of a new Unitas where order prevailed. A Nygaard for the people. None of her classmates at her private school echoed those sentiments. She'd seen him speak but had paid little attention to his fiery rhetoric. Nygaard would want to appear here, she presumed, to present himself as the one who'd brought order to Unitas.

Upon reaching the base of the stairs, they stayed behind the columns of Inquisition Grounds. The corpses of the last Republic soldiers loyal to Romis littered the street. Her mother inhaled sharply at the sight of the body of Julep, her father's second-in-command, tied to a light post as an example to anyone who dared to resist. Her mother was now panting, struggling to catch her breath. The flight from the Senate and the added element of carrying Finius left her depleted. Esna's father relieved her of Finius.

Esna, meanwhile, continued to humor Vensana. "You can't name your elosiv Vai. That's the name of a senator who passed the Senaz Relations Decree," she whispered.

"Why not?" asked Vensana.

"Elosivs are honorable creatures, but so are senators. They're two different things, silly. Okay, then, what else do you see? What color is your elosiv?"

"Purple. It's purple with little spirals of green," Vensana replied from the back of Esna. "Why are all these people sleeping?"

"A rare breed indeed," Esna said. "Those people are just tired. Let's get out of here before they wake up. How about you keep your eyes closed and tell me what else you see." She trotted faster behind the caravan of Anto and her family, with corpses smeared in every direction.

"I can't think with that sound." Vensana plugged her ears.

The sirens wailed louder. The family was closer to the Square of Roses. They stayed low behind some shrubbery on the south side of the square.

"Just keep them closed. We're almost there. If you're good, we'll ride in the magic green tunnel you keep hearing about."

A fire on the second floor of the Epoch Library continued to burn through one of the windows. The shrubbery hid them from plain sight as long as they stayed low.

"Everyone, down. I hear someone approaching," Anto ordered.

They immediately complied. Romis passed Finius back to Ansa and crouched forward in the front, ahead of Anto. He turned to his family and placed his finger over his mouth. Only Vensana was rambling.

"New game. You can open your eyes. I need you to now remember everything you see for the next minute. Don't say a word," Esna said. Not that there was much to see from behind the shrubbery, but at least it was safe. The green foliage hid the gruesome images from Vensana and Esna, who barely noticed that her sister was no longer shivering. The heat from the midday sun must have raised her body temperature.

Two members of the Infernum drew near. They were on patrol. The family was still out of sight, concealed by waist-high shrubbery lined with now trampled flowers. The sirens drowned out the restless movements of Finius and Vensana, who would not stop stirring.

"You dumb sack of nails. She wouldn't give you the time of day," one of them said.

"What do you know? She won't leave me alone," the other retorted. Both were wielding scepters.

The Infernum guards were directly across from Romis and Anto, with only the shrubbery separating them. Esna pulled her sister closer and placed her finger over her lips, making a soft shushing sound. She bobbed her head up just enough to catch a glimpse of her father and Anto waiting for the foot-patrol soldiers to pass before leaping out over the shrubbery in one bound and descending on them with a knee lunged straight to the back of their heads. The impact from the blow left the men instantly unconscious. It was an awesome display of agility that Esna could only hope to one day execute with enough training.

Romis couldn't jump as high or hit as hard as he used to in his youthful days. Still, the acrobatic feat of strength left Esna proud of her father. With Vensana unable to sit still, she took her hand to rise out from behind the shrubbery, gazing at her dad with admiring eyes.

"Your form is slacking on that knee takedown. Arched back. Force channeled through your core. Keep up, Anto," Romis said in jest.

"I am only as well taught as my teacher," Anto returned.

"Sir, these scepters. Look at them. They are much more advanced than anything we used in training and battles." Anto studied the scepter in his hand. Esna found it peculiar that the scepters her father had permitted her to train with had a different engraving at the base—a triangle, not the Republic Creed.

"This is not Unitas technology. I fear Nygaard allied with the Avondals to procure superior fighting technology. They are an intellectual people but of no courage to defy him," Romis lamented.

"Courage. Are we that much better?" Anto discarded the Infernum scepter, leaving it to lie in the bed of trampled flowers.

"We must continue to move. To the Empress Walk," Romis ordered.

The family slowly proceeded through the south side of Square of Roses. This place that had once been bustling with tradespeople, shops, and theaters had become a hollow ghost town peppered with the corpses of the few Unitas soldiers brave enough to fight to their last breath—adult men and boys no older than seventeen. Their blood, in drops and in puddles, stained the historic cobblestones of the square, trickling through the creases. The entrance to the Empress Walk was farther past the square. Phalanx who had recently come under the command of General Bruton were sweeping through the north side neighborhood of Sassine, except for two soldiers who kept guard at its doors. Romis and Anto kept an observing eye on any approaching Infernum thugs or soldiers. Scepters in hand, they treaded cautiously. Identifying anyone with a black hoodie from such a distance would be difficult.

The husky Infernum guarding the entrance seemed unfazed by the catastrophic scenes before them as they continued to monitor the Square of Roses. The family slid through the shadows of the square, remaining hidden behind the columns lining its periphery. Led by Romis, Anto and the family hopped from one column to another. They cleared each column like it was a milestone. The square led to a cobblestone road that led to a set of historical steps. A magnificent door, crafted from copper and brass, adorned the summit of the steps. The two First Rank soldiers were still beside it.

The sirens kept wailing.

"You wait here. Anto and I will approach through the side and surprise the guards," Romis said to the family.

"Anto, on my mark, we will leap up to those stairs and onto the guards. Understood?"

"Yes, sir."

"We're almost there. We'll be safe as soon as we are inside," Romis assured his family. He took baby Finius from Ansa, kissed him on his forehead, and returned him to her.

Esna watched her father and his most trusted soldier approach along the west walls of the Empress Walk. They stayed out of sight of the First Rank soldiers standing directly above them. Romis held out his hand for Anto to maintain his position.

Romis subtly nodded to Anto, and they hurled themselves upward to the platform with a mighty surge of brute force and agility. On their explosive ascent, they thrust the scepters straight into the unassuming soldiers, who never saw the sneak attack coming. It was an incredible spectacle.

Esna had kept Vensana's eyes covered the entire time, but she herself flinched at what had just happened. When she was eight, she'd insisted that her dad let her train with the Unitas Army. He indulged her incessant pleading. She would spend hours in the mirror perfecting her form and demonstrating it to her father when he came home from work. But never had she seen her father in combat. Never had she witnessed blood being spilled.

Romis and Anto rolled the bodies off the platform. They tumbled down into where they'd sprung from a few moments earlier. Esna's father hurriedly signaled for them to approach alongside the walls of the entrance. Led by Ansa, who was holding Finius close to her chest, Esna and Vensana hastily ascended the stairs. The family gathered outside the Empress Walk and were in plain view. Fortunately, they were not detected by Infernum or the First Rank Army.

"I don't know when we will ever return. I don't know," Romis said softly to Ansa. In his eyes, Esna could see the grief over his homeland. Ansa held his hand.

Anto assumed lookout while Romis turned the magnificent doorknob of the Empress Walk. It was crafted in the shape of an atlas of Earth. The blue, white, and terrestrial brown of Earth contrasted beautifully with the brass décor of the door.

Romis rushed his wife and children into the Empress Walk then slid in behind them. Anto quickly followed and closed the large door. Esna had never been inside the Empress Walk before. It was as massive as it was ostentatious. There were no other rooms but that one. It was a circular structure with marble floors. Columns with intricate geometric engravings lined both sides. A set of stairs led to an altar at the opposite end of the Temple. In the center of the ceiling, an oculus edged with bronze shed natural light into the interior.

There was a serenity to the temple. And then there wasn't.

In a flurry, Esna caught a glimpse of a scepter's tip thrust at Anto. He evaded the sudden attack just in time for it to graze his thigh. The attacker had drawn a sprout of blood from Anto's leg. Hiding behind the columns and against the wall, men in black fatigues drew their scepters on her and her family. Three Infernum quickly seized her mother, and another snatched Finius from her arms. Another grabbed Vensana, who let out a frantic howl. A large person bear-hugged Esna, picking her up off the ground. She could barely breathe.

"I have the eldest!" he shouted back in a husky voice. His gaze swept over her.

Esna displayed no revulsion toward this Senazi. She held his stare with a stonelike demeanor, tracing him to memory. He then contorted Esna to grip her from behind.

Her father overtook the first attacker, thrusting his scepter directly into his sternum in one swift blow. Romis was backed into the corner of the temple, surrounded by either a pack of Phalanx or Infernum with scepters pointed at him. Esna, either in her struggle to free herself or because this was all new to her, could not tell one from the other. The Phalanx must have been commissioned while her family had been in hiding over the past few days. All she knew was the Republic and the Republic Army.

Either way, they were enemy combatants, as Esna's father would have formally described them. He took one out in a whirl-wind blow of his scepter and hurled himself at the one holding his son. He punctured the man's leg with a vicious blow of the scepter, snatching Finius with his free hand. Anto finished off the four Phalanx with equal skill. He and Romis turned to the menacingly large man restraining Esna and the remaining soldiers who had fastened Ansa and Vensana in their grip.

A dozen more Phalanx flooded through the entrance of the Empress Walk. More formed a barrier between the family and the portal. The trap had been laid.

The sirens suddenly hushed. A fragile silence ensued.

A man in a rich brown silk robe descended from the raised plat-form, with a dagger hoisted on his hip. In the commotion, Esna couldn't tell if he'd been there the entire time or had just shown up. He was no taller than Romis, but his presence caused the Phalanx and Infernum to slightly lower their heads in deference. Ruffles from his robe rippled through the hush of the room. He raised both palms to insinuate that he meant them no harm.

"Marbas. Let them go. What do you have to gain by taking them?" her father pleaded, shielding his son protectively.

"Nothing and everything," he replied with a confident calmness. "Such an honorable man you are. Do they know how you expect to open the Empress Walk?" He was now speaking to Esna. "Without the Agoge, it requires the sacrifice of Senazi blood to open."

Esna caught her mother and father exchanging looks of dread.

"Oh, you have not told the children how this works. And what, then, when you spill your own blood to save your children? You would port them to Earth? For a better life? To be treated like second-class citizens? Is it worth it when you could have joined me here?" His stinging voice rang throughout the temple. Relaxing his shoulders, he turned to Esna's mother. "Forgive my ill manners, Ansa. I should have introduced myself to your children. I am Marbas Nygaard. Or, more formally now, Chancellor Marbas Nygaard, Custodian of the Lost Agoge, Field Marshal of the Phalanx, Supreme Leader of the Infernum, Lord of All Beasts on Land and Fish in the Seas, Conqueror of All Empires, and Father of Unitas."

Esna knew exactly who he was. The titles were new.

He swept his hand out in a rehearsed, regal way at the children. "Your father and I have a shared history of presiding over Unitas. It's a shame our differences have led us to this."

"You are a disgrace to Unitas!" Ansa shouted in revolt.

"Ah, disgrace. Interesting choice of words for the wife of a man who served at the whims of the decrepit Senate. You see, I am the only thing standing between the Senazi and our extinction." He met Romis's gaze. "You thought you could steal the Agoge all those years ago and then usher your family out of Unitas so easily, Romis. With whom as your bodyguard—Anto, this Viridian savage? Empress Sala should have finished your kind off all those years ago." He spat his words with disdain at Anto. "You steal the only thing ensuring the prosperity of our people from Unitas, and like the coward you are, you then seek to flee to the subgenes, who would just as soon destroy us if they could. This is your master plan for the security of the Senaz?" Nygaard mockingly clapped his hands in slow applause.

"You stole something from me." A sinister tone had replaced Nygaard's ridiculing laughter. "You will tell me where you and that other coward, Genuit, and his Legion Guard lackey took the Agoge. You see, Romis, I knew it was you all these years ago. You closed the door to every one of my inquisitions. It was all one big cover-up. Everyone I asked suddenly became a mute. Genuit with his senate grifters. You with the army. You had power, and look what you did with it. Now, after the Night of No Moon, power is in my hands. All will witness what I do with it." A sneer played on his upper lip.

Romis desperately tried to reason with Nygaard. "You know that Genuit would never disclose the location of the Agoge. Only he knows where it is. He could have destroyed it, for all we know."

Nygaard narrowed his eyes in unrestrained wrath and snorted with anger. Any semblance of composure he'd exhibited vanished. His indignation sent tremors through the temple. "Our people starve because we don't have enough to eat in Unitas. I grew up among them while you sealed yourself in the residences of Laurel Groves. We squeezed together in tight spaces with nowhere to go. Your Unitas squandered our wealth. Tore through our resources. All in the name of what? Progress? Is it progress when the most capable Senazis are equated with the worst of us—the thieves, the lazy, the handicapped?" Nygaard roared. "I gave you a chance to join me, and you betray the Senaz race."

"Enough of this. What is it that you really want, Nygaard?" Romis demanded.

Nygaard turned his gaze toward the altar at the far end of the Empress Walk. "We are all refugees of death. Except for one."

"Immortality," Romis whispered, narrowing his brows at Nygaard.

"*Li gal li Agoge,*" Nygaard responded. "As for your immortality, the great warrior Romis shall forever be a symbol of treason and deceit. Senaz children shall learn about you as the one who nearly brought about the ruin of our people through your treacherous acts. Your children—they shall be my slaves. Your wife—my men shall all have their way with her before discarding her to the alley dogs to feast on her defiled remains. That child you hold in your grasp—he shall know me as his father. I will raise him as my own and teach him to despise his biological father and scrape the filth of your treason from his skin. That braided-hair daughter—she will serve Unitas. And you—your body will hang in the town square to rot. The crows shall feast on you until the dirt reclaims the remains of your flesh and bones. And all will know of the fate of the great Republic Senazi warrior Romis."

Unable to restrain himself, Romis catapulted at Nygaard. Phalanx leaped before their Chancellor, forming a human shield. Romis directed a vicious blow through the neck of one, causing blood to splatter all over. He angled his body toward the other lone Phalanx on the left, a shorter combatant with massive arms who had no chance of surviving against a combat tactician like Romis. Esna's father struck a blow with his right fist then whirled the scepter into the Phalanx soldier's heart. It was a fantastic scene made only more impressive by Romis holding Finius with his left hand the entire time.

Romis suddenly stumbled. A stream of blood gushed from his ribs. It was only a few inches to the side of where Finius was cradled. In the rush to save his family, he had not felt the Phalanx's scepter pierce through him. Romis struggled to rise from one knee. His blood, mixed with that of slain Phalanx, trickled to the floor. Finius slid from his arms and down to his hand. Too weakened to lift his hand, the baby slid a little farther off his fingertips and onto the bloodied floor. Finius lay crying in a puddle of blood. Ansa shrieked.

Meanwhile, Anto was sweeping through waves of First Rank soldiers in the futile attempt to protect the family. Darius quickly released Esna and went to the aid of the other Infernum.

"Bruton—kill him!" Nygaard ordered in a shrill voice.

Anto called out, "General!"

Esna had never seen her father fall to one knee in battle.

"Anto—take my children to the light. Now, Anto. This is my last order." Romis pointed his scepter at the altar and summoned every drop of energy to shoot a faint light in its direction. The portal lit green instantly.

Within a few short moments, Bruton had picked Romis up like a child and raised him above his head. Nygaard watched with a vengeance. No smile appeared on his face. A profound darkness shadowed his eyes. He looked on with pleasure of what was to follow—Romis's death.

Bruton slammed Romis's weakened body to the floor. Ansa shrieked again in agony, "Romis!"

Throughout the unfolding madness, Esna was paralyzed with shock. No tears escaped her. She did not even whimper. She barely noticed Anto sweeping in to pluck her off the ground.

"Stop him!" Nygaard ordered. "Those children are to never enter the portal."

Esna snapped back from her trance to plead with Anto. "Please. Help my father. My family. Leave me here."

She knew it was useless. Her father had trained his soldiers to take orders from no one except their superior officers. Even in their last moments, they had to obey.

The energy of the portal grew more intense with each stride closer that Anto took. He lowered Esna, now an arm's length away from entering the portal. She didn't quite know where it led or how it worked. She just knew from her father that she would have to close her eyes and leap through when the time came.

"When you get to the other side, find shelter. We shall find you, young Esna."

"No! Please, no!" Ansa cried out.

Bruton was standing directly above Romis's bloodied body. The sun beaming in through the oculus emphasized Bruton's hideous scar. With Romis's own scepter firmly held in both hands, Bruton raised his arms to deliver the final blow to Romis.

Anto instinctively launched himself toward Bruton who easily dispensed with him with a swift blow, sending him to his backside, then returned his ravaging attention to Romis. From behind the green light, Ensa witnessed Bruton lifting his scepter to prepare for the final blow. It loomed fatefully over her father's depleted body.

Esna witnessed her father mouthing his last words as his gaze directly met hers, "Honor, sacrifice, loyalty," before Bruton's spear punctured the heart of the last noble Senazi General of the Army of Unitas in a swift, fatal blow. The great warrior Romis was dead. His lifeless eyes stared toward the oculus centered directly above him and up to the heavens.

"Esna, go—it's closing!" Ansa screamed from where Romis's slain body rested.

Droves of First Rank soldiers led by Bruton rushed toward Esna. The portal's green light was waning. Her mother screamed. Her sister wailed. It was just her, alone, and the approaching face of her father's killer. She took one last look at Bruton, committing his scar and every last particular to memory, before shifting her gaze to Nygaard to take one final look at him. Their eyes met amid the frenzy. Bruton was only a few paces away. Drawing her last breath in Unitas, Esna succumbed to the urge to charge at Bruton. At his soldiers. At every battalion of the Phalanx. She took one step forward and out of the shower of green. She wrapped her fingers tightly, creating a solid mass, and emitted a shrill roar directed at Bruton.

"No, Esna! No!" her mother screamed. "Go!"

Before she could lunge at Bruton, a bloodied Anto launched himself at her in one final swoop and pushed her back into the whirls of green energy. She was consumed by light. Her body disappeared into the portal. The green light was extinguished.

CHAPTER 20
WE RIDE OUT

ADA'S MOUTH hung wide open. Didi's lower lip quivered just slightly. Axel stared blankly. Ellen wiped a tear forming at the side of her eye.

"What happened to your family?" a subdued Ellen asked her.

"I don't know." Winter didn't look up.

"Bruton. That's the one who's here. He…?" Ada sank into her seat a little farther.

"Yes. That's him. Darius was there too." Winter looked back out through the storefront again.

"Winter, how did you survive all these years?" Axel's downcast face moved in closer to Winter.

"When the portal opened, I found myself not too far from here, actually. I was twelve. It was cold. I was alone. Afraid. I lived on the streets for a bit until I found a place. I had to live. I lied about my age and worked at a small restaurant for cash. The owner figured I was just another straggler from a broken home, so he let me stay in the apartment above it. I figured out how to use the internet and registered myself at Clifton High School using a fake address."

"You mean… you've been on your own this whole time?" Didi

said, finally shaking herself out of the shock of hearing Winter's somber account.

"Yes," Winter said, leaving the others anxious for an elaboration that did not come.

Ellen placed her hand on Winter's and squeezed it gently. Ada wondered if this was the first time Winter had felt the warmth of a caring touch since that ill-fated last day in Unitas when she'd guided her sister Vensana to the Empress Walk.

"That's why, in Mr. Paul's class, you left. It wasn't about the discussion. It took you back to your family. I am sorry I was such an insensitive asshole then." Ellen breathed a regretful sigh.

"Then?" Didi asked Ellen incredulously. "But seriously, Winter, how didn't anybody look into a twelve-year-old girl living on her own in an abandoned room?"

"When you look like me, you're just another box to tick. They figured I was another kid lost in the system," Winter said. "I was irrelevant. I felt like a speck of dust in the home that I'd left behind. Anyway, now you know."

"I don't think I've ever met anybody my age from Unitas. I have so many questions," Axel said with an eagerness that bordered on insensitivity. "I don't know any Senazi that crossed over after the Night of No Moon. What was Unitas like? Was the bread really as good as the elders say it was? Are the colors really brighter?" Axel caught himself in a moment of unrestrained excitement. "I mean, sorry. What happened to you was obviously awful. I'm going to shut up now." He sealed his lips with a touch of exaggeration.

"It's getting late," Ada remarked, sensing that Winter was tiring of the questions. "Let me grab my phone from Malek." She went to the counter.

"I've got it." Axel scrambled to reach for his pocket. "Is this enough?" He left a pile of bills on the table.

"It's more than enough. We ate shawarmas, not sea bass," Ellen said. "What? It's the steak of the sea, Diana."

Ada hunched over the counter to reach around for her phone,

where it had been charging. A slew of messages popped up from her father, her mother, and Roman.

Dad: *Ada where are you?*

Mama: *Why is your phone turned off? Call me.*

Dad: *Tried you again. Your phone is off.*

Mama: *Call me.*

Roman: *Dude, Mama and Dad are freaking out. Dad went to look for you.*

She was starting to punch a reply when her phone rang again. The word *Dad* appeared on the screen. A little ball of anxiety formed in her stomach. It was less than ideal to face her parents without at least rehearsing her story with Didi as to why her phone had been turned off all night. She found herself in a familiar yet unpleasant scenario. As with whenever she ventured out with Didi, she would have to wing it with her parents again.

"Hi, Dad. Sorry, my battery died."

"Are you okay? Where are you? I'll come get you." His shaky voice carried through the phone.

Ada leaned back on the counter, shuffling her feet. She stuck one finger back up to Didi and Ellen, who were outside, then pointed at the phone, mouthing, "It's my dad."

Startled, Didi mouthed back, "Yikes!"

"I'm good, Dad. We're just grabbing a quick bite and heading home now," she calmly responded.

"No. Do not come home. Meet me at this address: 1173 Tulip Tree Lane. Are you writing this down—1173 Tulip Tree Lane. Go there now." He repeated the address with more urgency.

"Tulip Tree Lane, the street over from us?" she wondered out loud.

"Did you write it down? Go to 1173 Tulip Tree Lane. Ten minutes. Go now." His voice was a bit raspier than usual. Somewhere in the anxiousness was a stern paternal authority she had never heard her father use before.

Her dad abruptly hung up, leaving Ada to deliberate the

address. Tulip Tree Lane was a block away. Ada and Didi often cut through there as a shortcut during rush hour.

"Ada, *habibi*. Take this for that girl. And here is an extra one for her," Malek said, snapping her back into reality. Malek was holding the other half of Winter's shawarma and a second wrapped shawarma for her as well.

"Amo, I think she only ordered the one. This one." Ada pointed to the shawarma cut in half.

"I know the face of someone who don't know when they will get their next meal. I had that face also too many times when I come to this country. Tell her I made too much by mistake." Malek nodded to the sandwiches.

Ada hesitatingly took the sandwiches. "Thank you, Amo, but you have a business to run here. You can't be giving away free food."

"Just remember. If you go to the well for water, and your heart is good, it will always replenish." Malek winked at her and returned to carving chicken off the spit.

When Ada rejoined her friends, she hardly noticed Didi holding car keys in one hand and the Aegis in the other, which Ada had forgotten to pick up from the table.

"So, is anyone dropping me off at home? No way I'm going back there to pick up my car tonight," Ellen asked, tapping her feet on the dilapidated sidewalk outside.

"That was my dad. He wants me to meet him somewhere," Ada said softly. "He wants me to meet him at…" She paused briefly to remember the exact address. "At 1173 Tulip Tree Lane."

Axel quickly jumped in. "That's Armor HQ's address. My address. Why is your dad…?" He looked at Ellen, then Winter, then Didi.

"I have no clue. I just know he told me to meet him there," Ada finally responded.

"Guess I'm taking you to that spot, then." Didi twirled the keys over her finger and proceeded toward the car.

"Uh, no, you can't go. I can't bring you all to Armor. I nearly caught a beating from Cisca when I tried to bring Ally Lindsey back there one night."

"Ally Lindsey? Didn't she decide in sophomore year to put a Von in her last name because she said she was of European nobility or something?" Didi asked.

"Her parents are from Myrtle Beach," Ellen added with a swipe of the hand.

"Yeah, not my finest moment." Axel slumped his head.

"And also, Axel, I have G5 clearance here," Didi said. "I knew about you and Cisca before Ada did."

"Wait, you knew about this?" Ellen asked, her mouth held agape.

"Yeah. Long story. Everyone, get in. We're Tulip Tree Lane-ing tonight. We roll deep in this." Didi tossed the Aegis to Ada, who stutter-stepped forward to catch it.

Ada studied the Aegis resting in her palm. Its weight was feathery. Its edges felt sharp but blunted, like a needle pressed gently against her skin.

"Cisca. I know that name," Winter said. "I've heard it before in Unitas. I was still young, but it sounds familiar." She stayed back, hesitating to get in the car.

"Winter, forget what I said earlier. You're welcome at Armor anytime. I'm sure they'll want to meet the daughter of General Romis." Axel gave her arm a reassuring squeeze without tugging forward.

Ada pulled her eyes down to the Aegis again.

"And the daughter of Ansa Amata," Winter curtly corrected Axel.

"Okay, I guess we're doing this." Axel glanced at Didi and Ellen and breathed a sigh of resignation.

The Aegis was calling Ada. There was something about this featherweight object resting in her hand –a silent connection. Her friends were still deliberating what to do next. She could hear them but wasn't listening. Ada unclasped the necklace. It was neither a conscious nor an unconscious decision. She brought it up to her neck by some function of her own will and something beyond her.

"So I am supposed to skip on home in these sneakers one size too large? I'm coming. This house had better have a panic room in case something else goes down tonight." She could hear Ellen's protests, though they seemed distant, almost detached from her.

"Ada, what are you doing?" was the last thing Ada heard Didi say before she clasped the necklace around her neck and was warped into a solitary darkness.

An image appeared. It was crystal clear. She saw the face of a man—a tribal leader of some sort—adorned with tattoos. He lay slain on the dirt. Dead—not from wounds but from a battle of some sort. The scene unrolled itself like a curtain peeling back the view. An uncountable number of corpses lay with pale magenta eyes resting open. Others had trickles of blood streaking down their noses. There had been a massacre here. In the distance, a lone figure lurked by at the precipice of a forest, staring hauntingly at her. Like a video, the scene turned her around to a group of people on the other side of a gate and a wall. They celebrated her, chant-ing, "*Malar di Unitas.*" Over and over again, the crest of jubilation grew as they repeated the words. Suddenly, the view was washed over with a film of faint green light. It was soft, subdued, until it grew fiercer, less restrained. What moments before had been a hue of peacefulness was now a blaze of rage. It wrestled with Ada, devouring her from the inside.

"Get it off of her. Now," she could faintly hear Axel say. "Hold her down."

Ada fell to the floor, screaming in agony. Her muscles revolted against her. Her limbs felt like they were ripping apart and sewing themselves back together. She convulsed against the coarse pave-ment. Her suffering felt like it had no beginning or end.

Until it ended. She opened her eyes, disoriented and panting, lying on the ground to find Axel clutching the Aegis. "What did I just see?" She panted. "Who were those people? What happened to them?"

"I… I don't know. What did you see?" Axel asked, placing his hand behind her back.

"I saw people. Massacred, dead, heaps of them….someone in the distance. Then this green thing, a flame, burned. At first, it was gentle then it overtook me. What was that?" she asked Winter.

Winter responded with a muted shake of the head.

Didi charged at Axel. "What the hell is that thing? Are you trying to get her killed?"

"He's not." Winter stepped in between the two of them. "That's not how an Aegis is supposed to work. You're supposed to communicate with others. Not…" She curiously gazed at Ada. "Not see things."

"I'm good, Didi. I'm good. Let's just get out of here." Ada took Didi's outstretched hand to propel herself off the ground. Didi gave her one last patient look, and Ada repeated, "No, really. I'm good."

"For the record, this is some messed-up stuff." Didi hopped into the car and once again alternated between pressing her foot on the gas and brake pedals in no particular sequence before turning the ignition key. Like someone who'd accidentally cracked a complicated math equation, she seemed surprised at the sound of the engine roaring to a start.

"We still going to Tulip Tree Lane?" Didi wound down the front window and drove out as soon as Ada had hopped into the back unassisted.

"I guess," Axel responded, settling into the front seat.

"We always knew you to be the weird kid, Ada, but tonight takes it to another level," Ellen said, squeezing into the rear seat between Ada and the window. Winter was on Ada's other side.

"It feels so…" Ada searched her mind for the appropriate word to describe the evening. Unitas. Her near-death experience. What she'd just seen when she put on the Aegis. She finally landed on the word, "surreal." She leaned on her choice of language, contemplating the evening.

"It's not. Unitas is real. But the Empress Sala of Legio – myth surrounds her." Winter chimed in.

"Who is she, anyway? And why does everyone bring her up like she's a god or something?" Ada asked Winter.

"Some thought she was a god," Winter responded.

"I've heard varied accounts." Axel chimed in.

"Ada. When is your birthday again?" Winter asked.

"September thirteenth," Ada cautiously replied. She knew there was more to the question. Winter was from Unitas. Winter was Senazi. "When was your seventeenth birthday, Winter?"

"It passed. This summer," Winter replied.

"Alone?"

"Alone."

"What was it like?" Ada asked with tenderness.

"It was… alone." Winter met Ada's sympathy with a hardness. "I preferred it that way. No formalities. It doesn't come on right away."

"How does it happen?" Ada said, seizing on the chance to ask a follow-up question.

"Well, you have instances of strength followed by bouts of weakness. It doesn't have to happen on that specific date, but around that time." Winter looked out the car window as they passed streetlights, trees, and paved curbs.

Ada glanced at Axel to confirm Winter's assumption.

He swallowed emphatically, shrugging. "I wouldn't know. I haven't hit my Age of Awakening yet. My birthday isn't until December." He fidgeted his hands on the center console.

"You shouldn't have to celebrate your birthday alone, Winter," Ellen said. "Unless you are Ada, and you decided to spend your birthday at the observatory because you wanted to look at constellations. So weird."

"Hey! Ophiuchus, the serpent bearer, is a rare sighting," Ada instantly answered.

"At least she didn't wear a swan dress to her birthday party like she was low-key trying to sneak into the MET Gala, Ellen," Didi quipped.

"Again, I risked death. I sacrificed my heels for her. I am shining bright tonight. And you will not dim my light," Ellen said.

"Pull into this lane. The house is set back behind those trees off the property," Axel instructed Didi as soon as they passed the street entrance to the house.

Didi slammed the brakes and backed up a few feet. Ada flung forward, catching herself on Axel's bicep. He grabbed her forearm to prevent her momentum from carrying any farther. They exchanged a fleeting glance. A natural stillness set over them. Ada cleared her throat.

"You still smell like alcohol and shame." Ada reclined back in her middle seat.

"Poor decisions were made tonight," Axel quickly responded.

Ada's heart forgot to beat as the gravitational pull of his lips drew her near to him. She could swear that Axel, too, was drawing closer to her. He tilted his head and held her gaze one second too long until Ada yanked her brows up and darted her eyes out the driver-side window. "That's my dad's car." Ada pointed to her parents' Toyota parked by the house. The Camry happened to be in her line of sight, saving her. The only thing is, she didn't want to be saved.

"Just tell him you were nearly abducted and killed by a race from another species. It plays well in this house," Axel cleared his throat, collected himself, and casually advised.

"This looks like the kinda spot someone goes when they don't want to be found," Didi said, gesturing toward the lone house surrounded by a thicket of trees.

"Everyone but Ada, stay here. Let us knock on the door first, and then I'll bring the rest of you in," Axel instructed the group.

"Tell me how you want me to sit in the dark on a farm while you bring Ada into this hideout lair? Hard no." Didi turned off the ignition and pushed the door open.

"I'm with Didi," Ellen said. "A broken clock is right twice a day." She pressed her lips together to form an insincere smile at Didi.

CHAPTER 21
1173 TULIP TREE LANE

THEY WERE deep into the property, under cover of large trees and overgrown shrubbery that swallowed any view of them from the road. The small, nondescript house had only one light faintly glowing through a first-floor window. The driveway was unpaved but had been traveled numerous times, judging by the apparent compaction of the trail leading to and from it. The property did not look like a homey residence. There were no deck chairs under the overhang out front, no landscaped flowers or planting to welcome anyone. A tractor out front looked like it had not been used for some time. The air ruffled the leaves, swiping at the distressed wood siding of the second floor. The branches whiplashed against the barely visible second-floor window.

"Let me do the talking." Axel led the girls to the front porch. The wooden panels under their feet squeaked with each step. Axel tapped the door with his knuckle in two successive beats—*tap, tap* —then paused before tapping it four times. *Tap, tap, tap, tap.* "Delivery." His voice bounced off the door and into the dark woods around them.

"Combo number four," a voice from inside said.

"Chinese hot spicy chicken on rice." Axel waited a few moments then turned to the group. "Protocols."

"Our cuisine goes back millennia, and you've reduced it to a combo number at a mall kiosk." Ellen hard-whispered.

A series of bolts and locks clicked and squeaked. Axel fidgeted from side to side, wringing his hands, putting them in his pocket, and taking them out again. Didi leaned against the post supporting the overhang above them, bobbing her head like she was listening to a beat that wasn't playing.

The door creaked open. A sliver of light migrated from the inside onto Axel and Ada, who were facing the entrance. Ellen was huddled closely behind them while Winter was out of sight.

A head poked out and swiped a sideways glance at Axel and Ada. "Ada!" she exclaimed then lasered in on Ellen. "Who is she?" Her wrinkles furrowed into her forehead. Each crevice held its own mystery of a life lived with dignity but now stripped of its purpose.

She nodded hospitably at Didi, who in return lifted her brows at her and muttered, "Sup."

"She saved Ada's life tonight. She escaped the Infernum," Axel quickly retorted.

"Let's not get carried away here," Didi muttered.

"Did you act with caution this evening?" The woman opened the door to let them in.

Winter stepped into the light.

"Flexible term, but sure. Yes, we were… cautious." Axel leveled a stern glare at the group behind him.

"Well, that's a creative interpretation of how things went," Ellen muttered.

"Forgive Axel. His etiquette requires finesse. I am Cisca Royas, former senator of the People's Senate of the Republic of Unitas. Special Advisor to Armor. Come in. You had a long night." She extended her hand to Ada to guide her into the house, and the others followed.

Standing in the foyer, Ada noted nothing exceptional about the interior. Its floors were just as distressed as the exterior, and the furniture seemed outdated and lived in. Scores of books and arti-facts were clumped in piles in various corners.

"Your father called us the minute this all happened. It is our eternal regret that you had to experience the dangerous misfortunes of this evening. Please, get comfortable in the living room."

"My dad?" Ada said slowly, unsure how to piece her father into all of this.

"Ada!" her father called from the second floor.

A rapid succession of footsteps rumbled above them. His feet ricocheted down the stairs. Clearing the final step, he extended his arms and hauled her to his chest, hugging her warmly. Ada burrowed her cheek so deeply into her dad that she could feel his heart pounding.

"Are you all right? Your lip. Are you hurt? What happened?"

"I'm okay, Dad. What are we doing here?"

"I should have told you. Your mom knew it would never go as planned." Her dad kissed her on the top of her head. "When we got word that Bruton was on his way, I knew something had happened."

"Dad?" Ada asked, astonished.

"I should have told you. I should have prepared you better for this moment." He fired his phrases indiscriminately.

"Dad, what are you saying right now?" She pushed him off her gently and looked her father over, hoping to find the answer somewhere in him.

"I know what they told you. Genuit did show up at our house seventeen years ago. But he didn't randomly choose our house. It wasn't by chance. Nothing in this world is. The truth is, I asked him to."

"What?" Ada impulsively blurted, taking a step back from her father.

This was her father—the person who'd raised her, who'd loved her, who'd taught her right from wrong. Never once had Ada doubted that she was his number one priority. Now his revelation sent her spiraling into a whirlpool of doubt.

"I don't understand." Ada looked for the answers in her father's face.

"Sit down." He guided her to the couch.

She was so consumed with the questions pouring through her mind that she barely noticed Winter seated beside her. Didi plumped herself down on her other side. Her dad pulled a chair from the dining room table and sat directly across from Ada.

"Is there Wi-Fi here?" Ellen plugged her phone into a cord by the outlet in the living room.

"Yeah, the password is 'read the room.' All lowercase. The *Es* are 3s. Sit down, Ellen!" Didi barked.

Ellen perched herself on the couch's armrest by Didi.

"There's much I need to tell you." Ada's dad lurched forward and dug his elbows into his knees. "All I wanted was to leave that life behind. But our past has ways of catching up with us."

Each word Marcel spoke left Ada grasping for the next one. Cisca observed like an audience member at a play who had already read the script. There was no intrigue in her patient smile, only a look of expectation.

"Dad, what are you trying to tell me?" Ada asked.

Marcel hesitated and took a final, decisive breath. "Nearly twenty years ago, I was asked, in my capacity as General of the Legion Guard, to accompany a few Senators to Earth to renegotiate the Diaspora Treaty with Senazi choosing to live here—"

"I'm sorry—as the *what*?" Ada asked.

"Wait, you're the General of the Legion Guard? We heard stories about you. You were a legend." Axel excitedly drew closer to him. "Ada, I heard your dad once put down an entire rebellion in the city. With him and just three guards." He was now teetering on his tiptoes, animatedly raising his voice a few decibels. "Oh man. What's your body count like?"

"You're not the main character here. Ada is. Back to her," Didi said, and Axel shuffled back to his original spot, raising his hand in a halfhearted apology.

"It's true." Her dad nodded. "You are of Senazi blood."

Ada blew out a large swath of warm air and massaged her head like she was trying to find a place to deposit this insane revelation her dad had just leveled at her.

"I met your mom, and that was that. I didn't want to go back. I returned to Unitas and told Genuit, our elected Head of the Republic. He was the closest thing I had to a father in Unitas. After young First Rank party members burned the courthouse, he knew the unrest was only the beginning. So he let me resign from my duties to come to Earth and marry your mother. Nygaard and his allies were growing stronger. He saw the storm coming and needed loyal Senazis here. They could have used me there, but he needed me here in case more Senazi showed up."

"What do you mean you met Mama? She knows about this too?" Ada asked, raising her voice.

"Yes. She does. I told her I had to go back to the Senate to formally resign. Then I returned here. To New Jersey. To start a life with your mother."

Ellen remained by the outlet, scrolling through messages after her phone finally powered on. "Whoa, Ada, I know this is, like, a lot to process here, but your dad is kind of a badass. I always thought you were a bit basic—"

"Ellen, I can't even right now," Ada tersely said. "Dad, I… I just need some fresh air." She inhaled deep, forced breaths. "I'm sorry. I just need to step outside."

Ada got up from the couch, taking care to not brush up against her dad sitting across from her. She wandered toward the room's window before hurriedly shuffling the other way and toward the entrance door.

"Ada…" her father called out.

Ada turned to her father and everyone else in the room. Suddenly, they were all spectators—everyone except Ellen, who seemed quite content scrolling on her phone—and Ada was the sole actress on a stage she'd never asked to be on. Didi gathered herself to follow Ada out. But Winter hunched over to place a halting hand on Didi's lap. She lightly pressed Didi back down to the couch and then rose.

Ada needed to get out of this stifling mass. The air was thin, and every inhalation she took was labored. Stepping outside, she breathed in the crisp evening night.

Her solace was short-lived as Winter joined her at the front porch and looked out at the large black walnut tree. "In Unitas, we used to believe that trees cooperated with one other to keep each other alive. They exchanged carbon and nitrate in a competitive equilibrium."

"Meanwhile, here we think they're competing for sunlight, air, and water." Ada stared in the same direction.

"Can't be. It wouldn't explain how so many different species of trees have managed to coexist beside one another for thousands of years."

"If it's nature's way of telling us not everything is a zero-sum game, then maybe we should listen," Ada said.

"You don't want to hear this, but I would give anything to be in a room with my father. Even if it meant hearing infinite lies and having him crush my world over and over again in an endless loop." Winter continued to look out to the trees whooshing about in the fragile night.

"I don't know. I can't help but think the life they built for me was exactly that—built. It was a stage of actors and props."

Winter gave Ada a few more moments of silence.

"It's just that I'm really starting to wonder if we have any control over anything—over how we got to this point, right now— or if our lives are designed for us to play within like little sandbox-es," Ada said.

"It doesn't matter. What matters is you're here now, Ada."

"I get that we live with the decisions we make. But I didn't even make any decision to lead me to this."

"Yes, you did. In your sandbox, you decide the rules. You worry about what only you can control. I didn't get to be here with you—outside this gothic farmhouse on a dangerously unstable deck with premises liability written all over it—by feeling sorry for myself. I came here with nothing. I didn't even have my name. My real name. I had to shed who I was to survive. I went from thriving there to surviving here. The only thing that kept me alive wasn't hope. It was a desire for revenge—to see those who hurt my family feel the same pain I did. All of them. But that's not enough. It will never be enough. I don't have what you have. I don't have that." She jerked her shoulder back toward the house. "Your dad looks at you like you're the center of his universe."

"Even when we're not in the classroom, you still gotta make me feel like I have a lot of catching up to do to get to your level." Ada swung her head toward Winter.

"You've got a lot more than I have." Winter started to head back inside.

Ada hurried to grab Winter's arm before she could reach for the door handle. "Winter, you can't keep holding on to that hate. You don't need to be alone anymore. We all know you're strong as hell, but everyone needs a friend."

"It's the only way I know how to survive," Winter responded, her back still turned to Ada.

"Like you said, surviving and thriving are two different things. I see how hard you work at school. You want more than just to survive."

"What I want to is to see every one of those people who did this to my family burn. Unitas, the Republic, First Rank, Infernum, Armor—they're all the same if you lost everything."

"All this anger won't change anything." Ada tugged her arm a little more forcefully and turned her around just enough for the warm light from inside the house to contour her face.

"No, but it's all I have." Winter brought her eyes to meet Ada's, finally revealing their dance of melancholy.

"You know, a lot of people try to be strong even when they are not. And when that doesn't work, they try to be resilient. But that could only take you so far. So then they go with hope. A sort of shot-in-the-dark kind of hope. And when that fails them, they finally turn to love. And love never fails." Ada unfastened her hand from Winter's arm and placed it on her shoulder.

Winter's breath drew still. She glanced at Ada's hand.

"Nope. You're stuck with us now. Even Ellen is moderately a better person around you. Relatively speaking, of course. She hasn't called you a street urchin from a Dickens novel yet, so that's gotta mean she likes you," Ada teased.

Winter crossed her arms and quickly tried to deflect. "I must admit, things did unravel in the most unlikely way tonight."

"Or did they? These trees, they all need each other. Like a sandbox, you can either build castles or… I don't know, dig a hole and poop in it." Ada withdrew her hand.

"What?" Winter recoiled.

"I don't know. I was on a roll there with the whole strength-to-love thing and the trees talking to each other. Gotta know to quit when I'm ahead." Ada jabbed her fist playfully into Winter's arm before reaching for the door. She paused to look at Winter one last time. "Hey, thanks for this. I needed it."

"Me too." They headed back inside, leaving the rustling branches and trees to their solitary dance in the evening breeze.

CHAPTER 22
TRUTH IS A MOTHER

IT DIDN'T APPEAR that anyone had moved since Ada and Winter had left the room. It was as though someone had pressed pause on the scene and suspended time while Ada and Winter were outside.

Marcel inexplicably stood up. He forced his fingers flat on his thighs to stop them from fidgeting. Ada approached him resolutely this time and placed her hand in his. She guided him back to his chair then resumed her position on the couch between Didi and Winter.

"I'm ready to listen now. But if you're going to drop any more earth-shattering revelations, at least give me a three, two, one countdown to brace myself."

"Oh, yeah, we do this thing where we count it down to each other before dropping explosive gossip. Like, Ada, I have something to tell you... three, two, one—you're not a human," Didi said.

Her father looked tense, like he was steeling himself for the ensuing conversation. He took a deep breath, exhaled, and then the words began to flow. "For ten years, I served as General of the Legion Guard. I protected senators and citizens. I brought order to our city. The night before my last day, I was doing a routine walk-through with my subordinates. We were by the Empress Walk when I saw a man waiting nervously outside the gate with three elosivs.

"I decided to approach him to see what was going on. Before I could reach him, two men attacked me from behind. Fortunately, Huxos and I managed to fight them off. One of them drew a scepter on me. It was different from the ones we used. It was longer, lighter. I'd never seen that kind of technology in Unitas before. On its base, I noticed it had the triangle emblem of the First Rank. They were still a small faction then but were gaining support. I acted quickly and wrestled the scepter from his hand. In one blow, I drove the pointed tip of its blade through his heart. The other two quickly scurried away."

"Um, I'm pretty sure telling your daughter you killed someone totally necessitates the three-two-one rule. You can't just drop that without a spoiler alert," Ellen said from the far corner.

"Again, Legion Guard. So cool," Axel chimed in.

Ada's father had humbly lowered his head at Axel's praise. "Of course, Nygaard would deny his party had been at the Empress Walk. But we grew wary. Why would Nygaard take a strong interest in the Agoge? Only a Legio can host its powers. There weren't many Legios left after Sala's assassination by her daughter. She had many children, but many eventually mixed with Senazis from all over. That was her vision during the Golden Age of Unitas. I was the last of the Legio to marry outside the bloodline."

"What he's saying is there's a good chance you've got some inbreeding in your genes, Ada," Ellen said, keeping her focus on her phone.

Didi tilted her head in mild acknowledgment. "Not much of a golden age if her daughter offed her. But aight."

"Anyway, Nygaard's obsession with the Agoge grew. He tried once to venture into the Hills of the Fallen to search for its source. It's said that's where the Agoge came from. But the Viridians nearly killed him as soon as he stepped through the gate of the wall of Unitas. From that point on, we started learning about Senazis with any trace of Legio in their blood mysteriously disappearing. Nygaard's party of thugs were picking them off to ensure that none of them could ever host the Agoge in the future."

"What you're telling me is we... I'm related to this Empress Sala?" Ada tilted her head, narrowing her eyes.

"So, silver lining of the evening—you got royal blood. I mean, that's cool," Didi said.

"Didi is right. But that never mattered in the Republic. Sala's last act as empress was to abdicate the throne, relinquish her power and status, and give it to the people."

"Still counts," Didi retorted.

"I went back to Unitas one last time to formally resign as the Legion Guard. The situation had grown worse. We could all feel it. Brother was turning on brother. Grievances were aired on the streets. The First Rank held rallies in every neighborhood. Nygaard pointed the finger at the Legios. Newspapers, posters, and films portrayed us as enemies of the Senaz—as the ones who were secretly in control of the Republic. They said that we controlled wealth and profited off their hunger and that the Empress Sala of Legio was a power-hungry narcissist who would have oppressed us all had it not been for the valiant bravery of her daughter, Sania, killing her and sparing us of her oppression. The only thing was, there were hardly any Legios left. We were being scapegoated. I had left Unitas by then, but I am told that during the Night of No Moon five years ago, the First Rank weeded out and killed anyone with a drop of Legio blood."

Ada flashed a glance at Winter—the only one among them who had lived through the Night of No Moon.

"It is the day when Chancellor Nygaard dismantled the Republic for good and established the First Rank," Her father confirmed with a nod, closing his eyes remorsefully.

"I don't understand. What is so important about this Agoge? Why would Nygaard want it so badly?"

Cisca finally inserted herself into the conversation. "Because it gave Empress Sala power. It made her immortal until she died shortly after willingly giving it up to Unitas, where it used to reside at the Empress Walk. All to ensure that if the hordes from the Hills of the Fallen ever invaded, our people could flee to Earth for protection. If a Legio were to host the Agoge again, it would threaten Nygaard and the First Rank's rule."

"And that *if* is now a reality." Ada met Cisca with a half-smile.

"Yes, it is, Ada. Shortly after your father came to Earth for good, Genuit followed him here with the Agoge to transfer to you when your mother was three months pregnant with you. Since that day, the Empress Walk could only be opened with a blood sacrifice. Very few fled afterward without the Agoge. Many were children whose parents sacrificed themselves in the Empress Walk to open the portal."

"So why give it to me, then? Why could you not take it, Dad?" Ada asked.

"If you didn't host the Agoge, the Infernum would kill you without question. We had to buy you time. You are the last of the bloodline. You and Roman," Marcel continued.

It was at the mention of Roman that Ada realized her brother was just as exposed as she was, except he had no Agoge to protect him. "What about Roman? Isn't he at risk? He would be a Legio, too, Dad?"

"Yes, your brother can pass on the bloodline. It ate your father up to know that his son was exposed." Cisca answered on behalf of Marcel.

Her dad picked up where Cisca left off. "Genuit couldn't harness the Agoge's powers, but he could at least contain it when he went through the Empress Walk. It nearly killed him. We knew we had to keep it dormant. And as long as it was inside you, Nygaard would never try to harm you until you reached the age of awakening on your seventeenth birthday." Her dad sat down in his chair. He was still until a force within him brought his eyes up to meet Ada's. "I would do it again if I had to."

"Still, you knew we were in danger this whole time, and you did nothing. You just lied to me—about who you are, where you're from. I thought you were from Staten Island. That your parents died when you were young."

Tension crawled between Ada and her father and spread through the room to Cisca, Axel, Winter, and Ellen. It was one of those times when spectators were aware that they were privy to a conversation that should otherwise not have been held in their presence, and blame rested with them for not excusing themselves sooner from this intimate moment.

"It could have been worse. You could have actually been from Staten Island. Nause," Ellen chimed in.

"I did my best to give you a normal childhood. I left Unitas to get away from it all. But unfortunately, our past is always hopping along two steps ahead of us."

"Does Roman know?" Ada asked in a brittle voice. All those who were dear to her, from her parents to her best friend, were now entangled in this harsh break from her old life, like an iron curtain slamming down to divide the past from the present. Roman was her only bastion of sanity and normality.

"No. He knows nothing. He will find out at his Age of Awakening. But the later he finds out, the better," her father explained.

"And he will have to go through all of this?" Ada waved her hand back and forth between her and Marcel. "He'll resent everyone, including me, for keeping his origin a secret," she said, though she couldn't help but agree with Marcel that they should continue to withhold this information from her brother. "Things haven't been easy since Axel broke all this to me this week."

"Yeah, it was definitely a moment for her, um, sir." Axel seized on the small window of a chance to redeem himself from his earlier buffoonery.

"I know your life was upended when you discovered all this. Inconceivable truths are sometimes still truths," Marcel said.

"You should have prepared me for this."

"I never asked for any of this, Ada."

"Neither did I, Dad."

"Is it cool to call an Uber here? My mom is blowing up my

phone," Ellen said to everyone and no one. Only Winter perked up.

Cisca returned from the kitchen with tea in hand. "It's getting late. Armor is already monitoring your house for unusual activity, Ada. They will continue to do so around the clock."

Ada had noticed how Cisca had been keenly stealing glances at Winter the entire time they had been there. This time, her eyes were glued on Winter. "You—what is your involvement in this? I am certain I've seen your face before." She moved closer to Winter.

"My name is Winter. I attend Clifton High School." Winter delivered her answer in a monotonous way that came across as rehearsed.

Marcel also shifted his gaze to Winter, looking from her to Ada as though her presence in the room was tied to Ada's and vice versa.

"No, it can't be." Marcel exchanged a look with Cisca.

Cisca scratched the space between her nose and mouth pensively. "Is there anything else we should know?" she asked Ada and Axel.

"Nope. I think that's all." Ada sprang up.

"All right, everybody, let's *vamonos. Yalla.*" Didi popped out of her seat and swayed her arms back and forth, sparing conspiratorial glances at Ada and Ellen.

"Winter, why don't you split an Uber with Ellen, and I'll walk the girls home," Axel said.

"Give me your address, Winter, and I'll tell him to take you home." Ellen reached for her phone again. A childish smile formed on her lips.

"I'll find my way home. Thank you," Winter curtly responded.

"No way. You're not 'finding' your way home tonight," Ellen said. "I'll tell you what. I'll call the Uber to my house, and from there, I'll tell him to take you home. Does that work?" She unplugged the charger from her phone and carefully mounted herself beside Winter on the couch's armrest.

"I... I guess that's fine." Winter let a nearly unnoticeable smile escape before recomposing herself, placing her hands by her side, and stiffening her posture.

Two knocks on the door alerted everyone to the window, exposing the outdoor patio. Four successive knocks followed. Axel bolted to it to peep through. Marcel left his seat to stand guard between door and the couch where Ada, Didi, and Winter were still seated.

"Not my ride. It's showing it's still six minutes away." Ellen shrugged.

"Wait here," Axel instructed the girls and crept closer to the door. "Who is it?" He brought his head close to the door.

"Delivery," the voice said.

"Combo number four," Axel said.

"Chinese hot spicy chicken on rice," the voice responded.

"Can we just, I don't know, workshop alternative food items going forward, please?" Ellen rested herself on the seat previously occupied by Marcel.

Axel unlocked the door and turned the knob. The harmonies of the rustling leaves and the sensation of the breeze greeted the room. Ada slid behind Axel to catch a glance of whoever was at the door. The figure came into full view, poking a curved walking stick at the overhead beam supporting the covered porch. He wore a brimmed hat and a trench coat.

"You really ought to touch up this paint." He prodded with his stick to scratch off a small clump of distressed paint that had formed on the porch ceiling. "In any event, I saw the cars and figured our guests were finally here." He swooped inside and passed Axel without waiting for him to extend an invitation. His long trench coat fluttered behind him as if commanded to follow at a preset distance.

Cisca and Marcel gathered closer to the girls seated on the couch.

"Were you expecting me to show up on time?" The man raised his hand to his hat, bringing into view faint spots of green on his fingertips. His fingers flickered about on the brim of the lowered hat. With a wiggle, he drew down the sleeves of his coat and removed it. "Hello to you, Cisca."

He waved his hand around the house. A cheerful smile emphasized the lines on his aging face. The newcomer hung on to his coat for an extra moment before laying it on a side table with his hat. A tall man, he had to bow slightly to hug Cisca.

"Seventeen years. Seventeen years, you go away, and all I get is a hello?" Cisca hugged him tightly.

"It's good to see you, sister," he said in her embrace.

"I'll be damned. Genuit!" Marcel exclaimed. A glow spread through his cheeks.

"Marcelo, old friend. So our fortuitous arrangements spiral into one another like the northern lights of this fascinating planet." Genuit skipped over to Marcel to embrace him but suddenly stopped at the sight of Ada.

"I'ma need someone to translate what that means," Didi said, checking her watch.

"And you must be Ada. What miracle of chance it is to meet you in this time capsule when the misfortunes of ways have gripped you." He took her hand and studied her curiously, not the cursory glance an average person would take but like someone peering through a magnifying glass.

"I… yes. It's me. Pleased to meet you. Again. I guess. Now that I'm not a fetus." Ada noticed, again, the blotches of green on his fingers. She made no effort to pull back her hand. Instead, she awkwardly waved her free hand at him and concluded with an even more awkward thumbs-up.

"Interesting. Interesting indeed." He examined her further and finally pulled away.

"And as for you, Esna, it is due to a regretful call to heroism that you are here today. How the road winds and the ways clear for you to find yourself here in this most unexpected predicament. But then again, nothing is really serendipitous, is it? We are the continuous product of our actions." Genuit lurched his curved frame, dragged down by age, toward Winter.

Winter froze. "That name is dead. And so is Esna."

"It can never be. You are an Amata. Always and forever." Genuit swung his walking stick in a loop.

"By the Imperious, it can't be," Cisca exclaimed. "My eyes betray me." Her wrinkles creased even further. They played on her forehead like the guitar strings being plucked. She tilted forward to closely examine Winter.

"Esna. The daughter of General Romis. You are alive. Among us. On this…" Cisca bowed her head at Winter and pressed her three fingers to her chest to form the Republic salute.

"I am the daughter of Romis Amata and Ansa Amata." Winter repelled Cisca's amazement with coldness. "This is not Unitas. We do not need to extend our formality to a farmhouse in New Jersey."

"A name may vanish, but a legacy endures," Genuit said, ignoring her icy demeanor.

"I am not her anymore. Just like you are not Genuit, the great Senazi Head of the Republic, anymore." Winter glanced over at Ellen, who gave a slight nod.

"Our ride is here. We'll walk out to the main road," Ellen quickly said.

"Let me walk you girls home. Ada, you could use some fresh air. I'll drop off your car when I get back." Axel rotated his wrist toward Didi as though turning on the ignition. On cue, she tossed him the car keys.

"Ada of Legio, only light can banish darkness. Be wary of your light. It has built and destroyed empires." Genuit's advice briefly paused the commotion among those preparing to leave.

"I am not sure if it's mine to begin with." Ada looked down at her hands and outstretched fingers, from where the green light had beamed at the pool house.

"I fear the worst of this trial is yet ahead of you. We come and go. We are unremarkable. All but one of us." His gaze landed on Ada. *"Li Gal Li Agoge,"* he muttered.

"Genuit, she's been through a lot tonight. Let's get her home, old friend," Marcel said, placing his hand on Ada's shoulder.

"You're in it now. For better or infinite worse. And Nygaard and the First Rank and all of Unitas are in it with you." Genuit widened his stance and brought his hands together. "Keep her well, the lot of you. You there," he called to Winter, and she and Ellen paused in their walk toward the door. "Your past is your present, Esna." He pointed his stick at her.

"Right." Winter shook off his message and left the house. Ellen followed.

"I despair to think what else is left when youthful idealism shatters." Genuit tapped his walking stick lightly on the wood floors.

"Whatever. I'm over this guy. Looking like Father Time himself." Ellen's last statement snuck through the crack in the door before it shut.

"Wait. Hold up." Ada snatched the keys from Axel to follow Ellen and Winter. She jogged past them toward the Blaze and returned with a plastic bag with the sandwich Malek had set aside for Winter. "This is for you from Malek. First-time-customer special, probably." Ada extended the bag to Winter, who eyed it skeptically.

"I… I just remembered. I went there a while back. He did the same thing for me," Ellen stuttered, not shifting her attention from her phone.

"Thank you." Winter took hold of the bag. She and Ellen faded into the thickness of the dark road ahead of them until only the outline of their diminishing figures in the faint streetlight remained.

CHAPTER 23
THE WALK HOME

Didi was tapping her toes impatiently when Ada came back inside. "I'm not trying to rush things along here, but there's a *chankla* with my name on it if I don't get home soon." Didi waited in the foyer, not leaving any chance for another reconvening of those present. She then turned to clarify to Cisca for no reason, "*Chankla* is Spanish for slippers. But it's also Spanish for my mama administering a Boricua ass whoopin' with it."

"Are you sure you don't want me to take you home?" her father asked.

"I'm good, Dad. I need some air. The walk will do me good. A lot to process here." Ada gave her dad an embrace.

"Remember, Ada, your power lies in your belief," Genuit said, tracing the hairline cracks in the ceiling with his walking stick.

"Brother, you seem unconcerned with all this. The girl is in grave danger," Cisca said to Genuit.

"It is not our world anymore. It is theirs. We are merely spectators living out our last days as witnesses." Genuit continued to move his stick at the ceiling like an orchestra conductor tracing shapes in the air.

"Okay, well, whatever that meant. That's our cue. Let's roll out." Didi gently pushed Ada out the door and into the open night.

Axel pressed his hands together like he was in prayer and bowed to Genuit. He alternated between hurrying past him and bobbing up and down in an exaggerated display of respect.

"What are you doing? He's not the pope," Didi remarked.

After one final half-bow, he hurried along to catch up to Ada and snatched the keys back from her. He sandwiched himself between her and Didi as they journeyed along the driveway.

"Man, I need a dictionary to be around that guy." Didi placed her hands in her pockets and shivered.

"That guy is the reason we even have hope. Without him, the Agoge would still be in Unitas, and who knows what would have happened next." Axel kicked a small rock along his path.

"First, I find out I have an Agoge inside me. Now it turns out I'm part Senazi, and my family's been lying to me my whole life. Worst *Truman Show* ever." Ada looked up at the stars, wondering if one of those shining objects a trillion light years away could give some clarity.

"Ooh, this is like junior year when Silvia Perreira told Manny that he was the baby daddy, but he, like, totally denied it, and then one day, she brought the baby to school, and everyone was like, 'Awww, it totally looks like that *pendejo* Manny.'" Didi moved her hands animatedly as she recalled that story.

"Am I supposed to be Silvia or Manny in this scenario?" Ada raised her eyebrow at Didi.

"Manny. Minus the deadbeat-dad thing. His whole life was flipped in that moment. Yeah, maybe you didn't father a child, playing like you ain't the daddy, but you know, same thing. Or not. Whatever—I'm trying to make it relatable here."

"I can respect that. That Silvia was messy, though," Ada said, lobbing her remarks over a bewildered Axel and onto Didi.

"But we don't judge." Both girls threw their hands to the sky in their mandatory routine to exonerate themselves from the guilt of their untimely gossip. It was less animated and a little more forced than usual.

The girls stiffened when they noticed two men following them at a watchful distance. Ada, Axel, and Didi stepped off the driveway and onto the main road.

"They're Armor. Cisca probably ordered them to follow us," Axel said.

"So is this how it's going to be from now on—two of them back there?" Ada slowed her pace upon accepting, however reluctantly, that the people trailing them were not there to harm her.

"I don't know, Ada. They don't tell me these things. I try to blend in and make sure you're all right." Axel gave up on the rock he'd been kicking along the way.

"For real? By surfing down a beer-pong table with the homies at the party? Top-notch undercover work, bro. You got blending in down to a science," Didi said, prompting a giggle from her and Ada. "I'ma hop the fence and slip in through the back door. Maybe Doralis won't catch me rolling in this late." Didi bolted toward the wooden fence separating her backyard from the road. She climbed to the apex and twisted around to whisper loudly to Ada and Axel. "Get her home safe. Text me when you're home. Pray for me at the hour of my death by my mama's hand."

Didi disappeared over the fence and into her backyard and groaned through the sharp and jagged shrubbery.

"She legitimately frightens me." Axel shook his head.

"Oh yeah. Don't anger her. Once when we were at Jojo's, she stole his remote control for calling her his *bombomcita*. Do you know how dark you'd have to be to steal someone's remote control? The inconvenience of physically having to get up every time to lower the volume…"

"Remind me to keep all electronics stored away next time she comes over," Axel joked back.

"So tell me, Axel. How do you fit into all this? Armor? The Senaz?" This was their first time alone without her troubles weighing on them. Ada could have chosen to talk about anything—it didn't matter as long as they weren't talking about her and the massive truth bomb about her family lineage that her dad dropped on her earlier.

"I am not sure. Cisca found me when I was a child. Armor raised me here."

"So you don't know your mom and dad?" Ada quietly asked.

"Nope."

Ada struggled with how to ask her next question. "Would you ever want to go back?"

"I think about it every day. Only I don't know what that means. Unitas, to me, is an idea. It's an energy. It's what keeps those folks obeying the orders to march behind us." He flicked his head back at the two people trailing in the distance. "I wish I could divorce myself from my home like Winter did. She seems at peace with it. Being physically present in one place and emotionally present somewhere you've never been before—a place that exists only in the stories you've been told—is a curse." He continued to rub his arms for warmth.

"We all do what we do to give our lives meaning. Winter couldn't have survived here without meaning. And neither could you. I hope you see your home again." Ada slipped her hand under his arm and moved toward him.

The heat from his presence visited her on her skin. She felt the hairs on his arm standing up. He locked his arm, bringing her closer to him. Together, on a serene walk home, with just the two of them stripped of any imminent, lurking drama, their troubles cleared away. The exigencies of life did not exist for those few moments.

"Hey, I'm sorry for not being there tonight." Axel led her up her driveway to her home, like an usher locking arms with an esteemed guest and directing them to their seat.

"We all get caught up in the life we want to lead sometimes."

"I'm still trying to figure out my part in all this." He stopped shy of her front door.

"Your part or who you are in all this?" Ada asked softly.

"Who I could be," he responded, bringing his gaze to hers. The pulsating rhythm of his heartbeat surged through his arm and rippled to hers, like water seeking the path of least resistance.

Ada curled into his arm as if it were a cocoon closing them from the world's orbit, pausing time and space. If their reality seemed to rain fine-edged daggers, the two drawn together created the umbrella they needed to protect themselves.

"I have a feeling the way all this ends will look much different than the way it started," Ada whispered. Light reflecting from the headlights approaching from the other end of the street distracted them. Ada peeked over Axel's shoulder and quickly jerked away from him, leaving the emotion lingering between them. "That's my dad." She snapped her head back.

"Yeah, um, you have your Aegis?" Axel scratched his eyebrow and took another step back from Ada.

"Mm-hmm. It's in my pocket." Ada tapped her pants pocket.

"You don't plan on wearing it again? After, you know…" He pointed at the outline of her Aegis in her jeans.

"I don't know. It was a lot." Ada's hand rested on the front door handle as her dad pulled his car into the driveway.

Marcel approached them and dipped his chin subtly at Axel in thanks for his charitable act of walking Ada home. "You ready?" he asked Ada.

"Yes. I don't have my keys, though. They're still with Axel."

Axel fumbled through the keychain he'd just retrieved from his pocket. "I'll drop off the car as soon as I get home, sir."

Marcel stepped between Axel and Ada to unlock the door and let her in. Ada gave Axel a single wave, her lips pressed together in a forced smile.

"I guess I'll see you Monday?" She shyly backed into the house, averting her father's knowing gaze for a few tedious seconds before sneaking in an embarrassed glance and closing the door.

Her home was exactly as it had been when she'd left. Despite her life being flipped upside down after leaving the house earlier that evening, there was, at least, the familiarity of her house to greet her. From the scratch in the cabinet over the stove to the distressed armrest of the family couch, everything was as it appeared. No layers. No hidden truths.

"Ada! *Habibi.*" Her mom came rushing down the stairs, scrambling to tie her nightgown around her waist.

She pulled Ada in for an all-consuming embrace and breathed in Ada's hair. The mad dash and hug startled Ada to the point where she felt like an inelastic object incapable of moving.

"I thought the worst. The absolute worst. What happened to your face?" Her mom covered her mouth with one hand and then pressed Ada's lips with her finger.

"Ow, Mama. Easy." Ada winced.

"They did this, didn't they?" She scowled at Marcel in accusation.

"Mama. It's okay. I know. Dad told me. I'm… just exhausted right now. Let me go to bed and get some sleep, and we'll talk in the morning." Ada wrapped her arms around her mom and burrowed into her before withdrawing back up to her room.

Ada usually closed the door to her room, but that night, she left it ajar for a sliver of the light from the bathroom to enter. Her fingers hooked the Aegis from her jeans pocket. She brought it to her face and stared at it with the intensity of a nuclear scientist. The pendant had been there, in the other room, her entire life. It had been sworn to her like a name given to a child that would provide meaning and identity for the rest of their lives. Her thumb rubbed the soft intersection of the three lines.

"What are you trying to show me?" Ada whispered to Aegis as she unclasped the hook and held the pendant from both ends.

She breathed hard and brought the Aegis closer to her neck, not by conscious choice but absentmindedly, finally clasping it around her neck and closing her eyes.

The images came back—the massacre by a forest leading up to crests of hills, the faces of those slain on the soil. That one lone figure in the distance. Then came a temple, regal but homey, with columns lining each side. The sunlight entering through an opening of some sort glistened off the marbled floor. Children, many of them, frolicked, some playing while others danced and giggled. One among them stared at Ada with hard purple eyes. She could have been mistaken for a statue had she not occasionally blinked. A green flame shaded the visions. It was soft at first but soon began to sting. At the same time, Ada could hear distinct voices creeping in from somewhere else. Not from the temple or outside but from another, a different wavelength invading her mind. Murmurings swirled about. She followed the noise, moving out of the temple and into a dark expanse. The farther away she moved, the less painful the sting of that green light felt. Only the voices—that was all she heard until she glimpsed a fleeting outline.

The shuffling of her parents' feet heading back upstairs twitched her back to reality. Ada quickly unclasped the pendant and buried it in her hand. Her mom cracked the door open, letting in a little more light.

"Get some rest. We'll talk tomorrow. I love you." Zeina swallowed hard, looking worried.

"Good night, Mama. I love you too." Ada looked at her mother but was still focused on the images in her mind. Her mother returned the door to the same little sliver as before. Ada dug her fingers into her eyes to rub away the images. Breathing into her hands, she muttered, "What the hell was that?"

CHAPTER 24
THE SUN ALWAYS RISES

By mid-morning, Ada woke up doubting whether anything that had happened the day before was real or if daybreak presented a chance to erase everything and start over again. Ada reached for her glasses to find the Aegis still resting on her dresser. She stayed under the sheets, staring at the ceiling. Then she stretched and groaned, rubbing her aching neck.

Ada puttered out of her room only to be met with an enthusiastic crackle from Roman. "Well… good afternoon, Grapes! She parties all night and sleeps all day. I might turn out to be the golden child after all."

Roman resumed stuffing himself with a *labneh*, tomato, and olive sandwich, no doubt his second one. Unable to speak with food in his mouth, he widened his eyes and yanked his neck forward. He pointed at her lip and hunched his shoulders, awaiting an answer.

"Yeah, little accident last night. I fell." Ada pointed at herself.

"Looks rough," Roman said. "Want to play *Mario Kart* downstairs?"

Ada perked up. "Umm, yeah, but only if I'm Bowser."

"Dude, you're riding, like, a seven-race losing streak against me. Don't matter who you take," Roman said with a full mouth.

"Talk is cheap. Let's go!"

Her brother had already sidestepped her on his way to the basement. He deposited the last chunk of sandwich into his mouth, with half the edges protruding from his lips.

They spent the rest of the morning playing video games, a respite from the eventual grilling from Ada's parents that would surely happen at some point that day. Whatever truths and lies she had yet to learn could wait a little longer outside the fortress of being with her brother.

"Ada, are you hungry?" their mother called when they'd just wrapped up playing video games and were challenging each other to a shooting competition on a mini basketball net, like they used to do when they were younger.

"The point of the game is to get the ball in the net, not have it ricochet off the wall and knock over that stack of books," Roman teased Ada with every wild miss.

"Ada! Can you please come up?" her dad sternly said.

"Ugh, the bell tolls for me." She snapped her head back.

Roman shrugged and deposited himself on the couch to resume his video games. He reclined with the remote control in hand. "Can you bring me down some juice when you come back?"

Ada marched up the stairs like a gladiator awaiting their fated doom in the Colosseum. She made her slow procession to the kitchen, hoping time would naturally expire her parents' request.

"Let's get this out of the way. I'm okay," she said when she saw them. "I know all about the Infernum. The Agoge. And Armor. I know I have to be careful. So let's just have this conversation and say we had it."

"Can you please keep it down?" Her mother jerked forward. She pointedly looked toward the basement.

Ada resigned herself to continuing upstairs to her parents' room. They followed and closed the door. "I know you're angry," her mom said. "You feel lied to. But I hope you understand why we never told you. We tried our best to keep you safe." Her mom said in a delicate voice.

"Where did you put your Aegis?" her dad asked in equal softness.

"It's in my room. On the dresser." Ada paused. "Do you even know what that Aegis is?"

"It's for your own safety, Ada."

"Hm. And that's it?"

"Yes. Why do you ask?" her dad said, angling his head.

"Nothing." Before her dad could interrupt, Ada asked, "So what comes next? What do we do now?"

"We don't know what the Infernum's next play is, but they're not going to just stop," Marcel said.

"You both need to tell me right now," Ada said. "Is there anything else I need to know apart from me being a mixed race of species who can burst out a light from inside me? Anything about the Agoge? Anything about that Aegis?"

"No." Her dad exchanged a glance with her mom.

"So, nothing else I should know about the Aegis?"

"No, Ada. Is there something we should know?" her mom asked.

She met their question with silence, examining them both intently until she finally replied, "Nope."

Her dad took a beat then proceeded. "Look, there's nothing else we can tell you that you don't already know. I think we're past trying to justify our actions. Like Genuit said, you are in it now."

"And apparently, being in it means having my mom and dad follow me around with a cloud of dread hanging over everything I say and do. I handled myself when they tried to get to me. And last time, I wasn't even ready for them."

"It's not that simple," her dad said as her mom shuddered. "Nygaard and the First Rank do not tear down a Republic and build an invincible system by accident. They have perfected the art of sniffing out any potential threat. They will keep coming, Ada. We need to keep you safe."

"I understand I have to be careful, but I can't stay home, Dad. If they wanted to get me at school, they would have. But they know it's too exposed. They won't risk it, especially after my last..." Ada contemplated how to frame her powers that had blasted Lamia, Darius, and Mikey Fay at the pool house. "Episode. And I'm not hiding out at Armor in that decrepit farmhouse."

"She's right, Marcel. She needs to find safety in numbers," her mom said.

"Mama, what was it like meeting Dad back then? Did you know?" Ada desperately wanted to talk about anyone but herself.

"*Ya'ane* I knew. He was open with me very early," her mom replied confidently.

"And you were cool with it—with, you know, Dad being not from here?" Ada timidly asked.

"I was a foreign student. *Eno* how much different was I from your dad? We were both strangers in our new home country."

"When two people find each other, even different worlds can't keep them apart," her dad added, holding her mom's hand.

"But our love story cast a ripple effect to other worlds." She nudged Ada affectionally.

Ada thought of Axel then shook her head to dispense with the fact that he was the first person to come to mind when her mom spoke of two people finding each other and nurturing their love.

"But listen, Ada. You need to be careful, okay, *hayete*? We know this is your journey, not ours." Her mother resolutely reached for her hand, still holding Marcel's with her other hand, forming a chain of resolve that flowed from her father and mother to Ada.

"I know. Trust me, Mama. I learned that the hard way yesterday. They could have killed me." Ada squeezed her mother's hand back.

"Listen to me, Ayda..." Her mother pronounced her name in Arabic this time, emphasizing the *A* in the back of her throat, enunciating a guttural cooing. "You might be half-Senazi, but don't ever forget, your other half is Lebanese. We're hard to kill." Zeina fixed her daughter with a look that left no doubt.

"This is why I married her." Marcel formed a cheeky smile. "That and the fact that her three hundred nineteen cousins back home scare me more than any Nygaard and dictatorships in Unitas."

While Ada chuckled at her dad's exaggerated—but partially true—statement, his reference to her mom's side of the family triggered another question gnawing away at her. The question would occasionally slip into the forefront of her mind until a more immediate, more gripping, matter would push it back. This was as good a time as any to ask her dad about that tiny, seemingly immaterial thing on her expanding list of questions.

"Dad, why… where does Lorham come from?" she finally blurted.

Zeina rolled her eyes and gave an entertained grin, casting a glance at Marcel, who let a sigh of embarrassment escape him. It was the face someone made who had been reminded one too many times of their blunder and now had no choice but to accept his shame and own it.

"Long story short. When I came here all those years ago on official business from Unitas, I popped into that bagel shop down on Van Houten. Anyway, it was my first day, and I hadn't eaten all morning, hopping from meeting to meeting. So I looked at the menu and ordered the first thing I saw up there. A few letters were missing. I read it out loud to the cashier in the way I saw it. I told him I wanted a Lorham Sandwich. At that point, he and everyone working behind the counter started cracking up. How was I supposed to know it was a Taylor Ham Sandwich? The first three letters were missing. So, every time I went back, they would call me Lorham. It stuck, and I went by that afterward." Marcel brought his hands up to invite the expected judgment from his daughter.

"Wait. Wait. Wait. You're telling me we're named after a bagel? You went from Marcel of Legio, a name with a royal bloodline, to Marcel of pork roll, egg, and cheese sandwich?" She brought her hand to her mouth to suppress the bubbling laughter.

"Not you too. It's bad enough I still hear it from your mother."

Marcel flicked his chin at Zeina, who was also struggling to keep a straight face.

"Wow. Just wow. Because the letters were missing..." Ada walked away, grinning.

———

Ada spent the rest of the weekend playing video games with her brother, with the occasional fort-building exercise. The family slipped back into their usual routine of Sunday night dinner, in which Roman gloated about his weekly athletic achievements, and Marcel brought his son's inflated ego down a few pegs whenever he needed to be reined in. It was a necessary timeout from the anxiety of tomorrow – Monday morning – when Ada would be thrust back into the madness of a life still all too new to her. On Monday, she would have to leave the safety of her home to head to school. The danger lurked: Mikey Fay. There was no way she was going to tell her parents that an active Infernum was at Clifton High School. If they knew, they would have chained her to the radiator in the basement indefinitely.

For better or worse, she was in it – just as Genuit had told her Friday night. But if the time came, and Ada suspected that, in one way or another, it would, she would not have to face Mikey Fay and the Infernum alone. Didi, Axel, Winter, and Ellen would stand with her.

CHAPTER 25

NEW WEEK, SAME ME

"ROMAN! Let's go! We're gonna be late," Ada called from the foyer, twirling the keys on her finger. She tapped her foot and checked the time on her phone again.

"Coming. Coming. Just getting these last ten reps in!" Roman yelled from the basement.

"I still gotta pick up Didi and Axel."

"Axel? Nice! He's such a vibe." Roman came upstairs, zipping up his hoodie, slightly winded from the last set of push-ups.

"Ada," her father called from upstairs. "Can you come up for a quick minute?"

"Dad, we gotta go," Ada replied, hoping she could dip out before her parents gave her another one of those talks about how the entire weight of the world rested on her shoulders.

"Please come up," her mother said sternly.

Ada dropped her shoulders, exhaled a defeated sigh, and trudged up the stairs as her brother noted, "They're really on you these days."

"Yep," Ada answered.

Standing at the threshold of her parents' room, she rolled her eyes and muttered, "Here we go," then willed herself into their room. "Hello and good morning." Ada smiled through closed lips. "How may I be of assistance to you all?"

Her mother immediately cut through her sarcasm. "*Sma'eeni ya Ada,* we all know about the dangers outside this house."

"It's just as dangerous inside, Mama." Ada glanced over at the closet where the Aegis had been before it was stolen.

"We cannot stop you from going out there. This is your choice *fhemti.* All we ask is that you exercise caution."

"I came face-to-face with them. I know how dangerous they are. You don't need to tell me to be cautious. Believe me, I know," Ada responded in a soft, sympathetic tone.

"We understand. We would never hold you back," her mother said.

"Guys, when I was a kid, you always told me that I can be what I want if I dream it. 'Live up to your potential,' you would say to me." She met her father's gaze. "I'm still trying to figure out if this whole time, that meant more than what I thought it did. Because apparently, there's a lot of potential going on in here." Ada waved her palms in a circular motion around her chest and stomach. "I know you don't want to hear this, but it's my turn. You did everything to protect me until now. And I can't even imagine how hard that must have been. But this part here, I gotta go through it now, whatever that means or however it plays out." Ada beamed a genuine smile at her dad. "It's like the first time I rode that two-wheeler, Dad."

"At some point, I had to let go of the seat and let you ride." Her dad's eyes glazed over, and he swallowed.

"Hey, it's going to be all right. I've got this. We've got this," Ada said affectionately, corralling them in for an embrace.

"We've got this," her dad repeated with a little less assurance than Ada.

"Mr. Lor-Ham. Still can't believe we went from Legio to that," Ada muttered, breaking away and heading back down the stairs. She swiped her bag and hollered one last "Love you, Mama, Dad!"

before stepping out for the first time since she'd returned home that weekend.

With Roman in the car, Ada took extra care to survey her surroundings before pulling out toward Didi's driveway just as Didi was exiting her front door, hauling a dark cloud of despair. She dragged her feet with each forced step as if pulling an anchor of misery. Didi made a fist and pretended to stab herself in the sternum, sticking her tongue out in a display of acted suffering and rolling her head back to feign death.

"You look like you were just released from Rikers Island. That bad?" Ada said after Didi jerked open the door to take a seat in the back.

"It was a twenty-four-hour lockdown. No time in the yard. Zero phone privileges. Not allowed out for a whole week except to school." Didi was now lying on her back, taking up the entire back seat, with her legs bent and her head resting on her bag.

Ada breathed through her teeth. "Yikes. Sorry."

"My mom and dad wanted info on my accomplices, but you know your girl don't snitch. So I did the time. Might get a teardrop tattoo this week," Didi said to the ceiling of the car as Ada drove off to pick up Axel.

"You two were out pretty late on Friday. I'm surprised Ada didn't get sent to the slammer, too!" Roman noted.

"She must have struck a plea deal." Didi playfully punched the back of Ada's seat, prompting Ada to reach back and take a blind swipe at her.

"I was dealing with my own polycrisis, thank you very much." Ada retorted.

"What?" Roman asked.

"Polycrisis. It's when a bunch of crises come to together to form a gigantic hot fudge fiasco sundae of a crisis," Ada explained.

"I'm not even gonna pretend to understand you and Didi's language," Roman replied. "Why are we turning into here? This where Axel lives? That's one long driveway."

Even during the day, the house itself was mostly hidden from view by high cedar trees. At the end of the driveway, Axel was waiting with his backpack hanging off one shoulder, casually observing his surroundings. Seeing him sent shivers up Ada's arms, inviting the little hairs to dance gleefully.

A genuine smile splashed across his face when she pulled in, and it widened as she drove closer to him. The Blaze's engine sputtered, emitting a rattling that blared over to him and out to the surrounding trees. Axel appeared to Ada like a mirage in a desert that turned out to be real. She tuned out whatever Didi was sermonizing about in the back seat. It barely registered as white noise. Ada drew up next to Axel, who threw one last circumspect glimpse at her before pulling himself together. He made a fist and rubbed his knuckle underneath his nose in an attempt to seem casual.

"Hey… you." Ada could not erase her beaming smile.

"Hey." Axel returned her greeting with a puncturing stare and a grin.

"Yo, Axel, what's up, man? Dude, do you want to sit in the front?" Roman innocently chimed in.

"Nah, it's all good, man. You stay where you are. I'll hop in the back."

"Such a gentleman, Roman. Where was the offer to let a lady ride shotgun?" Didi drifted to make room for Axel.

"Hey…" he said to Ada.

"Hey…" Ada repeated.

Ada peeked up at her rearview mirror, where she could see Didi swiveling her dubious gaze from her to Axel. "Wait. Hold up. What's going on here?" She reached around the front seat to cover Roman's eyes and mouthed, "What?" to Ada and Axel.

Ada smiled like she was unsure whether to laugh or frown. "Okay, so who's excited for International Sudoku Day today? It's a real thing. Not a pseudo-ku. Get it?" Ada slapped the steering wheel in a bout of conjured laughter.

Roman groaned, making no effort to remove Didi's hands from

his eyes. "No, let me out here. I'll take the bus before I have to listen to one more of these jokes."

"Save a seat for me. That was straight-up unacceptable," Didi said, shaking her head and lifting her hands from Roman's face.

For the rest of the drive, Didi talked about the mundane minutes that blended into hours of her weekend grounded at home, deprived of her phone or any electronics, while Axel nestled himself deeper into the fold of his seat, looking out the window. They stopped their chatter when they pulled into the Clifton High School parking lot.

Ada's focus sharpened.

"Let me out here." Roman turned to address Axel in excitement. "See you around, Axel!" As soon as Ada came to a full stop, he shoulder-checked the car door open and hopped out.

"He's a good kid," Axel remarked.

"You think Mikey Fay's here today?" Ada said, keeping a watchful eye on Roman walking over to meet his friends.

"I can't believe I missed that—an Infernum, my teammate, among us this whole time." Axel was swiveling his neck around to scope out the school grounds.

"Safe bet I dodged a bullet with that one. Quick swerve out of that mess." Didi tapped Ada on the shoulder. "I mean, not as big a bullet as you dodged with, you, know, not being captured alive—erm, or dead—and all."

"Cisca would caution me about how the Infernum rotate their people for specific goals then rotate them out for another mission," Axel said.

Ada's phone vibrated in the cupholder. It was a message from Ellen.

Ellen: *Meet at east wing entrance. Winter is on the way. Also these sneakers are totally a vibe with my outfit today. Sorry not sorry.*

Ada: *Be there in five. With Axel and Didi.*

"That was Ellen," Ada said.

"What's that spawn of Satan want?" Didi asked.

"She's being Ellen. And she's waiting for us at the East Wing." Ada tossed her phone back into the cupholder.

"*Pobrecita.* Little El is scared to go into the school alone." Didi laughed.

As the three of them exited the car, the unlikely pairing of Axel and Ada drew scandalized whispers from students going in and out of the school building.

"What are they thinking?" Didi leaned in to ask.

"The same as last time. It's not quantum physics or literary prose," Ada said.

"You're still able to tap into minds?" Axel asked.

"Yeah, but I'm getting good at drowning it out. Sometimes I can focus in on one thought among many. Like a conversation at a party." She relaxed, informally strolling through the crowd. "It's not this that freaks me out. It's the Aegis. I put it on again on Friday night when I got home."

"What? Were you okay?" Axel asked.

"Yeah. I saw the same thing as before. The bodies slain. But then I saw a bunch of kids in a temple. They all had these eyes. Purple—like magenta. They were all laughing. Playing. Except one. She creeped me out. Then I heard voices, but they weren't coming from the temple. It was like they were outside of where I was."

"Voices? Interesting." Axel nodded thoughtfully. "What were they saying?"

"I'm not sure. But I saw an outline of someone, too."

Axel spoke in a low voice as soon as they passed a few students. "That could be your Aegis working. It's connecting you to other Senazis here on Earth."

"Okay. That's a development, I guess," Ada responded, spotting Ellen impatiently tapping her waist and swiveling her head from side to side.

"Ugh, there you are," Ellen said, pressing her hands to her waist.

"Why you wearing them joints? We didn't take them for you," Didi chided Ellen, pointing to her sneakers.

"Oh, Diana, even you have to admit these sneakers are quite the touch. I'm going for the whole J. Lo Fly Girls vibe today. Vintage, right?" Ellen kicked one foot up to show off the shoes Ada and Didi had given her on Friday night. "I didn't realize they were limited editions."

"Okay, first of all, no way. You are banned from ever comparing yourself to the Boricua queen, *la Reina* Jennifer Lopez. Second, you realize you're rocking looted shoes for clout?"

"I prefer to call it forced sharing," Ellen said, rotating the shoes from side to side.

"How ironically anti-capitalist of you," Ada said with a reserved smile. "While I do feel conflicted about all this, you are slaying this look. I expect these shoes back. Uncreased." Ada winked at her.

"Totes. I would never be seen wearing something twice, anyway." Ellen snapped her wrist at Ada.

"I suffer in your presence," Didi remarked.

"I told Winter to meet me here at eight a.m. when we took the Uber. She shouldn't be alone at home. I feel so bad for her," Ellen said.

"Cisca and Genuit kept grilling me about her back at the house. It's not every day that the lost child of General Romis turns up out of the blue—"

"And Ansa," Ellen interrupted Axel.

"Not every day the daughter of General Romis *and Ansa* turns up in New Jersey, one degree removed from the Agoge." Axel pointed to Ada to establish her as the common denominator, where all degrees of relation would start and end.

"I am the host of the Agoge? That's my identifier?" Ada asked, rather unimpressed.

"I don't run the branding and marketing department at Armor," Axel demurred, prompting Ada to rumple her forehead in thought. "We don't actually have a marketing department."

"Winter, how was your weekend?" Ada asked, genuinely excited to see her.

Winter had swept into the group unnoticed. She was wearing another black tank top with distressed gray jeans and black Doc Martens boots. Her confident minimalism was the antithesis of Ellen's loud and often designer-splattered fashion preferences. Winter met Ada's greeting with an obscure silence. Either she was unwilling to answer, or she didn't care to take part in social pleasantries. Or she understood that her presence among them should have been sufficient for everyone to understand that she'd accepted them as companions. Perhaps even friends. The only friends she'd made since she left Unitas.

"Winter, this you-not-having-a-phone business makes sense now. I can see why you would not want one when you're keeping a low profile, but I've got you this burner phone. I have a stash of them. It's important that we check in on each other." Ellen tossed a phone at Winter, who caught it and held it out like she was unsure what to do with the device.

"Why do you keep a burner phone around? What are you, a small arms dealer?" Didi inquired.

"No, it's for when I go overseas. Data theft is a real thing. Read an article," Ellen shot back.

Ada stepped into the middle of the circle formed by the group. "Okay, what happens now? Do we sit around and wait, or do we go to them?"

"What do you mean, 'go to them'?" a perplexed Axel asked.

"I mean, do we go after Lamia, Mikey Fay, whoever, before they get to us? Because I don't think they're going to just… stop, and this whole thing of Armor following me around is a bit creepy." Ada looked around to find no suspecting Armor members present.

"Who's *we*, Ada? A nobody Senazi?" Axel thumbed his chest. "A wanted Legio?" He pointed to Ada. "A lone Senazi?" He pointed to Winter. "Two humans?" He then pointed to Didi and Ellen.

In a rare display of agreement, Didi and Ellen exchanged dubious glances to show their disapproval of being written off as merely human in his grand calculations.

"Two fierce, strong, and wildly independent humans whom I respect and admire, but two humans nonetheless," Axel rapidly clarified.

"You still have that Aegis thing?" Ellen asked Ada.

"Yeah, and it's still creepy." Ada took a look around first before reaching for the Aegis. She presented it to the group as though it was no different from any other item someone would keep in their pocket—gum, a receipt, keys.

"Okay, please put it away. The first time I saw it, I nearly got abducted by a homicidal maniac. The last time I saw it, you were convulsing on the ground." Ellen placed her hand over Ada's to conceal the Aegis and pushed it toward Ada's pocket.

"Um, you mean first time you saw it, Ada was nearly offed by that sociopath Lamia." Didi shoved Ellen's hand away.

"Yeah, and what's worse is I lost a pair of heels," Ellen retorted.

"I'm serious," Ada said. "We need answers. We're sitting ducks if we do nothing. Ellen, it's not too late for you to back out now. The Infernum don't know who you are. Neither do they know about Winter. Axel and I are in the line of fire. And you can be sure Didi is on their radar."

"I mean, duh! They would assume that I don't really associate with whatever is happening here." Ellen motioned her opened palm at Ada's distressed, vintage T-shirt.

"Ada is right," Axel said. "Ellen and Winter, this isn't your fight. You need to keep us at a distance. Why don't you go inside before us, and we'll follow you later. Let's not be seen together, all five of us."

Winter finally spoke. "Who are you to dictate who my fight is with?"

"You can't fight the world, Winter. You will endanger yourself and Ada," Axel sternly responded.

"I lived this. You just learned about it from secondhand accounts." Winter shot him a scornful glance. "My fight is with the murderers who killed my family and took away the only thing that mattered. Who is your fight with, apart from your own struggle to give your life meaning when you neither know devotion nor suffering?"

Axel was stunned into silence. No defense came.

"Okay, came out of nowhere, but noted," Didi said.

"Damn. Takedown. Let's go, Winter." Ellen tugged at Winter's elbow, ushering her toward the entrance.

Didi watched them walk into the school. "How long do you bet it will be before Winter body-slams her out one of these windows?"

"Go to class and text me," Axel said. "I have a coaches' meeting this morning. We'll catch up at lunch. Be careful."

"Careful is my middle name," Ada said, imitating Axel's mysterious tone.

"I think you mean, *danger*, A. That's not how it's supposed to… never mind. Let's go to class." Didi led Ada away, and they headed inside together.

CHAPTER 26
WINTER – HER AND ELLEN AND—YOU KNOW—HIM AT CLIFTON HIGH

TROTTING up the stairs to the second-floor east hall, Ellen yielded to let Winter go first. Winter's usual all-black outfit contrasted with Ellen's. Normally, fancy fashion styles like the ones Ellen flaunted reminded Winter of the excesses of the Republic elites, with their hats and their coats. But somehow, she was fine with Ellen's flamboyance. Perhaps Ellen's style felt like homage paid to a time and place in Unitas that had been lost to Winter forever. In any case, there they were, walking alongside each other.

"So, is Johnson your real last name?" Ellen asked.

"Does Johnson sound like a natural extension to Romis and Ansa? Esna Johnson…" Winter laughed.

"I figured as much. I know a thing or two about double names. My Chinese name isn't exactly Ellen, either. But who's gonna know how to pronounce Tian here?" Ellen pronounced her name in Mandarin, transforming her voice tonally.

"Esna Afra Amata." Winter stopped in her tracks to extend her hand to Ellen.

"Tian Liu." Ellen reached out to shake Winter's hand.

They met again for the first time.

Winter had never spoken her name on Earth. She'd buried it the moment she passed through the Empress Walk. She had to kill her past to survive. No amount of dwelling on the scents and colors of Unitas would bring her back there. She was here. And her Senazi name was an anchor that could pull her into danger.

"So, why Winter Johnson?" Ellen asked.

The girls resumed their casual pace down the middle of the hallway while streams of students parted for them. Ellen's commanding social status and Winter's bold self-assuredness cast aside whoever was in their way.

"I found out it was a common name for people here who look like me. The less attention I drew to myself, the better. And as for Winter, well, I came here in January. And I was cold." Winter shrugged.

"I thought maybe it was because of your frozen and barren soul." Ellen winked at Winter, nudging her elbow playfully. Then she withdrew nervously, waiting to draw a lighthearted reaction from Winter's otherwise stone-faced expression.

Winter finally snorted. The girls shared a restrained laugh while they continued their seemingly endless walk down the hall, gravitating just an inch closer to one another, evicting the unnecessary particles of space separating them.

"So, Esna Afra Amata, were you something like a big deal back home?"

"Why do you say that?" Winter coolly asked.

"Nothing. I saw the way Cisca and Genuit looked at you. The way they spoke to you like you were royalty or something."

"Yeah, they come from a Republic that championed equality among people. Except for them—some people were more equal than others. They lived in their own elitist bubble. They grew disconnected from the masses. Even as a twelve-year-old, I never felt right at dinners, banquets, or award ceremonies when, on the way there, we'd driven by Senazis barely making ends meet. By then, the Republic hadn't fallen, but Nygaard was on the rise. With each election, more of his supporters would be voted in. And that's because the Ciscas and Genuits were more concerned with the ideals of liberty and justice than they were with the people who were only thinking about how to put a loaf of bread on the table for their families."

Winter stared off into the blank canvas of the blue sky beaming through the passing window of the hallway. "My dad was still the general of the army, but we could all feel that tide changing. Then, when the time was right, Nygaard did what he did." Winter couldn't bring herself to verbalize the killing of her family.

"That's… that's horrible," Ellen said, grazing Winter's arm with hers. "So Lamia and Darius—ugh, I get shivers thinking about them." Ellen shook out her shoulders. "I'm guessing they weren't royalty there either?"

"I'm guessing Lamia was orphaned like many Infernum taken from the 'Treasonous' parents, as they liked to call them, and Darius was probably of the working, poorer people. Nygaard and the First Rank gave them all someone to point at. He told them that people like me are the reason they're poor. Blamed my parents for being puppets of the Legios, the boogeyman he invented."

Ellen froze. "Damn. Don't look. It's Mikey Fay."

Winter clocked him, too. She couldn't tell if Ellen was still breathing through her pursed lips. "Be cool. Just breathe."

She held Ellen's hand and squeezed it. Winter had been there before, the last time she'd guided her sister through an impending danger. Now there was a world's difference, literally, yet the same danger loomed.

"He sees us. He's walking this way. Why's he walking this way? What do we do?" Ellen spoke through her teeth, not moving her lips. She picked up her pace, only to be gently tugged back by Winter, who showed no visible sign of nervousness.

"Just hold my hand." Winter scrutinized Mikey Fay with increased ferocity as he came closer.

A few students noticed the unlikely coupling of Ellen and Winter, but Winter did not even remotely care. She breathed maliciously through her nose, directing every last atom of air to shoot toward Mikey Fay with spear-like intensity.

"He keeps staring at me. Why's he staring?" Ellen said frantically through her clenched jaw.

Mikey Fay loomed more immense and threatening with each unavoidable stride in their direction. Except for his blue shirt and tapered sweats, Winter saw him not as he was in that moment but as the boy who'd been knocked unconscious in the pool house—an Infernum agent who should be spared no mercy.

"Hey, Cinderellen." Mikey Fay planted himself directly opposite Winter and Ellen, bringing them to a sudden halt.

His taller frame towered over them. His invisible shadow of arrogance cast a foreboding cloud over the girls. Ellen cowered ever so slightly into Winter, who remained upright, chest out, chin up, her look piercing Mikey Fay with the eyes of a hawk stalking its prey.

"I'm sorry… what… what did you call me?" Ellen asked.

Winter could feel Ellen's fear coursing into her squeezed hand.

"You forgot your glass slippers." He formed a wicked smile and gave her a penetrating look. "See you around. Nice shoes, by the way." Mikey Fay nodded to her sneakers as he shuffled past them, leaving his dark motive to fester in the residue of his presence.

Winter turned around to watch Mikey Fay walk off, tilting her head to the side and tightening her glare.

Ellen tried to catch her breath. "He knows. He knows I was there. Winter, what do I do?"

"Hmm…" Winter still did not take her eyes off Mikey Fay.

"What does this mean? Do they know where I live? Will they come for me next? I don't have an Agoge like Ada. I can't shoot that green-light thingy."

Winter finally concluded her watchful stare at Mikey Fay to instruct Ellen. "Just get to class."

Throughout it all, neither Ellen nor Winter realized they were still holding hands until Ellen released her touch by reaching for her phone to text Ada. She held her phone out for Winter to see.

Ellen: *Mikey Fay knows I was there.*

Ada: *The limited-edition sneakers were a dead giveaway?*

Ellen: *No. It was the heels that I left behind. He called me Cinderellen.*

Ada: *Say word! I would have cast you as Anastasia or Drizella. (It's Didi btw. I'm with Ada).*

Ada: *Ya this is Ada now. Hold up. Let me make a group chat.*

Ellen: *Meet after class. Asap. And please change the name of this chat group to anything but the Stellar Squad.*

Stellar Squad group chat (Didi): *Hmm. I'm kinda busy after that. I got a thing… a 2-for-1 tacky-hoop-earring sale. Sorry.*

Stellar Squad group chat (Didi): *And yes, hard pass on the name.*

Stellar Squad group chat (Ada): *Ellen what happened? (And you all fail to appreciate the double entendre. Get it. Stellar. Squad. Interstellar. Come on.)*

Stellar Squad group chat (Ellen): *After class. 2nd floor. By my locker.*

"Ellen. Put. Your. Phone. Down. Go to class." Winter spoke slowly.

"I told Ada to meet me here right after this class. Let's regroup when we get out." Ellen looked around and over Winter. She stepped away from the window as though the danger might fly in from the outside.

"Meet after class?" Ellen asked tentatively.

Winter remained noncommittal, avoiding Ellen's helpless stare. "Go to class," she repeated and walked off.

CHAPTER 27
BLOOD ON THE WALLS AT CLIFTON HIGH

Toward the tail end of Ada and Didi's first class of the day, AP Environmental Sciences, their teacher, Mr. Bhurjee, went off on a tangent about how rare earth materials needed to produce green energy would radically alter existing geopolitical alliances. Ada listened attentively while Didi's eyes flickered between him and the clock hung up behind him.

"Oil reshaped our national security strategy and alliances. I expect copper and lithium will do the same. Africa and Asia might become the new battleground of world power. And as usual, they will plunder its resources at the expense of their continental chess game…" Mr. Bhurjee concluded as the bell rang.

Ada and Didi gathered their belongings and nodded to one another. They bolted out of class with books in hand. When they arrived at Ellen's locker on the second floor, she was tapping her legs with her fingers like she was playing the bongos. From the opposite side of the hallway, Axel hurriedly sidestepped students, advancing toward the frazzled Ellen.

"Took you long enough. Where's Winter? I told her to meet here." Ellen scanned both sides of the hallway.

"Wow, Ellen, you look like you're about to start rocking back and forth in the shower in the fetal position. Get it together," Didi said.

"Diana, not now." Ellen's brittle voice revealed a vulnerability she usually kept concealed under layers of a crafted social status and curated social media posts. She had shed her bravado and was laid bare, exhibiting one emotion: fear.

Didi erased her condescending smile.

"Babe, are you okay?" Ada asked gently, not wishing to press any further past the fragile limits of Ellen's mental state.

"I'm okay." Ellen looked up at a few students who had slowed their pace to clock her panic.

"Hey, beat it." Didi feinted a punch in a boxer's stance at the students to make them scurry away like a flock of startled birds in a public square.

"Mikey Fay. He called me Cinderellen." Ellen gasped for air. "Then he looked at my shoes, the ones you took from Lamia, and was like, 'Nice shoes.'" She collected herself just enough to contin- ue. "Honestly, if Winter wasn't with me, I would have freaked out." She leaned her head back against the locker door. "Where is she? I texted her to meet here."

"They know. They know it was you who threw that rock in." Ada dropped her head.

"They probably found my shoes. Who else would wear couture to a high school party?" Ellen said.

"Really? Like, even in the middle of a full-blown panic attack?" Didi said under her breath.

"He was supposed to be at the coaches' meeting just now. He wasn't there." Axel stared off into the distant end of the hallway.

"Maybe he went back to Lamia. To report. We should follow him," Didi eagerly suggested.

"Yeah, if we can find him," Ada said.

"Don't you think we should consult with Armor?" Axel flailed his hands.

"They can't do anything for us. It seems to me they're a bunch of old guards who sit around reveling in their past glory. No offense." Ada swallowed the little ball of doubt and pushed it back down into the pit of her stomach.

"I'm with Ada," Didi said to Axel.

"They're the ones who want something from me. They'll have to come get it. Even Lamia said it at the pool house. They want me alive." Ada opened her palm to examine the lines across her hands, where her power shot from—the soft grooves that formed when she flexed her fingers.

"We can't just give you up to them," Axel said.

At the end of the hall, a tide of students surged out, scrambling toward them. Some shrieked in horror. Others shoved people out of the way. Teachers were trying, without success, to patrol the mayhem. The raucous students were rushing the second-floor exit like an excited herd running in an uncoordinated dash. Before Ada could understand what was happening, it was over. The last wave of students emptied down to the staircase, with a few straddlers trailing behind.

Ada met the curious gazes of Ellen, Didi, and Axel.

"All students to the muster points in the football field. To the football field." Mr. Sam Paul made a direct path toward them, herding the remaining few to the exit.

"Sam, what's going on?" Ada asked.

"Just head to the football field. All of you."

"Why? What happened?" Ada asked.

Mr. Sam Paul first looked around to ensure that no students remained in the hallway. "A student is dead," he said in a low voice.

Ada exchanged a bewildered glance with Axel. Didi and Ellen did the same.

"That's horrible," Didi finally said.

"Who is it?" Ada's gaze shifted between Mr. Sam Paul and the exit door.

"I cannot say anything past that. Please, everyone, get to the football field." He marshaled them to the stairs.

They complied without any further questioning. It could have been anyone. Theories of what had happened, and whether it was connected to them, were boiling within Ada. "Who could it be?" Ada finally whispered to Didi, unable to repress her curiosity any longer.

Didi shook her head subtly. She peeked over her shoulder to where Mr. Sam Paul was walking a few paces away. Ada took that as her cue to also commit to silence.

Meanwhile, Ellen arched her neck forward and in between Ada and Didi. "Where's Winter? She's not answering my calls." Didi gave another muted response, this time pressing her index finger to her lips.

They marched together down the stairs, following their teacher, who was leading them toward the football field. He waved them to the exit and veered off to the first-floor hallway to round up the remaining idling students. When they reached the football field, some students were being consoled by their classmates. One was wiping tears running down her cheeks. Another was crying into a friend's embrace. Some were investigating the reason for their evacuation, while others took this opportunity to throw a football around. Approaching police and ambulance sirens howled. Their red and blue strobe lights reflected off the school's brick building and windows as a whole cavalry of first responders pulled into the school from every entrance.

Ally Lindsay came stumbling out of the building, looking out to the crowd, barely able to keep herself upright. She glanced back at the school like the impending danger was closing in on her.

"Mikey Fay is dead. It's Mikey Fay. He's dead," she sobbed breathlessly as she approached her friends and collapsed into one of their arms.

A blank look struck Ada, Didi, and Axel. Not a muscle on their faces moved. Ellen, meanwhile, pinched her finger and thumb under her nose, covering her mouth as she smattered quietly to herself. She receded a little from the group, glancing around the field.

"Where you going?" Ada called as Ellen marched away.

Ada followed for no other reason than that she found it odd that Ellen would veer off from them, and Axel and Didi trailed behind her. She followed Ellen's gaze out at the bus stop across the fence. There, in the distance, Winter had slid onto the bench and placed her bag on her lap.

"Is that Winter?" Ada asked.

The bus was pulling onto the road toward Winter. She gathered her bag and rose in anticipation. Ellen sprinted toward Winter as fast as possible. Ada picked up her pace. Axel and Didi passed her before too long, now in nearly a full sprint behind Ellen.

"Ellen! Wait!" Ada shouted between each adrenaline-induced pump of her legs and arms.

"Winter!" Ellen called.

Winter looked over her shoulder. What struck Ada—midstride, elevated heart rate, and all—was not that Winter would choose to leave at this particular moment but how emotionally vacant she looked when she turned to face them dashing toward her. The bus slowed, released ghastly hydraulic steam, and came to a complete stop. The doors swung outward. Winter flung her bag around her shoulder and disappeared into the bus.

The bus door remained tantalizingly open for a few extra seconds. Axel had zoomed past Ellen at that point. He hopped the chain-link fence with acrobatics then dashed over the grass and reached into the sliver of space between the folding doors.

"Wait, sorry, wait, I need to get on this bus." Axel's hand was trapped in the small gap between the partially shut doors. He struggled to wiggle his way through, but his arm remained lodged there.

Didi and Ellen had also cleared the chain-link fence, with less ease than Axel but impressively nonetheless. Meanwhile, Ada was straddling the fence at the top, wincing from the pointed edges that poked into her thighs.

"Ow, ouch. Okay, here we go, Ada… one, two, three, and away we go…" She tipped over the fence and landed on the other side with a hard thud. Spitting out a few blades of grass that had stuck to her lips, she brought herself up, adjusted her glasses, and limped in discomfort toward the bus, which had finally opened its doors thanks to Axel, Didi, and Ellen imploring the driver to let them in.

Mikey Fay was dead. Winter was on the bus. Somehow, Ada shuddered to think the two were connected.

CHAPTER 28
GET ON THE BUS

ELLEN HOPPED on first and scooted past the bus driver.

"Excuse me, young lady—you need to pay first," the bus driver —a stout woman with short hair and an oversized New Jersey Transit dress shirt—said.

"Oh no, I don't do… whatever this proletariat chariot thing is, I'm just here to see a friend." Ellen flicked her wrist at the woman.

"This isn't the racquet club, lady. Either pay or get off the bus." The woman turned off the ignition and rotated toward the door to stand up.

"That's okay. I'll pay for her and for them," Ada intervened, depositing a combination of change and singles into the payment slot. She waved in Axel and Didi, who were impatiently waiting at the curb.

The bus driver gave Ellen one last scornful look before turning the ignition key. The whole time, Winter, who was seated in the back, seemed unbothered by the scene of her friends sprinting to catch up with her. Ellen tucked her hands closer to her chest, avoiding contact with anything, careful to only hook her one finger against a railing for balance once the bus accelerated.

"Yo, just grab a seat!" Didi hollered to Ellen from behind.

Ellen wiped her finger on the side of her jeans and finally

planted herself beside Winter. The others encircled Winter, sitting in the empty seats.

"Where are you going?" Ellen asked Winter, glancing back at the school football field, where teachers were trying to corral the panicked students into clusters.

"Home," Winter responded, looking out at the shrinking portrait of the field as the bus drew farther from them.

"Why?" Ada quietly asked. She looked at the group as if to extract that same question from all of them and deposit it into an offering basket to present to Winter.

Ellen brought her hand to her mouth in disbelief. "Did you… did you have anything to do with what just happened back there?" She leaned in to ask.

"He was a threat. I handled it," Winter answered robotically.

"So you…?" Ellen stopped short of uttering the words.

It was too late. Her half-question had removed the airtight lid from the pressure cooker of Winter's short-lived secret. Didi stumbled back into her seat.

"Whaaaat?" Didi soft-whispered.

Axel scratched the back of his head and blew air into his expanding cheeks before emitting a hushed "Oof," exhaling the remaining bits of astonishment.

Ada's reaction was muted but not because of Winter's actions. Nausea and surges of pain were stabbing her brain. For a few agonizing moments, she heard nothing but a high-pitched sound in her head. It would retreat and charge again. The pain was an unrelenting ocean of waves slamming against rocks. No one, not even Didi, noticed her ordeal. Ada took a deep breath and exhaled the pain as Winter folded her arms and took to studying the cracked rubber seals framing the window beside her.

"I did what had to be done," Winter added. "He would have done worse to you. And to Ada. Or Axel. Or Didi, if he knew she was involved. You know that. You saw them." She gave them a steely look.

"Winter, how?" Ada bluntly asked, pulling everyone's focus

back onto her. The sudden onset of her headaches had subsided, leaving her to manage the residual buzzing sensation in her head. "How did you do it?"

"I don't see why that matters right now," Axel said.

"Because it matters, Axel, that's why." Ada doubled down. "We're in this mess together. If Winter did it, then so did we. And we need to know how it went down."

"We ride together, Axel," Didi added.

"I followed him into the locker room," Winter said in a monotone. "Before your coaches' meeting. And then I snapped his neck." Winter's tone held no emotion.

"Oh." Ellen's brows flung up.

The others quickly checked their surroundings to ensure that no one was within earshot. They all retracted in choreographed disbelief.

"And I'd do it again. I'd snap his bones a million times over until they were reduced to ether." Winter looked down at her stable hands, bringing them to rest on the soft threads of her jeans, which were distressed and flattened from repeated washing.

"Winter, you can't go rogue like this. You're endangering every one of us," Axel said.

"No, she's not. She's protecting us. Protecting me." Ellen took Winter's hand.

"She's not wrong. Is it even murder if the dude ain't even human?" Didi said, striking a conciliatory tone.

"So we're less worthy of life now, Didi? Yeah, Mikey Fay wasn't a good person. I would have loved to beat him senseless for what he did to Ada. But what are you saying?" Axel drew closer to Ada.

"Okay, relax, that's not what I meant. And chill with the heroics. Your girl handled herself at that party. She doesn't need your help," Didi quickly retorted, mimicking a fireball-throwing motion with her hands.

"You're missing the point," Axel said. "He and I, we're no

different. He was probably…" Axel paused, deliberating. "He was probably an orphan like me. Life just drew different fates for us."

"Winter, you're not a vengeful killer. I understand why you did what you did. If I'd had the power in that pool house, I might have done the same thing," Ada said. The fact that she killed Mikey Fay was justifiable in a twisted, it-was-him-or-us kind of way. He was Infernum and would have offed Ada at the first command from the higher-ups. But the fact that Winter killed him with zero remorse was something Ada was still trying to process.

"Okay, so now what do we do? We have a dead body at school. Everyone is going to be asking questions. Ada and I were in class. Ellen, Axel?" Didi looked to them for confirmation.

"I was in class but, like, literally trying to not lose my mind," Ellen confirmed, cupping her free hand over her and Winter's clasped hands.

"I was at the coaches' meeting," Axel said.

"That leaves Winter. Were you in class the whole time?" Ada asked.

"I showed up a few minutes late. But otherwise, class," Winter affirmed.

"Okay, so it's not so bad—apart from us dashing like crazy out of the schoolyard, which I can see how that would be incriminating," Ada said, swaying her head from side to side.

"So where do we go now? It's too early to hit up Malek's. Any suggestions?" Didi asked.

"Ain't no way I'm going to Armor with this news," Axel said.

Ada didn't want to, but common sense kept pulling her glances toward Winter. Knowing Winter's story, she understood why Winter had been careful to keep her residence a secret. It would not have been hard to do. Winter had no friends and was generally a loner at school. Those who occasionally interacted with her could have easily assumed she evaporated into invisible molecules when the day was over, only to come together to create someone whose sole existence happened during school hours. Ada had come to suspect that Winter had no life to share with anyone outside of school. It had taken Winter's harrowing tale of her escape from Unitas for Ada to finally understand that to Winter, survival was her religion. And surviving meant staying undetected. If Winter had been so successful at keeping a low profile, it was only natural that they convene at her secret residence, wherever that was.

"Winter, you've stayed alive all this time by remaining anonymous. To do that, you had to have left no breadcrumbs behind," Ada said.

"Yeah, you're a ghost just as much as Lamia," Didi said.

"Yes, Ada. We can go to my place," Winter said, continuing to stare out of the window.

"Great! Now that we know where we're going, can you get off this bus and call an Uber?" Ellen sprang up. "How do you command that woman with the unironic mullet to let us off here?"

"You just snap your fingers at her and demand to be let off. Try it," Didi baited Ellen, who was about to snap her fingers when she glared at Didi skeptically.

"Is that your ironic voice? I can't tell. I don't speak public transportation—the language of entry-level bank tellers," Ellen said.

"Okay, I'm assuming Winter knows where she's going. Everybody, just chill, and we'll figure out our next steps." Ada rubbed her temples, failing to conceal her discomfort from another bout of headaches.

"You good?" Didi asked.

"Yeah, it's just my head. It's like I go deaf for a few seconds, and I hear this high-pitched sound." Ada closed her eyes and exhaled in a hopeless attempt to expel the pain.

"It will get better," Winter assured her in a flat tone, finally turning her gaze to meet Ada's.

CHAPTER 29
A TALE OF TWO COUNTRIES

The bus circled over the bridge and onto a forgotten street. "We're a stop away," Winter informed the rest of the group.

"Is this where the Empress Walk put you?" Ada asked, looking out at a large mural on the side of a brownstone.

"In this neighborhood, yes."

The Empress Walk had transported Winter from Unitas to Earth all those years ago. Now they all got there by bus, but it was so removed from Clifton High School that it might as well have been a portal to another world. They were no longer in suburban Clifton, as evidenced by another large mural on the side of a brick building, depicting a scroll with the words "Sinners. Saints. Street Philosophers."

"This is me." Winter plucked the cord along the wall of the bus.

"Ah, that's how it's done. Cute." Ellen stayed close to Winter as they moved toward the bus door.

As Ada and Didi hopped off, they nodded to the passengers waiting to board. "I bet they got some bangin' food spots here," Didi remarked.

"Down the street is Kenny's Grill. I work there summers and

after school for cash. That's where we're going. You okay, Sandro?"
Winter led them past a homeless man, who smiled at her.

"Ey, girl. Thanks for that late-night sandwich the other night."
He tapped his belly.

"Ada, peep Ellen real quick. She looks like she's about to break
out in hives." Didi pointed subtly at Ellen, making no attempt to
conceal her delight. "Not exactly Montclair, is it, Ellen?"

"Very funny, Diana," Ellen replied, rolling her shoulders in.

The cracks in the pavement wound through the uneven sidewalk that seesawed at each joint. Ada found this all endearing and
reminiscent of the summers she'd spent with her mom's family in
the charming markets of Beirut. Nothing about Winter's neighborhood was new to her. The fact that it was in America and close to
her suburban world was uncanny, though.

"This is it here." Winter yanked open a door, producing a
screech of rust grinding against metal hinges.

The door was adjacent to a weather-stripped yellow sign that
read Kenny's Grill. Graffiti peppered the steel shutters of the
restaurant. Winter led them up a narrow, dimly lit stairway to a
small landing with a distressed door. She pushed it open after a
few casual attempts to unlock it.

"This is the first time anyone has been here. Only the restaurant
owner downstairs, Kenny Frazier, has stepped inside," Winter
said, standing aside to let the others in.

Ada took a moment to survey Winter's home. The paint-
stripped walls were offset by the neatness of what little furniture
occupied the room. The apartment was no larger than a bedroom.
There was an incompleteness to it. A distressed couch and coffee
table faced them. A small mattress was elevated on a series of
rusted metal rebars. The sheets stopped short at precisely the same
parallel distance from the floor across the entire bedside. Two
small pillows were fluffed to the exact same height. In one corner,
clothes were neatly hung on a rack with missing wheels. Ada
recognized the series of black tank tops as Winter's. At the base of

the rack were curved wooden inserts that she vaguely remembered Winter making in workshop class in the tenth grade.

Apart from a picture frame resting on a repurposed night table by the bed, there was no other memorabilia. Ada squinted to identify the characters in the frame without being obvious enough for Winter to notice. It was a family of five—mother, father, two sisters, and a baby in linen clothing posing in front of a large estate home.

"You live here?" Ada surveyed the place for a bathroom or kitchen.

"I've been here since I was twelve. When I first got here, Kenny took me in. I worked for cash, and he gave me a place to stay as long as I kept an eye on the store when it's closed. He couldn't rent this place out because, obviously, no bathrooms or kitchens that meet code."

Ellen looked around the room in a melancholic spirit.

"Not what you're used to, eh?" Winter asked with a hint of concealed embarrassment.

"I am so impressed by you. You have no idea." Ellen shook her head in amazement.

The vibration of Ada's phone in her pocket tremored against her leg. It was likely a message from her parents, which she would get to eventually when she wasn't dealing with the bigger issue of actively aiding and abetting a homicide. Then it buzzed again. Her notifications were going haywire. She finally gave in and reached for her phone. What she read on the screen nearly sucked the air from her lungs. "Uh, everyone, we're on the news." Ada sat stunned, bound to the pull of her phone.

The others huddled around her screen, leaning in to read the small captions. Individually, their phones each started buzzing. Didi silenced the call from her mother. Ellen contemplated her phone for a few minutes but didn't answer it. Axel stared reluctantly at his, and his thumb was veering toward the green logo to answer the call when the news reporter on Ada's screen started saying something. Ada raised the volume to the maximum.

"It's our school," Ada noted, doing her best to steady her trembling hand. When it became obvious that the initial shock still hadn't worn off, she rested the phone on the small coffee table.

"Look at all these cop cars," Didi added.

"Wait, wait, shh—what's she saying?" Ellen fluttered her hands in a downward sweep like an orchestra maestro to silence everyone.

"Authorities are still searching for these five students who fled school grounds after the death of a student at Clifton High School. They cannot confirm that they are, in fact, accessories to the alleged murder of the student, which, authorities believe, was carried out by another student identified as Winter Johnson, seen in this CCTV footage entering the male locker room and exiting shortly afterward. Authorities urge residents to take caution, as the suspects may be dangerous, and advise residents to report them to their local police."

Their faces and names were plastered all over the screen for what seemed like an infinite amount of time.

"They think we did it." Axel covered his mouth in disbelief.

"Well, we did, Axel," Ada replied, circling her hand to all of them. "For better or worse, we're all complicit now."

"I can't go to jail. I look terrible in orange. I exfoliate at least three times a week. Commercial soap makes me break out." Ellen paced around in a circle, chattering to herself.

"Does anyone know you live here?" Ada asked pointedly.

"Only Kenny. But he's been looking out for me since I got here. I use a PO Box in Clifton to go to school there," Winter said with just as much directness. But in a sudden shift of mood, she slumped and broke eye contact with Ada. "There's one more thing…"

Ada held her breath.

"I took this from him." Winter slipped her hand into her bag and pulled out a cell phone with a white case.

Not one of them dared to touch the device. It was more than a phone—it was damning evidence that would incriminate them beyond any measure of defense if found in their possession. They drew closer to it with the trepidation of a bomb squad inching closer to an explosive device right before they set about defusing it. The phone took on a life of its own in Winter's palm. Didi retracted her hand as far away from it as she could.

"Are… are you serious right now?" Axel jabbed his finger at the phone. "Did you give this any further thought beyond satisfying your personal vendetta against the entire damn Infernum? You are a liability. And you're reckless." He was now squarely facing her.

"I might be a liability. But at least I'm not unreliable," Winter blankly responded. "Where were you when Ada was getting beat down in the pool house? Where were you when Mikey Fay threatened Ellen in the hall?"

"Don't make this about me, Winter. It's bad enough there's a manhunt for us. Now, you have in your possession the only piece of evidence to link us to his murder. I mean, what were you even thinking when you took his phone?"

"I turned it off as soon as I took it. There's a password on there." Winter offered the phone to any willing taker, unbothered by Axel's harsh criticism.

In the midst of the infighting, Ada brought her finger to her upper lip. A thought had come to her.

"This is good. We can use this. He's Infernum." Ada then rushed to continue her thoughts before Axel's interruption, which, judging by his open mouth and raised finger, she guessed would be imminent. "The Infernum must be communicating with him on his phone. We need to stay ahead of them." She plucked the phone from Winter.

"Exactly," Winter said, meeting Ada with a sly smile.

"Are you hearing yourselves right now? You want to take the contents of the crime and use it to commit more crime." Axel flung his hands up.

"I mean, when you put it that way, yeah, we do sound like

fugitives. But I gotta roll with Ada on this one," Didi said, keeping her shoulders shrugged.

"You can't be serious. You're not thinking this through." He sighed, trying to catch the eye of anyone who would agree.

"You're dangerously close to being voted off the island right now." Didi lowered her shoulders to wave him off with a flick of her wrist.

Still engrossed in the news report, Ellen remarked, "Either way, the phone is locked. We can't use it."

"There is one person who can unlock it for us," Ada said.

Ada struck Didi with a solicitous stare. She inclined her head at a slight angle. Didi mirrored her body language, tilting her head the same degree as Ada's. Her pupils widened with shock as soon as Ada offered a mischievous grin.

"No. No. No. Not doing it." Didi waved her hands from side to side.

"Come on, D. You gotta be a team player. Just swipe right on him this one time," Ada pleaded, holding her breath.

Ellen finally unglued herself from her fixation on the news report blaring from the phone for a second. "What's going on? Why does it feel like you're pressuring her into an unwanted sexual favor?"

"Worse. She wants me to take the phone to Jojo," Didi said.

"Oh, that's low, Ada. Way beneath you. Not beneath Didi. But you, yes," Ellen said.

"Come on. He's the only guy capable of doing all that tech stuff." Ada persisted.

"Jojo, the guy who once offered to make me a fake ID?" Axel asked, having returned from the bathroom, adjusting his belt buckle.

"Yeah, that's his low-hanging fruit. But he's into heavy stuff. Dude hacked into Walmart and reset all their prices to ninety-nine cents last year. Then he had a dozen artificial roses shipped to my house for... you guessed it, ninety-nine cents." Didi put on a facade of indifference.

"Dude, this is a polycrisis if there ever was one. We gotta full send." Ada had nothing else to play but this last card.

"How's this a polycri—ok, well, yes, it's a hall of fame polycrisis, but ah, why does it have to be me?" Didi threw her hands up.

"Ada's got a point here. Circumstances are dire. We've got no other rabbits to pull out of the hat." Ellen grinned, seeming to enjoy the pressure on Didi.

"To rope Jojo into this mess would expose us to further risk." Axel paced around the room. "Another person who can slip up if questioned. Another tool for the Infernum to use to go after Ada." He stopped by the counter where he'd started.

"We're running out of options, Axel," Ada retorted. "Anyway, as I was saying, we're suspected of aiding and abetting a murder, no offense." Ada quickly turned to Winter. "We're all in the news." She pointed to Ellen's phone playing out the reports. "We have an out-of-this-world race that wants to kill me. I feel like invoking a polycrisis full send is appropriate given the absolute madness we're living in right now."

"Fine. Fine, I'll do it. But all of you better throw up a statue for me when this is all said and done. Give me your burner phone that Ellen gave you." Didi snapped her finger at Winter.

"Can we please stop calling it a burner phone?" Ellen said, then went back to watching the news report. "It makes me sound like a drug dealer. And not the wholesaler-controlling-shipping-routes kind."

"What is this, a flip phone?" Didi examined the phone. "Whatever, it'll do." She punched a message. The others idled around her, with Ada elongating her neck to catch a glimpse.

Didi: *Hey, meet me at Malek's @ noon. Don't tell anyone or I will savagely mutilate you. It's...*

She stopped to reflect for a few seconds. "I can't write my initials. I don't want anyone to know it's coming from us." Didi finally let slip a painful sigh of defeat. "Ugh, I hate myself in this moment." She frowned while Ada made little effort to conceal her amusement.

"Write it, D," Ada said.

"Ughh, why is this my life?" Didi wilted in defeat before resuming her text.

Didi: *This is Bombomcita.*

"Yes!" Ada exclaimed, tapping Didi on the butt. Within a few short seconds, Winter's phone jingled with a new alert.

Jojo: *Girl you know what it is. Ride or die for my shorty.*

"I'm already regretting this." Didi snapped the phone closed and threw it back to Winter.

"Malek's? How are we going to get to Malek's?" Ada asked. "Everyone is looking for us. We can't take a bus."

"Look, I'm thinking on the fly here," Didi said.

"I'm not going back out there. Especially not on public transportation. What a harrowing experience." Ellen protested with a condescending frown.

"We can't take the bus," Winter affirmed. "We'll take Kenny's delivery van. He sometimes leaves me a pair of keys for pickups on the weekend."

"Now we have a getaway van. The final touch on our descent into a life of crime." Ada nudged Axel playfully.

"We're all swimming naked at this point. There's no going back," Axel said resignedly.

"I never meant for this..." Winter spoke to the lead-paint streaks on the ceiling. "To play out like this." She then nodded at Ellen's phone, which was still playing the news.

This time, someone was being interviewed. They once again huddled around her phone, their elbows grazing each other. "Ugh, her," Ellen scoffed.

Ally Lindsey was giving a tearful interview to the reporter on the scene: "He was always so kind. And so timid. He would never hurt anyone. Mikey Fay was always such a gentle soul. He was everyone's best friend." Ally Lindsay choked back a sob.

The reporter chimed back in, despondently this time. "Again, if anyone knows anything about the five still on the run and evading police, please contact the authorities as soon as possible."

Winter furrowed her brows. "The beauty of a lie is convincing yourself of its truth."

"They're calling us the five? What are we, a nineties boy band?" Ellen said with an exaggerated frown.

"Turn this off. This isn't doing any of us any good. And I look terrible in that photo. Makes me look large." Ada snatched Ellen's phone and turned it off.

It came on again—the headache causing Ada to contort her face in agony. She squeezed her eyes shut in pain. The others exchanged knowing glances but said nothing. All except Winter.

"It will come about quickly. And when it does, it will hit hard. Then it will all be over," Winter said frigidly, as only she could.

"I'll be fine. Let's just get to Malek's." Ada shook off her discomfort. She was the first to make her way to the door.

"The van is out back." Winter said.

Together, they followed Winter to the rear parking lot and hopped into the back of the van, whose swinging doors were barely opened to discreetly allow them in individually. Fortunately, there were no prying eyes in the alleyway that morning. And while someone in the neighborhood might have spotted them, the residents all abided by one timeless code: see nothing, hear nothing, say nothing.

CHAPTER 30
WE RIDE OUT

"I'll drive." Winter put on a New Jersey Devils baseball cap she found in the front seat of the van and tucked her head deeper into her chest to hide her face. The others sat on empty crates in the back, bracing themselves against the walls of the windowless compartment.

Ada noticed something different about Axel. His Aegis was no longer around his neck. She reached into her pocket again to feel about for her own Aegis. Axel adjusted his seated position as Ada shot a laser-guided glare at his neckline.

"They can't know I'm involved with this," he said. "My job was to keep you safe, and now I'm embroiled in a criminal scandal. This won't end well for me."

"Look at our guy going rogue! You belong to these streets now, papi!" Didi lightheartedly punched him on the arm, eliciting an annoyed flinch.

"Is this what you want?" Ada asked.

"What do you mean?" he answered curtly.

"I mean, everything you do makes me think you want more than to live in the farmhouse and keep tabs on a girl with an Agoge. Has anyone bothered to ask you what you want?"

Ada's question cut into Axel's otherwise controlled face as though he could no longer prevent the words from flowing out. "You have something I never had. A choice. Even Winter—she chose revenge. Ellen, she chose to save you at the pool house."

"A wise person once told me we always have a choice." Ada glanced up at the rearview mirror to catch Winter's gaze for a brief second. "We chose to chase Winter onto that bus. We're choosing to ride in this van. I'm choosing to bruise my thighs from bouncing on these crates." Ada hugged her knees. Her arm just barely touched his as she settled beside Axel.

"It still doesn't make them good choices," Axel responded.

"We're here." Ada poked her head out to check for Malek's storefront sign. "Pull into the back alley," she instructed Winter. Ada then leaned into Axel and said in a low voice, "Don't sweat Armor. We got your back. All of us."

They were aggressively jostled by the unfinished pavement of the alley. Ada wrapped her arm under Axel's to brace herself. That familiar feeling of being close to him grew within her. Her eyes swept toward him briefly before a wave of heat in her cheeks turned her attention elsewhere. Any random fixed object would do. In this case, it was the latch of the rear door.

"I'm…sorry," Was all Ada could bring herself to say. His breath was warm against her face.

"Yeah, no, you're, you're good." Axel was searching for Ada's gaze.

"Um, yeah, let's go do this…you know, Jojo." She scratched her head and shook off the flutters in her stomach.

Ada did not need any more *things* happening inside her. The Agoge doing, apparently, Agoge things – whatever that meant – the stabbing pains in her head and the anxiety from her new life on the run as a suspected criminal were enough on their own. But that feeling – that feeling of being drawn to Axel, his chiseled jawline, the way his bicep tensed when she touched it, the way he looked at her with so much care, kept creeping up on her no matter how much she pushed it aside.

And here, in this van outside of Malek's, she would have to push it aside a little longer to figure out their next move.

CHAPTER 31

JOJO DEEP IN HIS BAG

WINTER PULLED in as close to the back door as possible. One by one, they exited the van, climbing out through the front. Ada banged on the restaurant's steel door, causing a jarring clanging of metal.

"Who is it?" Malek's voice was muffled by the door.

"It's me… Ada," she responded one decibel higher than she would have liked to. Ada looked around to ensure that no one had heard her and lowered her voice. "It's the five of us."

The steel door rolled from the bottom up, revealing Malek on the other side, nervously flitting glances behind them. "Ada!" he exclaimed, scrambling to lift the door. He stepped aside to allow Ada and her friends in then gave an extra peek out of the door. "Ada. You're on the news. Everyone is looking for you and your friends. And for her!" He'd finally noticed Winter, who tilted her baseball cap over her face even lower, kept her hands in her pocket, and tucked herself behind Ellen.

"It's not what you think, Amo Malek. It's bigger. Much bigger," Ada said.

Malek scrutinized each of them as if trying to piece together why Ada and her four coconspirators were in his shawarma shop at noon on a Monday when the entire police force was searching for them.

"We just need your help. We're here to meet with someone who can give us answers. He should be out front," Ada explained then shuffled past him with Didi.

They crept through the kitchen and peered out to the main seating area, where Jojo was chilling with his backward hat, idling on his phone.

"Psst... Jojo," Didi called out. She and Ada were crouched behind the counter, hidden by a stack of plastic cups.

Stunned, Jojo's eyebrows flung up. Didi signaled him over, flapping her fingers to the back. Jojo complied and strolled as inconspicuously as anyone summoned by a wanted criminal could. He whistled to himself as he skipped to the counter to meet the girls.

"Why you skipping and whistling? That's literally what every person who's about to do something sketchy does in every movie," Didi hard whispered.

"I don't know. It just seems like something people should do when they're trying not to stand out. And why are you whispering? We're the only ones here." He looked out at the empty seating area.

"Because... are you on the news and wanted for murder, Jojo?"

"Well, no, but—" Jojo started.

"Listen," Didi hurriedly whispered to Jojo and yanked him towards the backroom. "As you can see, it hasn't been an ideal day. We out here on the move until we can figure out how to make this mess go away,"

"Okay, cool, cool. This is sexy. The whole renegade thing suits you well, m'lady." Jojo bit his lip and clicked his fingers rhythmically while swaying side to side to the faint Arabic music playing in the seating area.

"Jojo. No. Not now. This is important. And ugh, I can't believe I'm saying this, but we really need your help." Didi posted up next to Ada, Axel, Ellen, and Winter.

They were the five—the five people whose names were plastered all over the TV and phones. And they stared at Jojo when

Didi held out Mikey Fay's white phone without uttering a word. It simply rested in her hand like it had an independent energy of its own.

"Okay, this all seems *muy, muy importante*." he said in a heavily anglicized Spanish accent that drew a less-than-enthused frown from Didi.

"This is Mikey Fay's phone. We need you to unlock it," Didi said bluntly, shattering any attempts to cushion the gigantic ask.

Jojo remained completely still, giving no indication as to what he would do next. Ada's stomach tightened, bracing for a resounding no. The seconds ticked away. He continued to stare at the phone in Didi's outstretched hand.

After what felt like a time-stopped interval, Jojo shrugged and finally said, "I've done worse."

He whipped his backpack around and pulled out his laptop. In all the time Ada and Didi had known him, Ada had never seen Jojo so locked in.

"Get me somewhere to sit and a power source." He seized the phone from Didi.

"Use my office. I will make you sandwiches." Malek hurried the six of them inside. Ada flashed him a grateful glance, mouthing, "Thank you." Meanwhile, Didi patted Malek on the arm, and Winter gave him a grateful nod as she brushed past him on her way into his office.

"I'll need to brute force the pin code to decrypt the password in an encrypted storage," Jojo said, setting up his work station.

"So, is that English for 'it's doable'?" Didi asked.

"Basically, we're gonna guess the pin code at a thousand pin codes a second. Come on, now—your boy's hacked into the Pentagon from an iPhone. This is light cheese, baby. Jojo already in his bag. On his throne. You know how I do."

"Jojo, for real, you're up here right now." Didi raised her flat hand slightly above her forehead. "I'ma need you somewhere down here." She lowered her hand to around her chest area.

Visibly excited, he collected himself to extend his hand to Didi.

"My Aphrodite, enter my garden of Olympia," he said, his hand alternating between his computer and the empty chair beside him.

"Oh my." Ellen looked on, sporting an amused grin. "Isn't that… cute." She dismissively swirled her wrist.

"Can you just not be…you for, like, five minutes?" Didi plopped down in the chair, sighing.

"Okay. Let's do this." He stretched his fingers out.

They waited anxiously as the seconds that felt like hours ticked away. Codes and numbers that could have been hieroglyphics, for all Ada knew, scrolled down his laptop screen. Jojo flipped through opened applications and windows, sporting an arrogant smile. He was a puppeteer with his computer, controlling an object removed from him but that could just as well have been part of him.

"And voilà. Jojo is still undefeated." He pinched his shirt, turning to Didi to soak in whatever praise she would be willing to shower him with.

Overcome with excitement, Didi pumped her fist into the air aggressively and reached over Jojo to pull him toward her. Jojo's confident smile morphed into a nervous laugh. He leaned in closer to her. Didi remained oblivious to his approaching puckered lips.

"Ew, the hell are you doing?" She jerked back.

"Sorry. Got caught up in the moment. I thought maybe I could…I mean, I've kissed girls before, but you know. Not ones that look like you." Jojo gave a sly shrug.

Didi's eyes made a dramatic roll, and without any warning, she kissed him on the cheek, prompting a rush of blood to his face.

"Let us rejoice! For the course of love never did run smooth," Ada's proclamation was met with an approving nod from Ellen.

"Tell anyone about this, and you won't live to see another sunrise," Didi warned Jojo.

Ada reached for Mikey Fay's phone. They clustered around her in a tight group.

"Ew, who puts a picture of themselves, flexing their abs in the mirror, as their wallpaper? That should have been your first red flag, Didi." Ellen curled her mouth in distaste as they perused his phone.

Ada furiously scrolled through his messages. Jojo sat in his chair, shutting down his computer with an air of satisfaction. He tapped his laptop gratefully once it was fully closed and reclined back, resting his hands on the back of his head.

"Looks like our victim recycles the same shirtless photos to the usual roster of girls," Ada observed, scrolling down the list of messages.

"Hold up—let me see. I'm on his roster? Nause. I am questioning every life decision right now." Didi stuck out her tongue in a mock gag reflex.

"Oh please, we don't have that kind of time, Diana," Ellen said, savoring Didi's calamity with a snort.

"Wait, what's that message? Look, there. It's from an unsaved number." Ada scrolled back up. "That one right there."

They each leaned closer to read the number. Ada tapped on it to open the message.

"Subject confirmed," Ada read. "Subject in cargo pants, sneakers, T-shirt. Subject at rear fountain." She skimmed through the text. "Look, they respond here: 'Confirmed. Will engage.' Look. The date. These were from Friday night. The day of the party," she said, looking to the group for confirmation.

"They were clocking you, A," Didi concluded, rubbing her thumb into her opposite hand.

"Not shocked. Axel warned me. Winter told us how the First Rank operated in Unitas. Even Lamia told me that night that they were on to me." Ada skimmed through the thread of messages out loud. "Subject in pool house. Confirmed."

Of the five, only Ellen didn't bother to read any further messages on the phone. Her lips moved faintly in an internal dialogue with herself. She brushed away one notion with a subtle shake of her head, only to entertain a new one, tapping her tongue under her top teeth.

She finally said, "Okay, this is good, Winter. This is good.

Listen, I might be new to this, but if anyone here knows people, it's me. Mikey Fay might have been Infernum, but he's, like, a nobody. These messages are definitely giving underling vibes. And I know a thing or two about having underlings." She flattened her palm against her chest and dropped her chin boastfully, much to Didi's groan of annoyance. "Lamia is the one we need to figure out. I saw the way she talked to Mikey Fay."

"Look, they go on. Next day, they say, 'Do not engage. Chancellor wants subject unharmed. Power of Agoge unstable in her.'" Ada continued to rush through to the last text. "Confirm status," she read again. "Confirm status."

"Um, y'all, is there something I should know here?" Jojo asked hesitantly. He'd been witnessing the entire exchange with a helpless, confused look on his face.

"Mikey Fay is not who you think he is. He is not from Earth. And apparently, neither am I. Or Axel. Or Winter," Ada said.

Axel gave her a dumbfounded look after she so casually disclosed the secret that Armor had spent years devising protocols to protect. Jojo froze in disbelief as if waiting for a punch line, a giggle, or a confession that it was all a joke. But no one delivered the follow-up.

"I mean, I'm Puerto Rican, and she's Chinese," Didi offered in consolation, pointing to her and Ellen. "So we're not really from here either. If that… helps. Or not…" Didi trailed off.

"Yeah, no, I totally hear you. Not saying I don't hear you. Because I do. But what the actual hell?" Jojo asked pointedly.

Jojo looked to any of them to offer a clue about what Ada had just told him. They all held the line, not because there was an unspoken oath of silence but because there was nothing left to say apart from the notes in the margins about the First Rank, the Agoge and Ada being a Legio.

"Jojo, no, you cannot take the phone home with you to look deeper into its security protocols," Ada added.

"How did you know that?" Jojo asked. He gave her a dubious glance.

"She can do that too. She can read minds," Didi casually said, dropping what would have otherwise been a spectacular revelation a mere few days earlier if it hadn't been supplanted by more spectacular events, like a green flare and the fact that an entire alien army was searching for her.

"I'm getting better at it. I can shut it out now." Ada felt compelled to clarify even though no one had asked. "No, I did not catch a glimpse of your laptop when it was open. And yes, this is wilder than the time you hacked into the digital boards on the turnpike to write, 'You'll never get to work on time. Ha ha ha.'"

"Tell me how that was you who did that?" Didi jerked forward to ask Jojo. "Well played."

"Okay. How is this even possible?" Jojo asked. "Where are you even from? How did you get here? Did you use solar sails? No, too inefficient. Ion propulsion? No, using charged particles to propel spacecraft is still in its infancy. FTL travel? Hmm, maybe there is a way to travel faster than light. Is hyperspace real? I have so many questions."

"We're not sure. Winter is the only one who can remember traveling here. I was a baby and don't remember anything at all," Axel said.

Winter spoke up. "I think it works like some kind of wormhole teleportation. I've looked into it here on Earth, but all I could find were comic books and movies. I've read the scientific journals, but your knowledge of the Agoge in this world is nonexistent. In Unitas, we believed it had something to do with the empress's ability to manipulate the Emerald Elixir. But I could find nothing on it here."

"I'm calling it," Ada declared.

"Wait, no, Ada." Axel tried to intervene.

Too late. Ada had already placed the call on speaker and put her finger to her lips to shush everyone. Axel sighed, exasperated, then drew nearer to the phone. The hollow ringtone echoed, followed by silence. Another ringtone. Silence.

The third ring was interrupted by an unsettling voice that answered with an edgy and commanding, "Yes. Confirm status."

It was that voice—the same menacing voice. It rippled through Ada to conjure the same fear and anxiety she'd felt at the pool house. It sent shivers down her spine. Her hair stood on end. Ellen also trembled with fear, her breathing suspended. Ellen and Ada quickly cast a fleeting glance at one another.

"Yes. Status check." The cold and calculating voice again filled Ada with dread.

To the others, it could have been any random stranger. To her, it was all too familiar. Ada drew a deep breath, summoning every last atom of bravery. "Lamia, you came for the wrong person."

Silence fell. And so it dragged on, weighing heavy and touchable.

Finally, Lamia spoke. "Hmm, Ada of Legio. I should have suspected as much."

"Call your people off. Or they'll end up like Mikey Fay." Ada met Didi with an awkward shrug.

"What are you doing? Don't threaten them!" Axel whispered.

"So, you kill an Infernum, and you think we'll just scamper on home through the Empress Walk? Is this how you think it ends?"

Her question lingered. "I don't know," Ada finally responded. "But I know how it ended last time—with you and Darius under a box of shoes."

Didi air punched the phone to accentuate Ada's point. She nudged Ada aggressively.

"With you and who this time? Axel, that unwanted cattle orphan? Didi, the subgene? That other try-hard subgene, Cinderellen? And Winter? Or shall I call her Esna Afra Amata?"

"Subgene? What?" Ellen mouthed at Ada's phone, scrunching her face.

"They're trying to track our signal. Hang up," Jojo whispered.

He frantically typed into his computer, growing more frustrated with each failed command. Finally, he leapt across to Ada and ended the call. Jojo pulled a small pin from his pocket, removed the sim, and powered off the phone. It was a multistep series of actions that only he could make look like it took only one swift motion.

"'Try hard'? I wasn't the one pretending to live in a house that wasn't mine that night," Ellen said defensively. "And the hell is a subgene?"

"It's…what the First Rank calls humans," Winter replied, shaking her head slowly.

"Ew, master race vibes. Gross," Ellen muttered.

"So it is Lamia." Ada peered over at Ellen. Apparently, only the two of them had recognized her voice.

"You sure it was her?" Didi asked.

"It's her, Didi. First, she comes for me. Now she's threatening all of us."

"This will not be the last time we hear that voice," Winter added with a tiny ember of anger glinting in her eye.

"Aight… so there's a lot to unpack here," Didi said.

"Yeah, starting with: she knows who we all are." Axel rubbed the back of his neck.

"So, what do we do now?" Jojo asked.

"We? Nah, you're going back to school. Or home if the school is still shut down. We"—Didi motioned to the five of them, drawing a line demarcating Ellen, Axel, Didi, and Winter from Jojo—"are going to handle this."

"Nah, you got me twisted. We ride together now. Besides, I was dabbling with Chinese launch codes the other day. I'm sure this would register much lower on the list of offenses." Jojo casually brushed his shoulder off.

"No, he should stay, Diana. We might need access again." Ellen adopted a stricter tone, pointing to the phone by the table.

"Fine. But just, don't be, you know, you all the time. Just be normal," Didi said.

"My phone is blowing up with texts from my parents and brother." Ada glanced down at her phone and slipped her thumb over the side to silence the call again. After several hours of her family hopelessly trying to reach her, the action had become automatic.

"Are your phones still turned on? Are you serious right now?" Jojo's eyes nearly popped out. "Turn them off immediately."

"Um, excuse me, content and engagement for my followers. Duh!" Ellen held her phone out.

"Give me your phones. All of you." Jojo flapped his fingers at them.

One by one, they handed over their phones and watched him power them off and remove the sim cards.

With no phones and no connection to the outside world, they were on their own and up against a psychotic and cunning foe in Lamia, who seemed hellbent on delivering Ada to the First Rank by any means necessary.

Deep down, Ada knew it would not be the last time she heard Lamia's voice.

CHAPTER 32
THE CALL

JOJO FURIOUSLY WORKED AWAY on his computer. Mikey Fay's phone was connected to his laptop, sending information back and forth as Jojo's eyes glinted in the light from his screen. He would frantically type then lean back, scratch and shake his head, and lean forward again to repeat that pattern.

"I can't figure out the location of that phone call. It's like a security wall I've never seen before." Jojo huffed.

"You finally found someone with more walls to climb over than Didi," Ada teased him.

"Difference is that one is a fine quantum encryption I'd like to crack. This is just numbers on a page." He winked at Didi.

"Just so we're clear, comparing me to whatever computer thingy you're talking about doesn't really move the needle for me," Didi retorted.

"It's because it's not from this world, Jojo," Axel said. He turned to Ada. "Armor stood no chance against the First Rank's technology. That's why all we had was our Aegis." He reached for his pocket, where his Aegis was stowed away. Ada checked on hers, too.

"Probably Avondal technology. They have no courage, but

they've always traded their superior intellectual discipline for security," Winter remarked.

"Whatever it is, this kind of technology is next level..." Jojo trailed off in excitement at the endless possibilities.

"What are you trying to do exactly?" Axel asked, his eyes scrolling through Jojo's screen of numbers and letters jumbled together.

"I'm trying to access the phone that Ada just called. I can't get through."

Then it happened. The sudden buzz of Mikey Fay's phone tore through the already thick air of the room. The same digits that Ada had called flashed across the screen. Jojo leaped back from the device as if it was a live wire. Their heads all swiveled to the phone at the same time. They alternated between fixing their eyes uneasily on the tiny screen and exchanging glances.

Then, as if by some unverbalized agreement, they all turned to Ada and waited anxiously for her next move. The buzzing persisted.

"Wait—don't answer it." Jojo's fingers flew across the keyboard. "Let me scramble our location first. That much I can do on this thing." He punctuated his last key command and nodded to Ada, giving her the go-ahead.

Ada answered the phone, putting it on speaker. "Yeah," she answered in a cool, unfazed tone.

Didi quizzically shrugged, held out her hands, and mouthed, "Yeah...?"

"Cute. You scrambled your location. You and your little henchmen are full of tricks, aren't you?" Lamia said, skipping the formalities.

"You missed me? I'll give you the address, but please don't show up doing that thing with the words on the giant cue cards."

Didi fanned Ada with her hands in a theatrical display. Ellen shook her head and dropped it into her hands, groaning inaudibly.

"You cookin'," Didi mouthed to Ada, turning her fist as though stirring a pot.

"Funny girl. I may not know where you are, but at least I know who you're with. And while we're on the subject of your ragtag confidants – Ellen Liu, Diana Mendoza, Esna Afra Amata, or Winter, as you are seasonally known here, Axel of the Treasonous – are you willing to die for this girl? Because this is how it will end for you. This isn't your fight." Lamia had softened her sinister voice, but it did little to conceal the veiled threat.

Lamia's slow and callous delivery had shattered Ada's humorous facade. She now had to acknowledge the stark reality wrestling about in the back of her mind. It was a sobering truth that no quips or witty one-liners could cover up.

"None of you need to be as invested as Ada is in this whole ordeal. Diana and Ellen, you could walk away unharmed. Right now. Axel, you could return to Armor and live to fight us another day. I welcome the challenge. Esna, you could still carry that vengeance in your heart. You were alone before you joined these people, and you can carry on that way. We want nothing from you all. This only concerns Ada. All she has to do, to spare you all and herself, is deliver the Agoge."

Ada cast each of them a pained look. They would have to let her do this alone. There was no other way.

Ellen ran her palms up and down her legs from her waist to her knees. She tugged her shirt down and lightly patted her thighs one last time. She looked at the others, who watched on anxiously. Winter maintained a frosty demeanor. Didi tightened her lips, bracing herself for disappointment. Ada, meanwhile, gave Ellen an approving smile.

Then, Ellen slowly pivoted away from Winter and toward Ada. Her eyes were downcast and avoided meeting anyone's judging gaze. Axel nodded almost imperceptibly as if to acknowledge her decision.

She had done enough for Ada already. Ellen had selflessly thrown that stone through the window to buy Ada more time.

She'd risked her life that night, fleeing barefoot. She'd kept Ada's secret. Between the harmless jabs and banter, she and Didi never let their disagreements escalate. She hated to admit it, but Lamia was right: this was not her fight. It was time to let Ellen go.

Ellen seized the phone from Ada and spoke in a commanding tone. "My name is Tian Liu. Get it right. And I'm not going anywhere."

Ada furrowed her brows when Ellen firmly planted her feet next to Ada. The others were equally caught off guard.

Axel stepped forward to speak into the phone. "My name is Axel. Son of the Unitas Republic."

"My name is Esna Afra Amata. Honor, Sacrifice, Loyalty." Winter extended her last three fingers out, brought them to her chest, and gathered herself around the others.

"I am Diana Uscátegui Leyva Mendoza. *Ya tu sabe*. Ask about me." Didi pursed her lips in steely resolve.

"I am Ada of Legio. If you want the Agoge, you'll have to go through us," Ada finally concluded. It felt good – so satisfying – to clap back at Lamia and let her know that she wasn't afraid. More importantly, to let her know that no matter how big and bad everyone thought the First Rank was, how much fear they struck in the hearts of Armor and other Senazis, that they couldn't bully not only Ada, but also her defiant, stubborn, bullheaded friends who stood with her.

Didi promptly shushed Jojo before he could inject himself into the conversation.

"How sentimental. But I, too, can be sentimental, Ada." Lamia chuckled. "Someone here wants to talk to you." She raised her voice to speak through the distressed groans in the background. "Speak," she commanded in a menacing tone.

"Ada. Help. I... who are these people?" Roman's voice shot through the speaker.

Ada gasped in terror and seized the phone back from Ellen. Tremors shook her hands. She struggled to keep them steady while holding the phone. "Roman."

Didi covered her mouth, breathing heavily through her fingers. Axel stared vacantly into the phone. Ellen whispered, "No."

"Six p.m. Tonight. The mansion. Or he dies." Lamia delivered her threat with a chilling, detached calmness.

"Ada, help, please... Ada..." Roman's pleas transmitted through the speaker.

The obscure sounds of a scuffle ensued before the line went dead. All that was left was that deafening, suffocating hush.

"Roman! No, Roman!" Ada screamed into the phone with no one on the other line. She frantically tried to call the number back, shaking with each tap of the screen. No answer. She tried again. No answer. Axel finally intervened to snatch the phone from her. Short of breath, she could feel her heart pound with every beat.

"They took him. They took my brother. They took him." Ada spoke to everyone and no one.

"Ada." Axel reached his hand to her.

"They took him. If she hurts him, I swear to everything..."

Ada continued to wildly flit around the room in a panic. She swiped for the phone from Axel's hand, but he swooped it away. She fell into his chest, his shirt brushing away her tears. Axel wrapped his arms around her and let her cry.

"We're going to get him back." Axel brushed her hair as he continued to embrace her.

The others maintained a respectable distance, leaving Ada the space to drown herself in despair at the sudden shock of her brother being taken by Lamia. Didi dropped her head, exhaling in defeat.

"No. No." Winter was muttering to herself, looking at the ground. Then she decisively brought her head up. "They will not take another one. No. They will not do to you what they've done to so many. No." If vengeance had a portrait, it would be Winter as soon as she heard Ada's brother pleading for help. "We're going to get him back. For you. For Vensana and Finius. If I have to kill Mikey Fay again and a thousand like him, I will."

"No, it's too risky. I need to do this alone." Ada finally peeled herself off of Axel's tear-soaked shirt. She rubbed her puffy eyes with the palms of her hands and sniffed her nose clear.

"I'm coming with you." Winter came closer and held Ada's hand. Ellen was at her side. Didi tapped her chest with her fist in solidarity. Jojo took his cue from Didi and nodded at Ada.

"You not doing this alone, A." Didi said.

Meanwhile, Axel reached into his pocket to pull out the Aegis. Deliberating something, he pinched the clasp to open it on one side.

"We're going to need all the help we can get. The Infernum will have summoned everyone to the mansion. They won't take any chances." Axel wrapped the Aegis around his neck and firmly shut the clasp, leaving the necklace to dangle. He then closed his eyes and went into a calm, meditative state.

"What's he doing?" Jojo asked, looking to any of the girls for an answer.

"I think he's putting a call out for help from Armor," Didi said.

There was only so much running away Ada could do – from the mansion, from school earlier that morning, to Malek's. At some point, she would have to dig her heels in, turn around, face the First Rank, and go at them head-on. It was time to accept that although this was bigger than her – the Agoge, the First Rank, Unitas – she was still the host of the Agoge. No more running. It was time to act.

"No. It has to be me." Ada clutched Axel's forearm tightly before releasing it.

Ada's hand slipped into her pocket and retrieved her Aegis. She ran her thumb over its sharp corners. A subtle glimmer of light reflected off its surface. Then she unclasped it.

"You ended up on the ground the last time you tried it on." Axel swiped at her Aegis, missing it when Ada swiftly retracted her hand.

"I can do this. I *need* to do this. For Roman." Before anyone else could object, she slipped it around her neck, adjusted it to the right height, and fiddled with her fingers to fasten it securely.

This was her Aegis. This was the life and the world her father, Marcel, had come from. This was the apprehension of her mother all these years. This was Roman's blissful ignorance of it all. Revenge, hope, friendship—they all rested around her neck. Every rung of her journey so far had been etched into that Aegis.

A percussion rippled through Ada's body as soon as the clasp closed and the Aegis rested on her chest. Fleeting voices traveled in and out of her mind. Immediately, the massacre appeared before her. She held her stare at the figure by the edge of the forest. When she turned to look behind her, the masses were still celebrating. This time, though, she looked down at her hands. They were soft, youthful, glowing with a vibrant green that pulsated through their veins. They weren't her hands, but they felt like a part of her. Ada cast a final glance at the row of bodies. A soothing sensation crept in. The scene went dark. Slowly, voices and figures emerged from the darkness. A nameless collection of people she had never met was speaking collectively yet distinctly. Different frequencies tangled together. Sound bites flowed between them. She could not see their faces but detected their presence at different locations. Some were far. Others near.

The sensation overwhelmed her. Her eyelids were pressed tightly together. She swam through the vastness of the presence of others, a convoluted web of energy and auras. Some drew near, while others were farther away. Some were distressed, others safe. They varied, but all shared a common energy—Ada was repelled by each, as if each voice had put up a barrier between them and her. It was like crawling from one closed door to another, unable to make out muffled words of a conversation from outside a room.

"My name is Ada of Legio. If anyone can hear me, I need your help." Straining her eyes shut, she channeled the force of her thoughts into the Aegis and transmitted them out.

"Can anyone please talk to me? Please. I need your help." Ada sent her mental transmission into the void again. "Please. They took my brother. I have the Agoge. I am the host. They took my brother."

Silence. The once-active thoughts, voices, and feelings receded into nothingness again. She was all alone in her mind.

Until.

"We will fight with you, Ada of Legio," a lone voice beamed through the stillness.

"We will fight for you," another voice said.

"For the heirs of Unitas," another said.

"For my mother."

"For my father."

"For our brothers and sisters."

One by one, they all spoke up. A flood of green light erupted from various pockets of the darkness, surging toward Ada all at once, illuminating a spectrum of colors, thoughts, and voices, making its presence known.

Ada crumbled to the floor and staggered to her knees, opening her eyes. The searing pain she'd been experiencing all day came back with unmerciful oppression. A single red stream of blood poured out of her nose.

She could not hold back any longer. The pain was too much. She let out a loud shriek, collapsing and spasming. Her back arched in agony. Her glasses sat off-kilter. Then she thudded back down to the floor, and the pain vanished as suddenly as it had come on, leaving her depleted. All she could bring herself to do was barely keep her eyes open, staring up at the creases in the ceiling above her.

"Get her some water!" Didi screamed at Jojo, who paddled out of the backroom to look for a glass and a faucet.

"Ada. Are you all right? Your nose." Axel wiped away the smears of blood and smudged them onto his pants.

"Why does it keep coming?" She asked, retrieving her glasses.

"It must be close, then. Your awakening is almost here," Winter said as though Ada was a lab subject on which the formula had already been tested in previous experiments.

"We need to get to Lamia. We need to go." Ada struggled to get back up to one knee. Her joints were still unsteady. Beads of sweat pooled across her face and ran down her neck.

Jojo joined her at her side, bent to a single knee, and offered her a glass of water. She waved him off.

"Drink. It will help. Trust me," Winter said.

Ada took the glass. The water swirled from the unsteadiness of her hands.

"I'll tell them where and what time." Axel closed his eyes to retreat into the Aegis.

The others helped Ada to her feet, and she dusted herself off. Damp patches of sweat spotted her shirt. Blood smeared her collar.

They gathered themselves to leave through the back again. In her peripheral vision, Ada caught sight of Malek approaching, swinging a white plastic to-go bag with sandwiches inside. Handing it to Ada, he gave them all a weary look, the kind that a parent would make before their child left for their first overseas trip without them.

"Where are you going, *habibti*?" The aroma of shawarmas wafted between Malek and Ada.

"To finish it." Ada brushed by him and out the back door.

CHAPTER 33
WE PULL UP DEEP

Winter was in the driver's seat while the others sat in the back again. None of them struck up a conversation. Every so often, Ada would spare them a glance just to acknowledge their presence. They could have easily abandoned her, but they hadn't run. Each of them had elected to stay by her side and face Lamia and the First Rank together.

Ellen pulled her hair back to tie it in a ponytail. Winter growled in the front seat, fixated on the road like it was a gauntlet to barrel through. The only sudden movement came from Axel, who tore off his Aegis and squeezed it back into his pocket. Ada noticed but elected to not probe.

"Cisca and Genuit want us to wait," he said to the group as they bounced around in the back.

"Nah, we're off that," Didi retorted.

"I'm off that too," he replied.

A familiar sinking feeling crawled its way back into Ada when the van pulled into the block by the mansion. The walls Ellen had scaled only a few days ago seemed taller, more impenetrable. The gate where Winter had cast that final deathly glare at General Bruton was screaming with impending doom. Every curb and streetlight scowled at Ada.

But this time, the road itself was empty. The late afternoon sun reflected off the mansion. Absent were the thuds of music blaring. There was no pretense of hospitality—no valets. Only the puddles from the overnight rain showers gathered in the large decorative fountain. Its extravagant waterfalls had vanished. The front door of the mansion was shut and the front gate wide open.

Winter parked by the curb, not too close to the gates but close enough to not be visible from the driveway. This was ground zero, where Lamia had revealed herself as an Infernum mastermind and where Ada had discovered her powers. This time, they would be entering the throes of danger, fully aware of the perils.

Ada exchanged one last dap with Didi inside the van and slowly raised her head. She gazed at Ellen, Axel, and Jojo then hopped out of the back of the van.

Axel tugged at Ada's elbow to pull her back. "We still don't have a plan. We can't just walk in there and demand the release of Roman," he cautioned.

"What's there to discuss? They have him in there. We need to get him out." Ada shook off his light grip on her elbow.

"I'm with Axel here, A. What if they don't cut Roman loose? Or worse, they free him and snatch you up instead? They're gunning for that Agoge," Didi said, pointing both hands at Ada's chest.

"I agree. We need to think it through and…" Winter started but left her sentence unfinished when a small contingent of young boys and girls, roughly high school-aged, rounded the corner off the opposite intersection. Dressed in jeans, crew necks, and button-ups, they clearly didn't belong here. They could have been students. None of them stopped to marvel at the decadence of the mansion as they passed it. They were disciplined despite not marching in any clear formation. What they lacked in order, they made up for in a steady, quiet confidence.

With Ada at the apex, the others formed a semicircle. They stood on alert like a tribe of warriors prepared to hold their ground against an approaching battalion.

"Hmm," Winter murmured.

One, in particular, was sporting a flannel shirt with the sleeves rolled up, biting his lower lip. Another continued to nervously run her hands through her hair. There was a couple holding hands, anxiously squeezing them.

"They came," Axel finally stated. He offered his hands toward them in welcome.

Ellen monitored them warily. "Who are these people supposed to be?"

"They're Armor," Axel said.

"That's Armor?" Ada asked with a raised brow. "That's all of them?"

"Not really."

They approached Ada with guarded scrutiny. The one in the flannel shirt strained to get a better look at her, like someone studying a complex algorithm. Finally, at an arm's length away, he stopped. His group looked Ada up and down, from her hands to her chest and waist.

"Ada of Legio, we answered the call." The young man in the flannel shirt ceremoniously placed his three right fingers on his chest to form the Republic salute.

Winter recoiled.

"Honor, Sacrifice, Loyalty," he uttered the Creed while maintaining his salute, waiting for Ada or anyone with her to do the same.

He was striking and confident, sporting dark hair with prominent curls and thick, expressive eyebrows that drew attention to his eyes. His well-defined jaw gave him a strong and distinctive look.

"I am Santi," he continued.

Axel was the first one to respond to the salute. "Honor. Sacrifice. Loyalty," he repeated the Creed, fixing his three fingers on his heart.

"I'm positively underwhelmed," Ellen muttered just loudly enough to be heard by Santi and the others. She returned to assessing the walls and gate of the mansion.

Santi broke from his salute to cross his arms. Leaning back, he surveyed Ada and her friends. His eyebrows pressed closer together. If Ada didn't know any better, she could swear his first impression of her could be characterized in one way – a bit of a letdown.

"Not what you expected?" Ada said, finally verbalizing what was clearly written on Santi's slack lips.

"We didn't really know what to expect. We were taught that the host, wherever and whoever they were, is a worthy possessor of the Agoge. A Legio dedicated to the restoration of the Republic." Santi lowered his head.

"You sound disappointed…" Ada responded.

"I can't tell yet. The elders ordered us to stand down. They've been trying to reach you through the Aegis." Santi scanned her neck then shifted over to Axel, neither of whom was wearing the Aegis. His fingers traced the curve of his neck, finally hovering over the sharp angles of his pendant.

"You all are either really stupid or really brave—or both—to go in there alone." Santi eyed each of them as though he was looking for a hidden chest of weapons, arms, or anything that would suggest they were not planning to enter the mansion with just blind will and a hope in hell that they would come out alive.

"We're going to go with C—probably a little bit of both," Didi answered.

"If you go in there, they will mutilate you the first chance they get in order to get that Agoge out of you."

"I'll take my chances," Ada replied.

"If you barge through the gates, it will end in violence or death for you," Santi said, appealing to their common sense.

"Then we choose violence," Winter spoke up, causing Santi to jerk back.

A few people on his side gave approving smiles, while others whispered speculatively.

"Is that really the Amata girl?" someone said in a barely audible voice.

"Yes. It's her. Now, if you'll excuse me. They have my brother in there." Ada broke away, waiting for no one as she set off toward the gate. With each step, she paved the path for Didi, Winter, and Axel to follow.

"Are you people gonna stand there or, like, are you doing this or what?" Ellen snapped at Santi as Ada turned to glimpse her folding her arms and tapping her sneakers. "Look, I'm all for making an appearance, like the time I went to the US Open just to take a picture of myself holding a Honey Deuce, but sometimes, you gotta get with it or get lost. And this is one of those times."

"Not you, Jojo. You stay back and hold it down here." Didi held her palms out at Jojo.

He breathed a sigh of relief.

Santi gave Axel a pleading look.

"I've tried, man. You're not gonna get far with these ones." Defeated, Axel shook his head and raised his hands.

Led by Santi, the members of Armor ultimately pooled their courage to take their first decisive steps behind Ada.

Ada, Didi, Axel, Winter, and Ellen arrived at the gate. The mansion loomed before them.

"Full send," Didi declared while glaring out at the mansion.

"Full send," Ada affirmed.

CHAPTER 34
WE OUT HERE

The mansion was bland in the daylight, stripped of its allure from that Friday night. There was no lighting, music, or energy of partiers. It was just another structure with walls, windows, a roof, and a gate. Every one of these features was noticeably bigger than the other houses on the block. Still, nothing of the mansion would merit a double take from a passerby. It was like being at a club when the lights were turned back on at closing time.

"I don't want to think about how scared Roman must be right now," Ada said.

Axel grasped Ada's forearm. "Do not do anything brash until we get him out." Then he turned to Winter to emphasize his point. "That goes for all of you."

"If she hurts him…" A sudden quiver overtook Ada's hand.

"She wouldn't do that. They want you alive," Axel said.

"You haven't looked into her eyes like I have. She's pure evil." Another flash of pain stabbed Ada's head, making her steps stutter.

Didi reached under her arm on one side to prop her up. Axel, on the other side, shifted close to assist. Ada pushed the pain aside and marched around the fountain and toward the front door without their help.

The five of them stopped short of the door. It was massive, looming larger in the daytime when it was closed than it had when it was held open for them at the party. The door was adorned with crystal handles and hinges that shone under the sunlight, reflecting blinding rays, which only made it look even gaudier.

"Yeah, no, I'm not loving this." Ellen scrunched up her face.

They continued to stand until the door finally creaked open to reveal the face of a large woman, the same one who stopped them to inquire about Ada's bloody lip on their way out on Friday. An unpleasant chill escaped from the home. The air was suddenly less plentiful.

The burly woman scornfully eyed Ada and then threw a look at her entourage behind her. "You again. You are to come inside. Alone."

"No. Tell them to come out here. We'll be in the courtyard," Ada replied.

An unsettling look crept onto the woman's face, who turned to glance inside and then back out to Ada.

"At least you didn't boop her nose this time," Didi whispered in Ada's ear.

"We're winging this, aren't we?" Axel leaned in to ask her quietly.

"For the record, this strategy was ill-conceived and poorly executed, from what I can tell so far," Ellen said.

"Relax. We got this." Didi swayed from side to side.

Axel turned to Santi and Armor, who were awaiting at the bottom of the steps, to confidently inform them of the strategy. "This is all part of the plan." He turned back to Ada and whispered, "We don't really have a plan, do we?"

"No. No, we don't," Ellen answered before Ada could say anything.

"So now what do we do?" Axel asked, turning back to Armor and smiling measuredly at them.

"We wait," Winter said.

And so, they waited.

The afternoon September sun drew small beads of sweat on their faces. The haze drifted in the background, causing surrounding objects to blur and blend together. As the mist wafted through the air, it cast everything in a soft, diffuse light, creating an almost dreamlike atmosphere. Shadows of passing clouds played across the mansion walls, twisting and turning in the setting sun, while the colors of the sky bled together.

Ada continued to wait. Each passing second felt more fraught than the last as the tension built. The door, that crass door, finally slipped open, reflecting a shimmering sparkle off its crystals.

"I will handle it from here, Solana," Lamia's voice floated out before her silhouette appeared in the doorframe. That pompous posture—her shoulders rolled back and neck held high—was unchanged from when Ada had encountered her in the pool house. Ellen gasped. Winter took her hand.

Lamia's eyes bore down on Ada and then her friends. She then skipped past them to Santi and Armor and let out a brief derisive laugh, clearly unimpressed.

"Is this it? The Host of the Agoge, and this is everyone she can muster?" Another short laugh escaped Lamia. She glared down at them menacingly.

Ada wasn't about to break. Not after everything she'd been through and especially not after Lamia had taken her brother. She glared defiantly back at her. Didi blew out a large gum balloon, leaving it to flutter before popping it emphatically then corralling the splatter of the gum from around her lips to resume her exaggeratedly slow chewing while she eyed Lamia. Ellen met Lamia's glare while retying her ponytail and tugging at its base. Winter was a steel curtain, impenetrable to Lamia. Axel shifted his gaze between Ada and Lamia, occasionally puffing out his chest.

Lamia's tongue snaked its way to the top of her lips and swiveled it from side to side. She nodded and turned to whoever was inside behind the partially closed door then stepped forward, leaving a blank space between her and the door.

A rumble of footsteps echoed from inside. Then Darius flung

the door wide open, and Infernum followed him from the mansion one by one.

Ada and her group shuffled back, pushed down to the last step by the herd of the Infernum flooding out and marching directly at them. With each stride, the Infernum drove them back until they reached the center of the courtyard. More Infernum filed out of the mansion, wielding long spears whose tips brimmed with a static blue light.

A red triangle was engraved into the tip of their weapons. In unbroken discipline, the Infernum continued to flood out of the mansion, taking their positions around Ada and her friends and encircling Armor, who huddled closer to Ada. They were hemmed in on every side of the courtyard, encased by a swarm of the Infernum gripping their scepters.

Lamia moved through the circle and toward Ada, passing two Infernum who had parted to make way for her. An eerie silence descended upon the courtyard. Only the tapping of Lamia's shoes could be heard. *Tap, tap, tap*—the rhythm of her heeled shoes cut through until she came to stand face-to-face with Ada.

"Enough games, Lamia. Bring out Roman," Ada demanded, clenching her jaw.

"Not the funny girl anymore. I was starting to like that version," Lamia snarled.

"I think she's using her sarcastic voice." Didi leaned in to tell Ada.

"The five of you have been really busy," Lamia said, pointing her finger at them.

"And she can count," Ellen added, catching Lamia's tight glare.

"Go ahead and tell them what happened the last time you were a funny girl." Lamia motioned with her brows at the small swell still visible on Ada's lip.

"Oh, my lip? Yes, that wasn't nice of you. And now look what happened to your boy, Mikey Fay," Ada responded.

"A necessary death. He served his part with honor." Lamia paused to study Ada. She forced a contemptuous scowl. "No, you're not a killer. Neither are you or you, and definitely not you," she said to Ada, Didi, Ellen, and Axel. "But you…" She landed on Winter. "You, Esna, have that controlled rage. I know it when I see it. You can step outside of yourself and take life when the time calls." Lamia delivered her remarks slowly, calculatingly.

Darius, who was directly behind Lamia, said, "The daughter of Romis Amata. It can't be." His low voice trembled in disbelief as recognition dawned on him.

Winter glanced between Darius and Lamia. "You asked Ada how this would end. With your blood staining these stones." Winter finally rested her chilling eyes on Darius.

"Well, then, let's be sure to leave an eternal impression on these stones, shall we?" Lamia replied.

"Lamia, we must remain sensible," Darius said in a shaky voice, stealing glances at Winter.

"Where is my brother?" Ada said, dispensing with the banter. "Bring him out."

"So, Ada, if you say please and thank you, you're going to walk out of here with him?" Lamia held the tip of her tongue on her upper lip, leaving her mouth slightly agape.

"I am here, am I not? What else do you want, Lamia?"

"I don't care about you, Ada. Or your Agoge. Or your name," Lamia replied, staring into Ada's chest and stomach as though the Agoge was neatly stashed away behind a layer of skin and organs somewhere in there. "What I want is much bigger than you."

"Yeah, and what's that?"

"Glory," Lamia declared, her eyes fixed on a distant point in the sky as though she could see her destiny unfolding. "I am to return you to Unitas, Ada of Legio, for the Chancellor to extract your Agoge. And from there, who knows?"

"I don't know how to give that to you. I don't even know how I got it." Ada tapped her chest, presuming it was lodged somewhere in her.

"No need. The Chancellor has a plan. Apparently," she muttered that last part. "Or that is the directive," Lamia said without a trace of emotion, continuing to pierce her with black eyes. "You will come with us in exchange for your brother. They are expecting you in Unitas."

"No, Ada. Don't do it. They'll kill you for the Agoge if they have to." Axel reached for her arm, but she stubbornly pulled it away.

"Come, Ada. Let's avoid all this regretful waste of blood all in the name of ego," Lamia said with an undertone of veiled threat.

"Um, says the girl who wants 'glory,'" Ellen said, making air quotes. "No ego detected there."

"Ellen, is it?" Lamia turned to her. "Look at you. She latches on now that Ada is more than a common person. You're a social tapeworm." Lamia's words dripped with disgust.

Lamia's amused grin transformed into something sinister. "Enough of this." She raised her hands to form the First Rank triangle salute.

The Infernum took this as their cue to point their scepters directly at Ada, her friends, Santi, and Armor, ensnaring the group in a huddle. They all clustered closer together, emitting sharp gasps of terror. With a flick of her finger, Lamia commanded the Infernum to take one step in, tightening the ring around them.

"Fine. I'll go with you." Ada flung out her palms toward Lamia. "But bring out my brother first. I want to see him."

"Ada, no, this ain't it." Didi tugged at Ada's arm.

Lamia rolled her eyes and sighed. "Such a shame, this outcome. Me and you, we're not so different. You are convinced of the righteousness of your ways. As am I of mine. Who's to say we're not on opposing ends of a circle like the one we're in right now? All we want is what's good for everyone. You go about it from one side" —she nodded to the left side of the circle then to the right—"and I do it from this side. Only to meet in the same terminal place. At the very top."

"We're nothing alike. You are a power-hungry monster, and I just want my life back. Now, bring out my brother," Ada said, her nostrils flaring and her chin pressing forward.

Didi stepped up to join her at her side, as did Axel, Ellen, and Winter.

"Ada, don't do it. We can handle these clowns. A few people with sticks don't scare me," Didi said.

"Those are not sticks, Didi," Axel said quietly.

"You should listen to him. Because I'm getting tempted, subgene," Lamia said to Didi.

"You take her, then you take us," Didi snapped back, stepping up beside Ada.

"All of us," Axel added, stepping up as well.

"How noble. Foolish, but noble. Very well, bring him out," Lamia instructed Darius, who hesitated before complying.

"Bring out the boy!" he yelled back into the mansion.

"I feel like you didn't really have to delegate that one. You could have yelled into the house yourself," Ellen curtly said, casually taking one long stride to take her place by Didi.

"Desperate power move. Noted," Didi said.

"Enough!" Lamia shrieked.

"She said, with a shrill," Ellen muttered.

"To hide her pain," Didi added under her breath.

Soon, two more Infernum appeared from inside the mansion, escorting Roman out. He seemed to show no discomfort. No signs of torture or pain. The Infernum guided him down the stairs and pushed him inside the circle surrounding Ada and the others. Roman's head turned in all directions, scanning the threats of the Infernum with their scepters held to their eyes like snipers. Each tip of the scepter fizzled. As soon as he saw Ada, he hastened his staggered steps toward her.

"Roman! Are you okay? Did they hurt you?" Ada pulled him in, brushing him past Lamia. She hugged him tightly then pushed him away to check for any signs of injury.

"Didn't I say that all we want is what's good for everyone, Ada?" Lamia said incredulously, giving Ada a pointed look.

"I'm okay. I... Ada, you have to get out of here." Roman

clutched her arm tighter. "These people want something from you. I heard what they're going to do to you if you—"

"I know. I'm going to take care of it. Listen, as soon as I go in there, I want you to run as fast as you can. Okay? You run as fast as you can." She embraced him again, running her hand through his coarse hair like she'd done when they were young.

"Touching. Now, come with us," Lamia said in an icy tone devoid of any empathy or emotion. This was another transaction to be carried out. The currency was Ada and Roman.

A low, sinister voice from the top of the steps shot through the crowd. "Not yet."

Lamia rolled her eyes and curled her upper lip. The cocoon of people wrapped around the source of that voice opened up. The sunlight dug into his scar, bringing it into prominent view.

"I have me some unfinished business of me own." General Bruton trudged down the stairs, tracing his scar with his thumb. "I reckon you'd be comin' to visit your mother in her nameless grave pit. And that scum father too." He cut his words at Winter.

"I 'eard your dear mum screamed bloody murder when my Phalanx had their wicked way with 'er. Your old man, he whimpered like a wee boy when I drove my scepter through him. And now it's your turn. You reckon you'll squeal or scream when it's your turn to die, eh, Esna Afra Amata?" Bruton ran his tongue through the crevice of his front teeth and crudely spat out a vile splatter of saliva at Winter's feet.

"Bruton." Winter stiffened her lip. "Thank you."

"Er...?" Bruton said, raising an eyebrow. "Grateful little scum you are," he said, posturing through Winter's cryptic retort.

"Until now, you were only an idea to me. But now here you are, in the flesh. A monster I can kill with my own hands." Winter spoke in an eerie monotone. It felt like Winter could have darkened the rays of the sun from where she stood or wilted the plants and leaves in the courtyard.

Winter forced her lip into a rigid line. She was locked in a tense standoff, facing General Bruton with an unyielding stare, with Ada between them. Eye to eye, as if Ada were invisible, they neither flinched nor backed down.

"Yeah?" he grunted. "And did I fall short of your expectations in the flesh? Or is the monster as big and bad as you had always bloody dreamed?" His towering presence leaned over Ada toward Winter, suffocating the space between all three of them.

"It won't matter in the end. I've thought of so many moments like this. How they would play out."

"Tell me, how does it play out, Esna?" Bruton's harsh voice switched from stern to mocking.

"In your death." Winter met his gaze. "Only the question is, would I plunge a knife straight into you, or would I take your life with my bare hands? The ways change, but the outcome is the same. Always the same. You die every time."

Lamia shot a quick conspiratorial glance at Solana behind her. They shared an amused look. Ada stood in the middle, ready at a moment's notice to yank Winter back in case things got testy. Winter took one quick step toward Bruton, ready to charge, before Ada raised her hand in front of her to check her. Not that she sympathized with Bruton or with anyone complicit in the taking of her brother. Winter could have ripped his head off for all she cared. But for the moment, she couldn't risk any flare-up until Roman's release was secured.

"Not here, Winter," Ada whispered through her gritted teeth. "Not yet."

Winter growled through tightly sealed lips as the Infernum steadied, pointing their scepters at them with laser-like focus.

CHAPTER 35
SHOWDOWN

"THAT'S ENOUGH OF YOU. Fall back, you treasonous filth," Lamia spat her words at Ada and the others, stepping between Winter and General Bruton and attempting to sweep Winter away with her forearm. Winter intercepted her hand and twisted it down in a swift defensive maneuver.

"You have received training. Impressive," Lamia said, sporting a cunning smile and arching a brow. "It's a shame that won't save you from the tips of these scepters aimed at you."

Before Winter could react or Ada could intervene, a deafening call reverberated from the gates of the mansion, capturing the attention of all.

"Bruton!"

The Infernum swiveled their scepters toward that roaring voice. From behind the gates, a pack of people emerged, brandishing what looked like scepters of their own. Only theirs seemed older and less sophisticated.

Ada recognized the voice that called out to General Bruton with unmistakable ferocity. It was her father. He stood by the gates, joined by Cisca, Genuit, and a smattering of elders. For the first time, he appeared to Ada not as her dad but as an officer,

Legion Guard Marcel of Legio. He was strong, defiant, and primed for battle.

"Kill them all!" Lamia ordered the Infernum.

In a split second, Lamia lunged at Ada and wrapped her arm around her neck and arms, pinning Ada in place. Lamia hastily shuffled backward then swiveled Ada around like a human shield. Sprays of blue lasers fired at Marcel and his company, who took shelter behind the columns of the gates, returning fire to the Infernum exposed in the open courtyard.

"Roman, go!" Ada yelled to her brother, who was staggering aimlessly out in the open.

Infernum and Santi's Armor volunteers scrambled in all directions, attacking each other. Some Infernum were diverted by Marcel's company behind the gates. Blue beams from the scepters flew in all directions in a chaotic display of color, illuminating the early-evening sky. A few combatants from both sides fired their weapons, and others resorted to hand-to-hand combat. Punches and grunts mixed with the subdued laser noise of the scepters. The scene was utter pandemonium as people fell to the ground, some injured and others lifeless. Bodies were scattered everywhere.

Amid the bedlam, Lamia continued to overpower Ada with her superior Senazi strength. Despite Ada's fierce kicking and fighting, she was dragged back toward the mansion by Lamia, who had one hand around her throat and the other wrapped around her waist.

As they shuffled closer to the mansion, Ada again, called out to Roman. "Run! Roman, run!" Ada yelled as she continued to be pulled away by Lamia's unyielding grip. He remained rooted to the spot, looking unsure about what to do in the gunfire and turmoil.

Not too far off from Roman, she saw Ellen curling into a ball, still in the place where Lamia had just plucked Ada from. Ellen was rocking back and forth and flinching in horror at each sickening thud or scream of agony from another fallen body. Off in the distance, Ada vaguely spotted Winter searching for someone in the melee.

"Bruton!" Winter yelled out.

General Bruton passed Ada, either not noticing her or simply choosing to ignore her as he was whisked by guards back into the mansion, keeping his head low to avoid detection or a stray laser shot or both. The fight raged on, with laser beams ricocheting off nearby surfaces and the occasional scuffle breaking out.

"Axel! Help!" Ada called out.

Axel had leapt into action by disarming one of the Infernum of his scepter. He swung it forcefully to strike the Infernum with its base. After studying it for a few seconds, Axel then pointed the weapon at another Infernum, only to shoot a blank.

"Ax—" Ada tried again, but Lamia covered her mouth, leaving Ada to pant through her nose, kicking her feet and flailing her arms.

"Tug the base—with your hand!" Cisca bellowed at Axel as she poked her head around to fire off another shot.

The violence intensified. The searing shots of the scepters whizzed by, striking anyone in their path. Axel gripped the base of the scepter and pointed it at an Infernum who was about to direct his shot squarely at Didi. He released a swift blast, piercing his opponent's chest, prompting him to fall instantly. In the tumult, Didi's eyes widened at Axel.

"Take cover!" Axel shouted. "Ada!" He caught sight of her off by the stairs to the mansion, with Lamia still covering her mouth. Before he could pursue her, blue beams whizzed by him, forcing him to duck behind the fountain in the center of the courtyard.

"Ada, hold on!" Didi shouted, meeting her eyes.

As though Didi had just had a revelation, her eyes widened at the sight of the scepters by the fallen Infernum. She picked one up and tossed another toward Ellen, who was nearly hyperventilating as she cast her eyes on the scepter laid before her.

Didi reached out a hand, offering calm in the face of the mayhem. "Just breathe, Ellen. Look at me. Breathe. You got this." Another shot landed close to Ellen's foot, prompting Didi to duck reflexively. *"Oye, hijo de pu..."* She shouted at the shooter who was raining beams at her and Ellen.

Before Didi could aim her scepter, Winter appeared out of nowhere, hurtling toward Didi's shooter with incredible speed and power. With a mighty strike, Winter smashed into the Infernum with such force that he was knocked out. It all happened so quickly that Didi was left stunned, scepter still in hand. Winter was on a rampage, landing blows with her fists and driving the scepter through Infernum.

"Is this not delightful, Ada of Legio? Let chaos reign," Lamia whispered in Ada's ear.

It was madness, and Lamia seemed to enjoy it. Ada turned her head to regard the glint of pleasure in Lamia's eyes.

"What?" Ada struggled to say.

"Anarchy breeds ascent," Lamia said with a cold, calculating snarl.

Shaken and afraid, Ada tried to process what was happening—Lamia with her foreboding declarations and the mania in the courtyard. Infernum exchanging fire with the elders of Armor. The younger members of Armor fighting the Infernum. In the middle, Ellen huddled into herself, finally bringing her head up to witness the mayhem.

Ada and Ellen locked eyes briefly. Ellen's lips were moving, muttering something to herself like she was possessed. And meanwhile, Lamia was still dragging Ada backward toward the mansion. She lifted Ada up one step with little effort despite Ada struggling with all her might.

Clutching the scepter, Ellen struggled to regain her footing amid the battle scene that whirled around her. She aimed the scepter at Lamia, the blue tip facing Ada. The Scepter trembled in Ellen's hand. Then it steadied. She focused her aim squarely at Ada and fired, barely missing Ada. Instantly, Lamia released her grip, and Ada fell to the steps.

"Ahh." Lamia winced, holding her arm. Streaks of blood spouted through her torn sleeve.

"Your mother's a subgene, bitch." Ellen yelled.

As Lamia crumpled to the ground, wounded from Ellen's shot, another Infernum sprang into action to avenge his comrade. He lunged toward Ellen.

"Come get it!" Ellen dared the Infernum attacker. She was ready, drawing her scepter into position.

Ada knew that Ellen fenced but hadn't realized she did it this well. Ellen looked comfortable with the scepter in her hands. She skillfully batted away the attacker's weapon, sending it flying. With a clean strike to his torso, she forced him to the ground. He writhed in pain.

"Know your place. Hashtag sword slay." Ellen regarded the fallen Infernum beneath her with a haughty stare.

As Ada struggled to regain her footing, she heard Santi, somewhere, yelling out, "Ada! Get to cover."

Ada scrambled to duck behind the potted plants elevated on a concrete bank by the stairs. Out of the corner of her eye, she spotted her father engaged in fierce combat, occasionally poking his head out from behind the column of the gate, aiming and firing at an Infernum combatant with military discipline. She barely recognized him—the way his frame was perched forward, the oneness he had with his weapon in hand, or how his trained eye calculated the movements of the enemy and the trajectory of his shot. With each hit, he demonstrated the patience and precision of someone with seasoned combat experience, not the father she'd always known.

Her heart pounded as chaos reigned. Amid the shooting, Roman was stumbling into the open. He looked lost until he spotted their dad motioning him to the far end of the gate. Roman must have seen their dad, as he picked up his pace and began to sprint toward him. Meanwhile, from the corner of her eye, Ada could see Lamia, still on her backside, homing in on Roman with a scepter aimed straight at him.

Ada sprang up from behind the concrete landscaped bank, sprinting toward him, shouting, "Roman! Get out of the open!"

She looked back at Lamia, whose scepter's sizzling tip was ready to fire. With the base of the scepter digging into her shoulders, Lamia focused her aim. *"Pora toras,* Ada of Legio," Lamia shouted, letting out a shrill, mocking laugh.

With all her strength, Ada jumped on Roman and tackled him to the ground to shield him from harm. They were a mere few feet away from their dad.

It was too late.

She felt the impact of the laser ripple through Roman. A trickle of blood spread across his shirt.

"No!" Marcel's voice erupted from behind the gate. He rushed forward to take hold of Roman and dragged him back to cover and out of the driveway.

Breathless and shaking, Ada stayed at her brother's side. She saw fear and pain in his eyes. With tears streaming down her face, she cradled Roman in her arms. Marcel rushed to his side. He ripped open Roman's shirt to identify the point where Roman had been struck. He hastily tore open his own shirt, sending buttons flying in every direction, and rolled it up. Marcel used his shirt to apply pressure to the wound above the right rib cage.

Ada could see the vibrancy of life seeping away from Roman's eyes. The vivid color on his cheeks paled. His breathing grew more labored. He never took his eyes off Ada. Her brother. Her source of innocence and pride. The kid who'd followed her around when they were young and looked up to her, even when he was too proud to admit it as a teenager, was lying mortally wounded on the ground, a casualty of a war he had nothing to do with.

"No, Roman. No. Breathe. We're going to get you to a hospital. Stay with me," Marcel urged him. There was a fragility in his voice, a mournful tone he could not conceal. He continued to apply pressure.

"Grapes. I tried. I tried running as fast as I could, Grapes. I ran as fast I could… I tried…" Roman trailed off, his breath coming in shallow gasps.

"You did great. You did amazing. It's a little cut," Ada said, struggling to take control of her quivering voice and shaking hands. She held his hand tight. Hers were covered in the blood of her brother.

"No. No, Roman, stay with me, son." Marcel's voice was choked with despair, urging his son to keep his eyes open and hold on for just a little longer. "Stay with me, son." Marcel flipped Roman's hair back off his forehead. He caressed his cheek in a desperate attempt to find life anywhere in Roman's face.

He was gone. Roman was dead.

Marcel sobbed uncontrollably. "No. No. Roman." He continued to urge him back to life.

Ada withdrew into herself, and a rage took hold of her. That scowling, unmerciful face of Lamia with her scepter pointed at Roman—the way her mouth had snarled in absolute disregard for his life. She'd done this. She'd shot her brother. She'd killed Roman. All because she hadn't gotten what she wanted. And what she wanted was glory. At any expense.

Ada could sense it—the feeling that occasionally simmered and subsided with each throbbing headache that had visited her these last few days. It was either grief or something else. The gnawing headache seared into her one last time, reaching a crescendo.

Then, the pain vanished. The high-pitched noises and stabbing pangs were gone. With every other sensation stripped away, all that remained was a seething desire for vengeance. The sight of her dead brother festered into a raw, unquenchable fury that left no room for anything but revenge.

They killed Roman.

Lamia. The Infernum. Bruton. All of them would have to answer for their crime.

Ada blinked quickly. In that fleeting freeze-frame with her eyes closed, she'd receded into the depths of her mind. She'd been a bystander to a scene. The image of the massacre by the forest she'd seen when she wore her Aegis came to her. Only this time, it was more vivid. As clear as the battle in the courtyard of the mansion.

As real as the death of her brother. In that vision, a green flame flickered.

Finally, that flame exploded in an ethereal light.

Her hands shook violently. That imagined green flame in the deep confines of her mind manifested itself on her fingertips. The color glowed and swirled between her fingers. It intensified with each passing breath. Ada looked at her hands, too consumed with grief and rage to consider anything else. The last vestige of reason had been extinguished when her brother took his last dying breath.

"Lamia!" Ada screamed out in the direction of the mansion.

"Ada?" her father's voice from somewhere behind her barely registered.

"Stay with Roman, Dad." Ada replied over her shoulder.

The flaring light intensified with each passing second. Ada charged over to the middle of the open gates, exposed to everyone in view—Infernum and Armor, friends and foe. Those who were engaged in a vicious battle with one another stopped to marvel at the scene of the girl in the green flame in the driveway.

"Lamia!" Ada unleashed another primal, savage cry.

Her glasses were off, but she could see Lamia with absolute clarity squirming on the steps from her wound. Lamia rose to her feet, urgently ordering everyone to retreat.

"Fall back. Everyone out, now!" Lamia commanded.

The Infernum scattered in all directions. Lamia limped toward the mansion, repeating her orders to retreat.

"Ada, wait." Didi rushed to keep up with Ada, who was methodically putting one foot in front of the other toward the mansion door.

Winter shoved away the last Infernum within her clutches and hurried toward Ada. Ellen followed. Axel sped up to her but stopped short of Ada, looking spellbound.

With one resolute step after another, Ada marched toward the mansion. The iridescent flame blazed from her very being. If it looked surreal to those around her, it did not to Ada. Through the opaque green flame emanating from her, she only cared for one thing—getting her hands on her brother's killer – Lamia.

"What…what is happening right now?" Ellen marveled.

"I-I don't know…" Axel stammered.

The shimmering radiance flowed from Ada.

Ada?" Didi said.

Ada heard them loud and clear. But she was focused on one thing only—her brother's killer.

"Lamia!" she called out again, with flames shooting from her pores. She was wrapped in the tendrils that curled and twirled.

Lamia slipped inside the mansion.

"It's happening," Winter said.

"Ada, can you hear us? Ada!?" Axel asked frantically in response to Winter's cryptic declaration.

"The Agoge. It is the Agoge." Winter tugged Axel back to maintain an even greater distance from Ada. At her side, with scepters firmly in their clutches, Didi and Ellen did the same.

Her friends, the Agoge, Unitas, this otherworldly light blanketing her—none of it mattered. All that mattered was getting her hands on Lamia.

They marched up the stairs and stopped before the shut crystal-plastered door of the mansion. Ada studied it through the transparent glow of her presence. She effortlessly pushed the door off its hinges, sending it flying inside. The door clattered to the ground, and for a moment, all was still.

"Did she just…?" Didi asked in disbelief.

"Ada, can you hear me?" Axel asked, his voice rising to jolt her out of her trance.

"Lamia!" she called out again, filling the mansion with an unmissable tremor.

No one was to be found. The mansion was eerily empty. There was no sign of Lamia or the Infernum. Ada stomped over to the center, underneath the chandelier.

All that was left were scraps of loose-leaf papers scattered across the floor. A cup of tea rested on a coffee table by the corner.

The furniture was askew. The kitchen was littered with abandoned clothes, dishes, and books.

"I don't get it. Where could they have gone?" Axel asked.

"They went back," Winter muttered to herself, moving closer to Ada, ignoring the luminance flowing through her.

"Back where?" Didi asked with caution.

"Back to Unitas. Through the Empress Walk," Winter concluded.

"No. No. She won't get away with it." Ada's hands compressed to create a solid mass.

The light fluttering around her sparked. Its once graceful twirls spun violently. The enchanted radiances of the light morphed in ferocious flames.

The others watched the spectacle in terror and awe. The light seemed alive and at one with Ada, writhing and twisting. The flames crackled and hissed, sending more little green embers shooting into the air. They cast shadows of the others that danced across the walls. Ada and the light took a life of their own.

"What is she doing? Ada, what are you doing?" Ellen shrieked.

"Ada, stop!" Didi put her hands up guardedly.

"It's too bright—I can barely see you!" Axel strained to look away from the blinding light.

With a sudden burst of energy, the green light burned brighter than ever, illuminating everything around them with an other-worldly glow. In one fell swoop, it engulfed them, sweeping through them, swirling all around them, blinding them. Ada could see nothing but the color surging. The flare consumed her as she melted into it. The world around her disappeared, replaced by a shimmering sensation.

"What the hell is happening?" Didi asked somewhere in the distance.

Just as quickly as it had started, it ended. The tumult subsided, leaving everything eerily silent and still. Gone was the mansion— the gaudy floors and ornate pillars. Ada glanced down at her hands, stained with the blood of her fallen brother, to find that the light flowing through and around her had disappeared. She brought her face up to her friends, who were equally perplexed. They were still there. Disoriented, she reached out to touch Axel to see if he was an image or a real person.

Ada, Didi, Axel, Ellen, and Winter found themselves the middle of a magnificent circular structure that had a massive dome at the ceiling with a circular opening allowing the sun to flood the room with its rays. It was a vast rotunda. Columns were erected at the sides. They were at an elevated altar of some sort.

Then Ada heard sirens wailing in the background. She looked at her friends again. Ellen and Didi said nothing. Total silence. Axel brought his hands to cover his mouth in disbelief.

Winter pulled her arms in, taking in the space. "No. It can't be," she murmured. Her gaze shifted to the light drawn into the center through the oculus.

Outside, the sirens wailed.

"Ada? Where. Are. We?" Didi finally asked, still casting her eyes around the space.

Winter, her voice tight, looked up at the oculus and uttered a single word. "Run."

You're all absolute legends for giving this book a chance. Book two — Insurrection—is on deck. New worlds, new adventures, new villains, same Ada and the crew. This time, friendships will be tested and lives will be altered forever. Ada knows what she must do, but it will come at a great cost.

Let's get it, people.

THANK YOU

Thank you for taking this ride with me to read Heirs of No Empire: Origins. If you get a minute, hop on over to any of the platforms to leave an Ada-style feel-good review. If you felt "positively underwhelmed," like Ellen would say, leave a review anyway. It's all love on this side.

Stay up to date for all things Heirs of No Empire on our Discord group text channel. You know we had to call it the Stellar Squad. Hit up our shop for all things Heirs of No Empire.

See you on the other side in Book 2 - Insurrection. In the meantime, full send.

ABOUT THE AUTHOR

I am an immigrant kid who grew up between Lebanon and Canada. At some point - in my infinite wisdom - or lack thereof, I decided to go to law school and become a lawyer. Maybe it was personal ambition. Or maybe it was my Lebanese parents giving me three sole options in life: doctor, lawyer, or failure. It was a toss up.

When I wasn't doodling or questioning my existence at my big boy law job desk, I was imagining worlds, their political structures and power struggles, heroes and antiheroes. Safe to say, that part - the serious suit and tie phase of my life didn't last long. Although, I must say, my suit and tie color palette combos were on point. So I started writing down these worlds and, like that episode of the Simpsons where Lisa puts a tooth in a Petri dish with cola and wakes up to it being a full-blown civilization, my worlds began taking on a life of their own. Even when I owned my own business afterwards, I'd find some time in the day to check in on my worlds so I could tell my kids another "chapter" for bedtime stories. P.S. The three of them were the first ever fans of Heirs of No Empire. The story was conceived for them.

Half of me is an avid reader of history and political theory, the other half loves a good Sci-Fi novel, the other half is big into comics and the other half still loves 90's and 00s rap music (trust me, the math adds up).